Pulchritude[1]

... an ugly tale of beauty

by Ana Mardoll

Title: Pulchritude

ISBN: 978-0-9849822-1-9

Author: Ana Mardoll [4]

Publisher: Acacia Moon Publishing [5]

Lawyer: Brooke Mixon [6]

Editor: Elaine Kennedy [7]

Character Artist: Emily Vreeland [8]

Cover Artist: Clarissa Filice [9]

Cover Fonts: Black Jack [10], Shonar Bangla [11], Estrangelo Edessa [12], Calibri [13]

Edition March 2012

Your generous support of indie authors
nurtures creativity and allows it to thrive.
Thank you!

Ana Mardoll ♡

Technical Details

Length: 60,000 words

Audience: This work is written primarily for an Adult and Young Adult audience.

Triggers: This work contains potentially triggering content, a list of which is provided on the Trigger Warnings page. Please note that lists of triggers may be seen by some as "spoilers" for book content.

Format: This book was created in doc format [14] by the 52 Novels design shop [15].

Distribution: This work is available through multiple distribution outlets. A list of these outlets and a sample of this work are available on the author's website [16].

Derivative Commercial Works: This work is licensed under the Creative Commons Attribution-NonCommercial-NoDerivativeWorks License in an attempt to strike the best balance between consumer freedom to use-and-distribute and consumer protection. In other words, this means you're welcome to copy and share this book freely.

The author is open to the possibility for derivative works (both non-commercial and commercial), including "fan fiction" works, and encourages anyone interested in such a project to contact the author for a license waiver. Thank you.

Table of Contents

Note to the Reader

Dear Reader,

Thank you for opening this book and providing me with the chance to entertain you. I hope that you will find this novel as delightful to read as it was for me to write. Please feel free to contact me for any reason at AnaMardoll@gmail.com or on my website at www.AnaMardoll.com. If you enjoy this book and would like to donate to support my writing efforts, there is a donation link available on my website.

The world you are about to enter is fictional and fantastical. Scattered pieces may be recognizable from our history, but a number of details — including the racial makeup of the setting — are entirely ahistorical. I have also attempted to give each narrator their own voice, and to allow them to present the truth as they see it. My hope is that you will enjoy reading their sometimes unreliable accounts and will arrive at a truth that has meaning for you.

Thank you again,
~ Ana Mardoll

To my dear Husband, who carries me when I cannot walk, holds me when I cannot sleep, and comforts me when I cannot smile. You are my hands, my heart, and the source of my deepest joy.
Also, to my cats, who hiss at my dear Husband for being so unreasonably tall.

Chapter 1 - Rosella

Rosella eyed the darkening sky appreciatively as she walked the dirt-packed road. The sky had threatened rain all day, and she was thrilled to see thick thunderclouds rolling overhead as dusk approached. She hadn't planned on a downpour, and did not have the necessary skill with weather to create one even if she had, but a storm would add a nice touch to tonight's events.

She had been walking for weeks since she had awakened from her winter sleep, traveling through the country with no real destination in mind, until a night spent in a country village had planted in her mind an idea that promised to be amusing. The village itself had been disappointing: a small collection of straw-thatched houses inhabited by a handful of land-bound serfs and itinerant workers. The villagers had been deeply suspicious of her, but the gossip they had been willing to share was of the recent death of the local lord and the upcoming nuptials of his heir. From the shabby condition of the village, Rosella gathered that the elder lord had been an impoverished country prince. No doubt the lord's extensive debts would pass to his heir along with the usual prestigious titles and enviable blood-relationships to distant emperors.

The politics of the situation had been breathtakingly dull, but Rosella's interest was piqued by the news that the young heir, now in his second or third decade of life (she had never been very good at remembering mortal ages), would soon be receiving guests to announce the news of his wedding. Opinions were varied on what this event would mean for the villagers, with speculation ranging over the prospect of holidays, stag hunts, and almsgiving. Yet for Rosella the possibilities of the event were perfectly clear. She set out from the village the next morning without causing even the slightest bit of mischief in the village, her feet almost dancing with anticipation.

Now the sky was darkening with the coming of evening and the threat of rain, and she was certain that she would arrive just in time for the festivities. A dozen carriages had passed her on the road during the day — frilly, gilded things with spoiled nobles on the inside and weary coachmen on the outside — and she had whiled away the walk with thoughts of which carriage she would follow out after her dramatic exit tonight. Of course, such thoughts were getting ahead of herself. Rosella glanced at the sky again and fervently hoped that the foul weather wouldn't cause her newest target to relent and offer her succor. If that happened, her fun would be thoroughly spoiled, but she could always stay in the area and try again in a few months if another opportunity arose. Time meant little to the *fata* [17], and good amusement was worth a little extra effort.

The road crested a hill, and Rosella paused to take in the view of the valley below. The forest that had been closing in thickly on either side of the road stopped abruptly here. The land in the little valley had been diligently cleared away to make room for a small country castle and a few surrounding orchards and fields. The castle itself was unimposing, its squat towers built with stone blocks cut so roughly that heavy drafts and thick damps would be as familiar to the royal family as to the poorest of their serfs. From her vantage point, Rosella could see in the dim evening light servants milling about the castle courtyard and lighting torches in the newly-budding orchard.

A brown hare, freshly awakened and caught in the grip of his spring frenzy, sprinted wildly across the meadow that spanned the short distance between castle and forest. Once within the shelter of the woods, he halted and his long ears twitched once in Rosella's direction. She stifled a laugh as his eyes warily scanned the area where she stood. After a short moment, his ears won out over his eyes and he sped off into the woods. Rosella smirked; she knew that if the animal had seen anything at all, it would have been only the slightest of shimmers in the air. She had a great deal of practice at fooling mortal eyes.

As the thunder rumbled overhead in earnest and a chill wind started to blow, Rosella decided that it was time for the game to begin. The fairy woman stepped out from under the shelter of the trees, shedding her invisibility and shaping around herself a new form. Had anyone been there to watch, they would have seen a battered old woman dressed in the poorest of rags emerge slowly from the forest. Her ancient face was lined with the indelible marks of hard living; her back was humped and she walked bent at the waist. Her movements were painfully slow, as though years of heavy burdens had left her gait hobbled. As she picked her way along the side of the road, brambles ripped and tore at her tattered hem and at the stained rags tied over her feet.

Rosella gritted her teeth and leaned into the gathering wind, struggling toward the castle courtyard. She could not feel the pain of the brambles, nor was she bothered by the bite of the wind, but she knew from experience that it was important that she *look* as though she suffered from such realities. Anything less than a flawless performance could alert the target to her true nature, and humans were always on their best behavior when they suspected a *fata* was in their midst.

A smile curved over her lips, safely hidden from sight by the straggled hair plastered to her creased face. She couldn't help but be pleased with

the perfection of her disguise. A good disguise was built from so much
more than the magic that shaped it, and it was always the little details that
made the piece complete. Rosella excelled at the details that many of her
fellow *fata* did not bother to notice when they played among humans:
the unmistakable odor of sweat, the papery skin of weathered hands, the
tremulous shaking of a body gone too long without food and warmth.
The key was to make the disguise as pathetic as possible without being
so wretched that only the sadistic would turn her away. The goal was to
maximize her righteous fury while minimizing the chance that a target
might slip the net. She carefully leaned into another cold gust, relishing the
enjoyment she always felt when on the hunt.

No one could begrudge her for finding amusing ways to pass the
centuries. It wasn't as if the humans didn't have free will in the matter;
she never used her power to *force* them to turn her away. It was true that
she allowed herself multiple tests to truly gauge their mettle, and indeed
one young duke had proved a challenge that spanned nearly a decade,
granting her succor eight times before failing her ninth test. However, if
one possessed a pure heart, then a hundred tests would yield the same
result, and she would leave them forever with her blessing. It wasn't *her*
fault that eventually they all gave in to their pride and arrogance.

She was halfway between the forest and the castle when the downpour
started in earnest. Staccato bursts of rain whipped at her frail form as
she hobbled along the road. The sharply pelting drops churned the dirt
road into sticky black mud that clung to her clothes with thick tenacity.
A carriage, late for the engagement party, drove by too quickly on the
slick road and sprayed a coating of mud over her. Peering out through
the patina of slime that now covered her face and tangled hair, Rosella
carefully memorized the shape and color of the offending carriage. *"Well,
that answers the question of who to visit next,"* she thought triumphantly.
Everything hinged on getting tonight as perfect as possible.

Through the thickening rain, Rosella could see the gilded carriages
dotted around the castle courtyard as the latecomer took one of the few
remaining places near the castle doors. The sight of the carriages lifted her

spirits higher, for the engagement party was why she had chosen tonight, and why she knew her trap was perfect. The game was always so much more fun when it was played for an audience, and her targets were always especially ill-mannered when other humans were present.

By the warm light cast by the open castle doors, she saw servants scurrying between the carriages, handling luggage, and tending to weary animals. Other figures milled more slowly about the sheltered courtyard. *"Beggars, like myself,"* Rosella absently guessed. A wry smile crossed her lips a moment later at the thought that these humans might have anything in common with herself. Perhaps she'd played this game a little too long if she'd begun to think such ridiculous thoughts. Maybe it was time for a long rest, but it was so hard to give up the game when it was such wonderful fun.

Rosella watched the figures in the courtyard, noting with considerable interest that none of the humans ever crossed the threshold of the imposing castle doors. As the servants labored with luggage and the beggars milled about seeking employment, both groups studiously avoided the light spilling from the main doors. Instead, they slipped into the dark shadows on either side of the castle. Rosella decided that some back kitchen door or stable entrance was what the commoners were expected to use, and she was certain that breaking this protocol would be a perfect start to the evening. She allowed herself a very small giggle as she lowered her head and trudged on toward the beckoning doors.

Her favorite game was about to begin.

Chapter 2 - Ezio

Ezio sighed with pleasure as a gust of cool air burst through the open castle doors and swirled around the stuffy hall. The older matrons glared fruitlessly at the disturbance and shuffled closer to the fireplace, clutching protectively at their elaborate hairstyles. His own hair fluttered pleasantly with the wind and he felt relief at having the sweat lifted from his brow. There had been a few unhappy mutters about leaving the doors open as the latecomers to the party were welcomed and the servants finished their preparations in the dining hall, but no one had been brazen enough to complain directly to the prince. Ezio almost wished that someone *would* complain; a full day of receiving distant relatives had put his nerves severely on edge, and he could use a good excuse to vent his frustration.

Standing close enough to the main doors to be the first to welcome any latecomers to his engagement party, Ezio crossed his arms over his chest and surveyed his guests with resentment. The muggy weather had caused many of the velvet tunics and brocade gowns of the party to be stained with sweat and the stench made Ezio gag. Idly he imagined hurling this fact as a choicely-worded insult at the clump of ladies gossiping by the hall hearth, and wondered how they would react. Ezio turned back toward the cool breeze and tried to banish his irritation so that he could be appropriately pleasant for the dinner announcement. *"You're just tired,"* he coached himself. *"Get through tonight and everything will be fine."*

"Quite the crowd," a voice murmured appreciatively at his side. Ezio glanced to his left to see his younger brother, Flavio, standing quietly by with a full wine glass in each hand. "The castle hasn't seen so many guests since the funeral."

"Quite the expense," Ezio retorted grumpily, taking the proffered wine glass gratefully. "At least when Father died, a week of seven-course meals wasn't expected." He wanted to bite his words back as soon as he'd said them. It wasn't appropriate to his station to speak of such crass matters, but his anxiety had made him more candid than he should be. He drained the wine glass in a single gulp and reminded himself to maintain decorum.

"Nothing but the best for Cousin Adelina," Flavio countered mischievously, breaking into a wide grin. He dropped his voice to a whisper. "Her dowry will more than make up for the initial investment. I should consider myself lucky to wed even the handmaiden of such a distinguished lady," he reminded Ezio with a teasing pout.

Ezio shot a disapproving look at his younger half-brother, but then smiled in spite of himself. Flavio had been born on the wrong side of the blanket, and with his bastard blood he would never rise higher in the world than his current position of captain of the castle guard. His position was cold comfort, since the castle guard consisted of no more than a dozen young men tasked to ensure that the servants didn't walk off with the kitchen silver and expected to join Ezio for his morning hunts in the forest. But Flavio's self-effacing charm made him impossible to dislike, and if Flavio harbored any bitterness at being eclipsed by his half-brother, he never showed it outside of the occasional good-natured gibe.

An elderly man — a distant uncle or cousin, Ezio wasn't certain —

broke off from one of the groups engaged in conversation and wandered over to congratulate the prince on his good fortune. Ezio received the well-wishes with as much politeness as he could muster, but he could feel his frustration mounting. His betrothal to Adelina would be announced at dinner with appropriate etiquette, but Ezio could see no reason why he should pretend to be in raptures at the thought of marrying his dowdy cousin. The marriage was a profitable one for both sides — her family would be absorbed into his royal titles, and he would be so enriched by her dowry that he need never again worry about matters of expense — but it was tiresome to protest a heartfelt passion for a woman that stirred in him only indifference.

The thought of his disappointing betrothed drew Ezio's mind back to the greener pastures embodied in her younger sister. He waited until the old man wandered off in search of more spiced wine before casually picking up the thread of conversation with Flavio. "I wouldn't sell yourself so short as to settle for a handmaiden. I'm confident that my bride's family will see the benefit in joining Lady Imelda to my distinguished Captain of the Guard." He glanced sideways at his younger brother, hoping to gauge his reaction to this proposal.

Flavio looked startled for a moment, but his face quickly smoothed over into a bland expression. "That would be quite an honor," he said in a neutral tone.

Ezio smiled in satisfaction at his own planning. His marriage to Adelina might be necessary to pay his father's debts, but there was no need to limit himself to the cold marriage bed offered by his homely cousin. Imelda had only a fraction of her older sister's dowry, but she was as beautiful as her older sister was drab, and gaining her as part of the bargain lightened Ezio's spirits considerably. A match between Flavio and Imelda would take the burden of the youngest daughter off the family's hands, and Ezio was confident that his brother was shrewd enough not to interfere with the prince's seduction of Flavio's pretty new wife — not when there were dozens of pretty chambermaids and local shepherdesses to tumble instead. *Father always insisted that princely tastes had to be discerning,* Ezio mused, though Flavio's low-born pedigree proved that Prince Domenico had rarely followed his own advice.

The storm was picking up outside. A particularly strong gust of wind swept through the castle doors, bringing with it a spray of rain and a deeper chill than before. Several of the ladies gasped in alarm as at least one elaborate hairstyle crumpled in the face of the evening winds. Even several of the gentlemen looked disconcerted and moved further into the dry hall.

"Shall I close the doors, Your Highness?" Flavio asked, his voice uncharacteristically formal.

Ezio hesitated — he had rarely seen his unflappable younger brother speak so stiffly, and wondered what could have occassioned Flavio's sudden annoyance — but after a moment he nodded. "Yes, we might as well move to the dining room. The servants should be ready by now, and I don't think any more relatives will be arriving at this late — what is *that?*" he asked in sudden puzzlement.

Something was moving up the steps of the castle, but it was impossible to make out any details in the fluttering torchlight that reached out into the night. Through the curtain of rain, the figure was a short, brown blur; Ezio imagined the shape as a young orchard tree come to life and lumbering slowly up the castle steps. He took a step closer to the door in curiosity just as the apparition stepped over the threshold of the castle and resolved itself into nothing more exotic than an ugly old woman.

The woman walked bent at the waist so that she was forced to crane her head up to see where she was walking, and her sight was impeded by the stringy hair that clung wetly to her scalp and partially covered her face. Despite being drenched through with rain, a thick coat of slimy mud coated the woman's dress and hair, and Ezio found the look and smell of her to be instantly sickening. "It's a beggar," Flavio murmured in answer to the prince's earlier question, though now that she was fully bathed in the castle light, Ezio could see the obvious for himself.

"The storm always brings them out," Ezio said with irritation. "They're supposed to go around to the servants' entrance. Get her out of here before the guests see her." Dark mud was already dripping from her on to his fine rugs, and Ezio grimaced as he mentally calculated the cost of cleaning them.

Flavio strode over to the old woman and Ezio carefully cast a glance back at his guests. Thankfully, they were too absorbed in their own conversations to have yet noticed the social gaffe standing on his doorstep, but he needed the woman out of sight before the ladies went into hysterics upon seeing her. The filth caked on her was enough to put his guests off their dinner. *"And no one knows what diseases beggars carry these days,"* he thought with a grimace. He looked back at the woman and saw with mounting annoyance that Flavio was having trouble convincing her to leave quietly.

"—but I have nowhere to go in this storm. If I could just have a night's shelter," the woman pleaded in a shrill, nasal voice.

"And you *can* have shelter," Flavio said, his voice soft and reasonable but with the air of a man repeating himself, "but we need you to go around to the kitchen entrance. You can't come in *this* way, little mother," he urged with gentle firmness.

"But it's so cold out there," the woman argued loudly, "and so dark! I'd never find my way in this storm, and who's to say your kitchen will let me in? Please let me stay *here* where it's warm!" She looked about wildly, and Ezio flinched as her rheumy eyes landed on him and took in his rich clothes and royal jewels.

"Here, I'll escort you myself." Flavio sighed, stoically resigned to escorting the woman through the rain, but she was staring intently at Ezio and seemed not to hear him. Flavio reached out to take her by the arm and guide her outside, but with a burst of energy, she jerked away from his outstretched hand and lurched forward to grasp at Ezio's arm. The prince pulled back in disgust, but the old woman was surprisingly deft and clutched at his sleeve with her dirty gnarled fingers.

"You, sir, good lord," she pleaded, smiling up at him with a mouth filled with rotting black teeth. She struggled to lower herself into a kneeling position, and her iron grip on his sleeve pulled him down so that he was forced to lean over her as she knelt in supplication. Ezio tried again to pull away, but to his astonishment found he could not. Flavio shook off his surprise and sprung forward to take the old woman by the shoulders to wrest her away from the prince, but the moment he touched her twisted back, she shrieked in pain and Flavio quickly pulled his hands back as if burned.

The scuffle had not gone unnoticed by the dinner party; Ezio could hear gasps of shock mingled with peals of high, nervous laughter from his guests in the hall. He felt blood rush to his face in embarrassment, followed by a deep rage at being so thoroughly humiliated in front of his guests. Oblivious, the grime-caked woman plunged ahead with her supplication. "Please, good lord, give me shelter from the storm," she begged in her shrill whine, smiling expectantly up at the tall man helplessly leaning over her.

"Unhand me," he hissed at the woman. He tugged his arm back again, but she stubbornly gripped at the fabric and he could not pull free.

"Please, good lord—" she whined again, repeating her plea, but Ezio felt a rising panic and could stand no more. With his free hand, he struck the woman hard across her face. She cried out in a feral yelp of pain and dropped his arm, crawling backward away from him and kneeling so deeply in supplication that her face touched the floor rugs.

"Prince Ezio!" a voice shouted behind him in alarm. Ezio recognized the voice of his father's old advisor Guerrino, but could hardly hear for the roar of blood that pounded in his ears as he glared at the prostrate woman. Furiously, he wiped his filth-stained hand on the shoulder of his ruined sleeve and struggled to collect his temper.

Her pleading voice rose up to him, muffled by the weight of the carpets, "In the name of charity, please give me shelter," she begged. Even muted by the rugs, her nasal voice grated on his nerves, as did her insolence when she dared suggest, "If you cannot afford me charity, I beg you give me honest work in your home as payment for lodging."

Time seemed to slow in that moment. Ezio could see Flavio, still standing uselessly by the castle doors, struck dumb by the strangeness of the situation. He could feel his guests behind him, and sensed their disapproval at this disgusting intrusion and their mockery at seeing him in this ridiculous situation. He could hear Guerrino running towards him, his meddlesome help utterly unwelcome unless he could somehow magic the beggar woman away, and her mud and stench along with her. Ezio could make out the watery eyes of the old woman as she peered up at him through the thin curtain of her dirty hair, waiting for his reply.

"Payment?" he sneered at her, his voice booming through the hall. "You could labor for the rest of your life and not begin to cover the expense you've caused!" He gestured expansively, taking in his smeared silk sleeve and the caked muck on his rich floor rugs. "Get out!" he ordered, pointing to the castle doors, "Get out and stay out! A night's sleep in the rain may at least scrub the filth off you!"

Out of the corner of his eye, the prince could see Guerrino skid to a halt at his side, panting from the exertion of running the length of the hall. The agitated advisor immediately began an incoherent babble between gasps for breath, *oh no please stay no no he didn't mean please madam please stay*, but before Ezio could react to this bizarre behavior, his attention snapped back to the old woman. No longer cowering fearfully on the floor, she had rocked back on her heels and was actually *laughing* at him. Her laughter was deeper than Ezio would have expected from such a small woman and as her mocking peals rolled over him, Ezio was convinced she must be insane. He took an apprehensive step backward — it wasn't safe to stand so close to a mad woman — but she gestured sharply, and he found himself rooted to the ground, unable to move.

"No, my little prince, I don't want you running off just yet." Her mouth moved in time to the words, but the voice was strangely foreign to the prince. Deep and sibilant, it belonged to a much larger creature than this frail old woman, and was laden with an accent so thick and unfamiliar that it was a moment before Ezio could understand the words. In a single fluid motion, the woman rose from the floor and stood tall and straight before him. Her entire body — her papery skin, her stringy hair, her tattered clothes — shimmered and glowed with an unnatural light. Ezio gaped in astonishment as pieces of her began to flake off and fall from her body, the little thin wafers disappearing before they touched the ground. Beneath the flakes, where there had been black mud and drab skin, there shone through vivid bursts of color: verdant greens, dark crimsons, and deep browns.

As fragments of the old woman swirled in the air like dry leaves, a new shape began to take form before Ezio's astonished eyes. It was a woman, but unlike any that he had ever seen. She was at least a head taller than himself, and she stared down at him with an imposing countenance that somehow combined cold anger and childish amusement into a single expression. She was clad simply in a loose green gown, but the material shone in the torchlight as though the cloth were really thousands of tiny emeralds. Dark vines stood out against her deep olive skin and climbed over her dress and down her arms like sleeves, each vine sporting dozens of thick red roses and bright green thorns. Her face was unlined and smooth, but her bearing was too harsh to be lovely and she seemed anything but young. She looked wild and untamed, like an ancient goddess of the forest.

Ezio was still frozen to the spot, but beside him Guerrino seemed to have regained some of his composure. He bowed deeply before the strange apparition and when he spoke, his voice trembled apprehensively. "Good mistress *fata*," he began respectfully, "Please forgive this grave misunderstanding—"

The woman cut him off with a sharp gesture, and the old man's mouth clamped shut with an audible click of teeth. Ezio felt a shiver scramble over his spine as he realized that her imperious gaze had never left his face, and that her eyes were bright with excitement. "Prince," she addressed him loudly in that deeply accented voice, "you have failed my test of character." She gestured contemptuously to his guests in the hall behind him; from the complete silence, he supposed they must be frozen from either magic or terror. "You play the host for your rich friends, but you turn away those most in need of your charity. You complain of the expense of the poor while you revel in your own riches."

Her expression darkened, and Ezio trembled as he remembered that he had struck this powerful creature. Slowly, with a show of consideration, she plucked from the vines covering her arms a single sharp thorn. The *fata* stepped forward gracefully until she stood over Ezio and he found himself staring helplessly up into her haughty face. She raised a hand to his face, and cupped his left cheek with her cool fingers. Her touch was almost tender, but then a sharp pain shot through him as she pressed the thorn into the flesh of his cheek. The thorn dug deeply into his face, but the pain spread through his entire body: a strange sensation that ran cold through his veins and left him feeling deeply nauseous. Triumphantly, the woman stepped back from him and the spell that had rooted him so firmly to the ground left with her. Unable to stand, Ezio collapsed to his knees, his palms pressed into the rug and his stomach heaving violently.

"For your crime, I curse you, prince," the *fata* intoned softly, her voice twining like vines into his ears. *"You shall take a form as beastly without as you are within."* The coldness that had shot through his veins turned to fire. Sweat stood out on his skin and he felt a burning pain spread through him to the tips of his hands and feet. He felt an overwhelming urge to scratch his arms: if he could just scratch away all his skin, then the heat would leave him and he could be cool again. Driven by compulsion, he raked his fingers down his left arm and was astonished to see how long and sharp his nails had suddenly become. They were sharp enough to cut through his sleeve at the elbow and puncture his skin, but as his nails dug into his arm he felt no pain and no blood welled up. Instead, the skin peeled away as easily as the shreds of his silk sleeve, and beneath the skin was a thick mat of coarse hair.

Shock and confusion sent him into a frenzy. He dug and tore at his arms, his legs, and his scalp with the strange claws that extended wickedly from the tips of his fingers. Everywhere he scratched, clothing and skin peeled away to reveal thick animal hair matted over a tough hide. Still the hot pain flowing through his body did not cease; Ezio writhed on the ground in agony as he felt his bones crack and shift into new formations. Mindlessly, he felt the strangeness of new joints and could not understand the sensation of weight that descended upon him.

Her voice cut through the haze of pain, seeming as much in his head as it was in the air around him. He felt the burning recede as she commanded, "You must find that love which is willing to sacrifice everything."

His eyes had been clenched shut; Ezio opened them warily and looked around in shock. He lay sprawled on the floor of the hall, lying on his back before his tormentor. The hall was subtly changed to his eyes: it was smaller, narrower. His brother Flavio had backed against the castle doors and was staring at him in undisguised horror. He swiveled his head to stare at his guests, but the moment he turned in their direction, the entire company panicked; several of the women shrieked or fainted, and at least half the men took off in the opposite direction at a full run down the hall. Only Guerrino seemed unafraid: he stood at the side of the hall, shaking his head slowly as though trying to wake himself from a dream. Ezio looked back up at the woman and though she still towered over the room, he was confused to see that she, too, seemed subtly smaller. Then he looked down at himself and, as his mind registered what it saw, he began to scream in terror.

His body was no longer human. He was covered from head to toe in coarse brown animal hair. His arms and legs were longer, and his legs lay jointed deeply at the knees, as though he were a goat or a satyr stepped from one of his classical tapestries. Where his feet had been were now horse hooves; his furry hands still ended in fingers, but deadly claws extended where his neatly-trimmed nails had once been. Within his peripheral vision he could see that his nose had elongated into a strange snout, almost like a jaguar, but with small boar tusks protruding on either side of his mouth. Even Ezio's screams were inhuman, a terrifying mixture of a cat's screech and a pig's squeal.

The *fata* began to move her hands in a complex series of gestures. Ezio immediately fell silent, but he realized after a moment that the silence was produced only by his own fear and not by any magic. Helplessly, he wondered what new spell was being worked as a strange tickling sensation swept over him, but when his gaze darted around the hall and over his own bizarre body, nothing had changed. The woman finished her elaborate movements and smiled coldly down at him. "Without such love made manifest," she said with an air of cold finality, "before the last estate-rose dies, a beast you shall remain."

With a triumphant smile, the *fata* flung up her arm in a final flourish and her entire body exploded in a shower of red rose petals. As the petals floated slowly to the ground, Ezio realized that she was gone. A painful emptiness washed over him; the overwhelming feeling that everything was horribly wrong and if he could just wake up from this nightmare, then it would somehow be all right again. He felt himself faint from shock, and as he lapsed into unconsciousness his last thought was that he didn't *have* any roses on his estate.

Chapter 3 - Guerrino

Guerrino saw the *fata* vanish in a shower of rose petals, and knew he could not be dreaming. His mind would never have been creative enough to supply the detail of the petals, fluttering gently in the wake of such violence. The prince, horribly changed, lay sprawled on the hall floor in a deep faint. He looked for all the world like a strange amalgamation of animals, and was completely covered in thick hair beneath the tattered remnants of his clothing.

Behind him, Guerrino could hear the rush and clamor as the guests fled in panic to their rooms. He quickly realized how easily that fear could turn to violence. Any violence directed towards the prince could easily spill over on to nearby scapegoats like himself. *"I need to get the prince out of the hallway,"* he thought, his panic rising. If they were both hidden away, there was a chance they would not be looked for.

"Help me," he ordered the trembling Captain of the Guard, as Guerrino knelt to slip his arms under the prince's heavy shoulders. The younger man, barely out of boyhood, only stared at him in mute incomprehension. "We have to get him out of here," Guerrino urged. He tugged at the prince's prostrate form in demonstration, but the useless boy merely shook his head in terror, backed out of the castle into the rain, and darted off into the night.

Guerrino sighed in frustration and tugged at the prince more forcefully. The prince had not been light as a human man, and the addition of a thick coat of fur, heavy hooves, and boar tusks had not made him grow any lighter. Fortunately, Guerrino had been a strong man before his life with the royal family, and age and easy living had not softened him too much. With a great deal of pulling, and stopping for a few short breaks, he managed to drag the sleeping prince into the side hallway that led to the stairs of Guerrino's personal tower. He met no one along the way; the shrieks and clamor drifting through the drafty walls seemed confined to the guest chambers and servant quarters.

At the foot of the tower stairs, he laid the prince out on the hall floor and paused to catch his breath. Guerrino decided he could not drag the sleeping prince up the spiral staircase without one or both of them getting seriously hurt; the climb was too steep and the stairs too sharply cut. As he evaluated their tenuous situation, he noticed the prince stir fitfully on the stone floor. He aimed a tentative kick at the prince's leg and the prince's eyes flew open in panicked response.

In the dim hallway, Guerrino was disconcerted to note that even the prince's eyes had changed. The pupils had expanded so that his eyes were almost completely black, ringed by only the smallest sliver of their previous brown coloring. Those black eyes glinted in the weak light of the hallway, making the prince look wild and unhinged. "Your Highness must come with me," Guerrino ordered in a stern voice, and the prince was too befuddled to do anything but obey him. Clumsily, he staggered to his new feet, and Guerrino ushered him into the stairwell.

The two men climbed the stairs silently and with great difficulty. The prince's clawed fingers dug into the stone walls for support, and Guerrino kept his hand on his back to steady him. Twice, the prince's hooves slipped on the steep stairs and he stumbled; the second time, his claws swung out instinctively and nearly raked Guerrino across the chest. Trembling with exertion and fear, Guerrino coaxed him into taking the steps on all fours and that went better.

When they reached the top of the stairs, Guerrino slid around the prince to open the wooden door to his chambers. He ushered the young man into the room and the exhausted prince collapsed into a faint on the floor. Guerrino stepped over the inert form and barred the door. He placed his fingers firmly on the wooden bar and concentrated. *"What power is in me, so seal this entrance,"* he pleaded, pouring as much raw power as he could muster in his exhausted state. Once he was sure it would take a battering ram to budge the wooden planks, he gingerly moved over to his bed and lay down fully clothed. He glumly hoped that he could gather his energy before the eventual search party was organized, but he wasn't optimistic.

Guerrino shifted on to his side. In the dim light of the guttering candles he scowled at the misshapen prince. When he'd promised Prince Domenico that he would look after his son, Guerrino hadn't imagined the boy would be stupid enough to bring something like this on his own head. After Domenico had saved Guerrino from the noose and brought him to his court to practice his craft in safety, Guerrino had done his best to earn his keep. He had dispensed advice to his benefactor and his son, and taught them what he could of the invisible world and of the spirits that could bring them help or harm. *"Clearly, the oaf didn't listen to my teachings,"* he thought sullenly, glaring at the prince. Guerrino could not fathom what had caused him to strike the *fata*, but he seemed lucky to have escaped with all his limbs intact, even if they *were* greatly changed.

"I thought after Domenico died I might retire to the country," Guerrino thought mournfully. That dream was shattered; he was now in more danger than ever before. He had managed to build a respectable reputation in the elder prince's household as an advisor but now that magic had struck the castle, people with long memories would recall his questionable past. He sighed and closed his eyes, but sleep would not come. Every sound that

floated up from the castle below caused his muscles to tense as he waited for the end.

As the candles died out into the night to be replaced by the rosy glow of dawn, Guerrino began to realize with relief that he had been overly cautious. The dreaded knock on the tower door never came, and the only activity in the castle seemed to be that of people fleeing as quickly as possible, with as many of their possessions — and, he guessed, as many of the *prince's* possessions — as they dared stop to pack. Unless his ears deceived him, the first of the carriages rattled hastily out of the stone courtyard almost as soon as the storm gave way to sunrise. This departure triggered a wave of desertion as each panicked voice below vowed not to be the last to leave.

From the tower window, Guerrino cautiously watched the last of the guests leaving in the cold morning light. The stillness that descended on the castle convinced him that he and the prince were completely alone. The ground was a morass of mud and fallen branches, but no one had wanted to stay long enough for the roads to dry. From his vantage point in the tower, he could see two carriages stuck fast and he smiled thinly at the sight of the beleaguered drivers laboring to pull their heavy coaches out of the deep mud. No doubt the castle servants spreading out over the estate lawn on foot would find employ in the services of the stranded nobles, as it would be cheaper to hire a score of servants to *push* the carriage home than to abandon the expensive vehicle on the road.

He squinted into the sunlight and realized with astonishment what the final spell of the *fata* had wrought: a tall, unbroken hedge of dark thorns and thick brambles now ringed the edges of the estate. The hedge was covered in a thick profusion of roses, and pushed against the tree line of the forest that stood between the valley and the outside world. The sight was stunningly beautiful; hundreds of bright red roses sparkled with dew in the morning light. It would be impossible to count the vibrant blossoms, but Guerrino eyed them sadly, wondering how long it would be before the last rose died. Even if he hadn't heard the curse of the *fata* or felt her parting spell sweep over the estate, he could have had no doubts as to the origin of the roses, for only magic could produce such flawless flowers, to say nothing of their rapid overnight growth. *"They represent the limit of his time,"* he thought glumly. Such were the ways of the *fata*.

He wondered anxiously how the departing guests would get through the rose bushes, and if he should warn them against damaging the blossoms, but relaxed after a moment's consideration. The superstitious guests and servants were already terrified that merely staying another night in the castle would bring curses on their own heads. Certainly they would avoid disturbing plants so clearly grown with fairy magic, and would carefully pick their way through the single opening where the road ran through the thick hedge.

A low moan sounded behind him and Guerrino turned from the window to see the sleeping prince stir fitfully. The creature moved jerkily, and again came that strange moan: not quite feline, not quite porcine, but definitely not human. Guerrino hesitated to disturb him, but he felt alone in the abandoned castle, and imagined that now was as good a time as any to wake the young man.

"Your Highness?" he called softly, backing a little further away from the restless form. Those claws were deadly, and he didn't want to be on the receiving end if the prince suddenly started lashing out at nightmares. "Your Highness," he urged a little louder, and the young man moaned again, stirred, and slowly opened those wild eyes.

"Where ... where am I?" the prince asked in dazed confusion, as he pushed his spindly body from the stone floor and managed slowly to bring himself to his feet. Guerrino noticed that the sleepy young man seemed to be moving entirely on instinct; his movements were far from graceful, but were definitely more fluid than they had been last night during their struggle up the tower stairs.

"You're in my room, Your Highness," Guerrino offered cautiously, still keeping his distance. Drawn up to his full height on those thin goat-like legs, the prince was now two heads taller than Guerrino. His waist, arms, and legs had all lengthened significantly, and his muscles ran like thick cords over thinned bones and under coarse hair. Guerrino guessed that a single swipe of those long claws could disembowel him; a closed punch would probably kill him outright.

"I ... Your room ..." The prince's voice trailed off in confusion. Distractedly, he touched his throat with the flat of his fingers, as though he could not understand why his voice sounded so deep and full of gravel. His black eyes wandered the room restlessly until they fell upon a shaving mirror that Guerrino kept by a basin near the far window. The prince stumbled awkwardly toward the little mirror, but even from a distance he could see his strangely changed reflection staring back at him. He whirled around to face Guerrino, eyes wide with panic. "My dream!" he howled in despair.

To Guerrino's relief, the prince dealt with this distressing realization by sinking slowly on to the floor and wrapping his arms over his head. Rocking back and forth, with deer-like ears poking between his folded arms, the young man looked touchingly vulnerable. *"He doesn't understand what has happened,"* Guerrino thought, moved to a touch of pity for the miserable young man. "Your Highness," Guerrino said softly. His voice trailed off; he couldn't think of anything useful to say. He stepped closer to the poor creature, one hand reaching out to touch his shoulder comfortingly. "It will be all right," he offered, lamely.

"All right?" The prince's head shot up and swung around to scowl at him. His eyes were narrowed with sudden rage and his voice was like the deep guttural growl of an angry cat. He struggled to his feet, and Guerrino had to tilt his neck uncomfortably to maintain eye contact with the towering creature. Claws spread, the prince gestured at his own terrifying form and demanded, "How is *this* going to be 'all right'?"

Guerrino stared at the prince, silently seething. *"Fine. You are a spoiled ingrate with no one to blame but yourself and you are most likely stuck this way. Is that what you want to hear?"* He had to bite his lower lip to keep from voicing his immediate reaction; snapping at the young man would not be the wisest course of action. He briefly considered backing away from the prince, but immediately decided that this show of submission would only fuel the prince's agitation.

Fervently hoping he was not making a mistake, he adopted his firmest voice and said, "Your Highness, remember your childhood lessons. Do you recall my teachings that *fata* walk the earth cursing mortals who offend them?" This was uncomfortably close to blame, but his scholarly tone produced the desired effect. The prince's animal face furrowed in concentration and he nodded slowly. "Anyone can be cursed," Guerrino continued in gentler tone, "for almost any reason, but the curse always has a counter-curse: a way to return everything to its natural state."

His words jolted the prince out of a trance. Those black animal eyes went wide with excitement, and he stepped forward uncertainly on wobbling hooves. "You mean everything can go back to normal?" he asked, his excited voice carrying an undercurrent of pleading.

Guerrino grimaced with irritation. *Now* the boy wanted to be told that everything would be all right. He answered cautiously, "If we can figure out the counter-curse to your curse, yes. The process is not usually simple, though." The prince's face fell — obviously he'd been expecting some immediate solution — and he sank glumly back to the stone floor, his long arms wrapped around his knees. Guerrino hesitated and added, "The counter-curse is laid out in the language of the curse. Therefore we will write down the language of the curse as nearly as we can remember it."

Guerrino moved briskly towards his worktable, hoping to convey with his body language a feeling of purpose. *"At the very least, it will give him something to focus on,"* Guerrino thought. He carefully opened the grimoire that lay on his worktable, and flipped to the empty pages at the back. The prince rose to his feet unsteadily and slowly came to stand behind Guerrino so that he could watch over his shoulder. Seeming lost for something to do, the young royal reached out his fingers to the edge of the open page, but after a despairing frown at his elongated claws, he awkwardly tucked his arms behind his back in a comical posture of study. As though it were the most natural thing in the world, Guerrino picked up a slender quill and inscribed in long, neat letters:

You shall take a form as beastly without as you are within.

You must find that love which is willing to sacrifice everything.

Without such love made manifest before the estate-roses die, a beast you shall remain.

When he had finished writing, the prince stood in silence for such a long time that Guerrino finally cleared his throat and said promptingly, "I believe that was the substance of it."

"I think so too," the prince said quietly and Guerrino turned to see that his eyes were closed in concentration, his head cocked slightly to the side as if listening to some faraway sound. He suddenly broke from his reverie, his eyes flying wide open with excitement. "But don't you see?" he urged cheerfully, "This is perfect!" Guerrino frowned in confusion as the prince continued excitedly, "We were just about to announce my engagement to Adelina. All we have to do is move forward with the wedding as planned."

"Your Highness," Guerrino said slowly, hating to interrupt. The prince's excitement was so brittle that it could snap into a rage at any moment. "Your Highness, I don't think that Adelina's family is still interested in the marriage."

The prince stared at him, his face frozen in an excited smile that was especially disturbing on that beastly face; sharp teeth were visible under the feline nose and extruding tusks. "What?" he asked Guerrino, his voice sharp with denial. "No, that's impossible. Her parents want my titles and Adelina will understand once you explain the curse to her. Then we'll fall in love and everything will go back to normal."

"Lady Adelina and her family," Guerrino said, emphasizing the words carefully, "left the castle this morning, at sunrise." He braced himself for another emotional outburst, but the prince only seemed perplexed by this announcement.

"They're gone?" he asked, wonderingly. "I didn't ..." his voice trailed off. "Well," he said finally, speaking hesitatingly, "the curse didn't say it had to be Adelina, right?" Guerrino nodded cautiously. "That's fine, then," the prince decided briskly, "I'll just have to marry one of the servants. It's a drastic step, but probably the best option under the circumstances."

It was all Guerrino could do to not press his hand to his forehead to massage the headache that was forming under his temples. He was certain that the innocent gesture would be taken as a sign of exasperation by the agitated prince. With a composed tone, hoping he wouldn't sound as frustrated as he felt, he said, "Your Highness, all the servants have left along with the guests." The prince blinked at him, uncomprehending. "We're alone," Guerrino said bluntly.

The prince's eyes widened as he considered the implications of this announcement. When he spoke, his voice held an edge of panic. "What do we do?" he asked quietly. All the haughtiness had fled from his voice, and now there was only fear. "Do we ... should *we* leave, too?" he asked.

"You can't leave," Guerrino said, as gently as he could. "Anyone you met, in your current state, you must understand ..." His voice trailed away. The prince stared at him with blank eyes. "You'd be viewed as a monster," Guerrino finished awkwardly. "You'd be killed."

"A monster ..." the prince murmured, and he ducked his neck, crouching into his body as though to make himself smaller. He began to pace the room in panicky little steps. Suddenly he stopped and turned to Guerrino, pleading, "So we just stay here? Alone?" His voice was almost bleating with fear. "How will we survive?"

Guerrino stared at the prince sadly. He had been asking himself that question all night long, even as he coaxed the prince up the stairs, while he barred the doorway with wood and magic, and as he'd wracked his brain trying to remember the *fata's* curse as accurately as possible. Suddenly very tired, he walked over to the bed and sank down onto it, resting his arms on his knees and dropping his head into his hands. He could feel the pleading eyes following him. *"He's on the verge of hysteria,"* Guerrino realized.

This wasn't the life Guerrino had planned. When Domenico died, he'd hoped to live out the rest of his life comfortably with a pension from the young prince, maybe even moving away to a country cottage under a new name. In a single night, all his plans had been undone, and now his future looked bleak. Even if he ignored his debt to Domenico in favor of pragmatism, where would he go? He was no longer strong enough to earn his living as a field hand or hired servant, and he didn't dare return to a life of living by wits and magic. *"One shot at the hangman's noose was enough,"* he thought ruefully. If it weren't for the curse, he could have found a place in another royal household, but no one would be his benefactor after last night's debacle.

He looked up at the prince, who was once again sitting despondently on the floor with his head in his arms. Wearily, Guerrino weighed the prince's own options. The young man couldn't possibly leave; he'd be eventually seen and then hunted like an animal. Nor could he stay on his own. Even if the servants hadn't raided the castle larder, there hadn't been much left after the harsh winter, and Guerrino was doubtful that the prince could forage enough to survive. *"Even with only one person to feed, the stores will run out fast,"* he thought.

Guerrino gazed out the tower window. The roses were still there, winking at him in the morning sunlight. The thought crept into his mind that the situation could last only so long: either the prince would find a lover to break the curse, or the time limit would run out. *"If we can trap a woman here and coax her into falling in love ..."* He glanced at the prince again, and doubts swirled in his mind. Yet if they could, the curse would be broken and the prince would be restored to himself. His claim on the land would be honored, and Guerrino could have an assurance that he would be provided for. And if not ... Guerrino chewed on his lip, considering his alternatives and weighing the danger represented in those sharp claws. *"I can always leave later,"* he decided. And it would be much easier to leave when the prince had calmed down somewhat.

He rose to his feet and the prince looked up at him with wet black eyes. "It will be all right," Guerrino said firmly, echoing his earlier attempt at comfort. "We will stay here at the castle together, and wait for an opportunity to break the curse. A woman will come to the castle eventually — if nothing else, the beggars can't stay away forever — and when one does, we'll be ready."

Relief was visibly etched on the prince's beastly face at this announcement, but still he hesitated. "What will we do in the meantime, for ... for food and things?" he asked plaintively.

Guerrino pursed his lips in frustration. He supposed a 'thank you' would have been too much to expect from the prince. He pushed his irritation away; it would do no good right now to dwell on his ingratitude.

He walked tiredly over to his workbench where his grimoire still lay open. "Fortunately, Your Highness," he said stiffly, "I know quite a bit of magic."

Chapter 4 - Bella

Bella gingerly touched the dark circles under her eyes and frowned. Her reflection in the mirror frowned back at her and she quickly reverted to a neutral expression to smooth out her creased brow. *"Bad enough that the storm disturbed your sleep enough to leave those dark circles,"* she chided herself automatically. *"There's no need to compound the problem with an ugly scowl."*

She reached for the tin of cosmetic powder on the vanity table, but noticed as she removed the lid that the tin was nearly empty. She sighed and mentally added cosmetic powder to the growing list of things she needed to ask Father to buy, once she could catch him in a good mood. Briefly she wondered if she should forgo the powder today and stretch her supply, but if she was going to ask Father for favors, it was all the more important to be as pretty and pleasing as possible. With the tip of her finger, she dug out what powder she could and spread the light substance under her eyes before carefully replacing the cover and setting the tin back on the table.

Bella fought the urge to chew her lip, reminding herself that she was trying to break that habit. The list of items she was running out of was growing quite long. Yet every time she had tried to broach the subject, Father had made it clear that he was not in the mood to listen. *"He's been so cheerful since Venizia paid off his debts,"* she thought doubtfully but, even with him calling her his 'little princess' again and laughing all the time, he still seemed distant.

It was nice to see Father smile again, but Bella had expected that his remarriage would return everything to the way it had been four years ago, when Mother had been alive. Back then, the family had accounts with the village stores and Father paid the bills without question. When Mother died from the winter illness that had left her weak for months, Father sank into debt and depression. Their accounts had been closed, but he and Bella had gotten through the worst of it. Now that finances were back on a solid footing, Bella couldn't understand why things hadn't gone back to the way she remembered them.

"Isabella!" The call came from somewhere down the hall, in what Bella was beginning to recognize as her new stepmother's no-nonsense tone. She pursed her lips in annoyance and decided not to respond. Deliberately, she began to brush her hair, trying to decide whether to braid it or leave it loose. "Isabella?" The voice was closer now. *"I'll braid it,"* Bella decided firmly, blocking out the noise. The air was so thick from last night's rain that, if she didn't pull her hair back soon, it would be curled and tangled by evening.

There was a light knock on her door before Venizia strode into the room. Through the reflection in the mirror, Bella saw her stepmother enter but she didn't turn around to acknowledge the intrusion. Instead, she drew a long ribbon from the drawer of her dressing-table and began carefully braiding it through her thick honey-blonde hair. "Isabella?" her stepmother asked in her lightly accented voice. "Are you all right? I called, but you didn't hear me." Venizia's tone was polite, but skeptical.

Bella met her stepmother's gaze through the mirror's reflection. "I didn't realize you were calling for *me*," she said simply, with a light shrug. Casually, she returned her gaze to her own reflection as she concentrated on weaving the ribbon through her hair. Her hair was so much like Mother's, long and thick. *"I wonder if Father will even notice that I'm wearing one of Mother's gowns today,"* she thought sadly.

Her stepmother frowned in irritation, and Bella studied Venizia from the corner of her eye. She was fairly certain that Father loved Venizia for more than just her fortune, but she hadn't figured out what had compelled her father to marry the wealthy widow so soon after meeting her on one of his trade visits to the city. *"I wonder if he likes her because she looks so different from Mother?"* she thought. Venizia was lovely in her own way, as were her daughters, but her deep black skin was a sharp contrast to Bella's own paleness.

"Excuse me, *Bella*," Venizia said, carefully enunciating the sobriquet. "I am sorry. I forgot that you prefer not to be called '*Isabella*'."

The apology was stiff and tinted with obvious exasperation, but Bella felt that she owed it to her father to be gracious to his new wife. She smiled and acknowledged the correction by turning around to face her stepmother. "Can I help you?" she asked politely.

Venizia hesitated for a moment, while Bella held her smile in place and tried not to sigh impatiently. The ends of her unfinished braid hung loose down her back, and she could feel the whole thing beginning to unravel. *"I'll have to start all over again once Venizia leaves,"* she realized.

"Your father has business in the village today, but he says he has an important announcement to make tonight at dinner," Venizia said, a little briskly. "He asked me to make sure that the whole family will be at the table."

"Oh." Bella blinked in surprise. That was unusual; ever since he started working again, Father rarely made it to dinner, and he wasn't especially given to formal announcements. Her stepmother seemed to be lingering for some kind of answer, and Bella found herself filling the awkward silence. "I wasn't planning to stay late in the village today. I'll just make a few quick social calls and be home in plenty of time for dinner." Her voice trailed off and she wondered why she was volunteering any of this. It certainly wasn't Venizia's concern how she spent her time.

"Thank you," Venizia said with a hint of warmth and a tiny smile. "I'm sure your father will be pleased." She turned to leave, but paused at the door. She looked back at Bella, and raised a hand to absent-mindedly push her dark curls away from her face. "Bella," she asked tentatively, "Would you like me to braid your hair for you?"

Her smile was kind, but Bella was so surprised by the unexpected offer that all she could do was shake her head. Venizia smiled again, a little awkwardly, and left, closing the door gently behind her.

Bella waited until her stepmother was gone before turning back to the mirror and beginning the process of brushing out her hair and braiding it again. Butterflies churned her stomach as she worked her fingers through the snarls in her hair. What could Father possibly have to say to them that would justify a formal dinner announcement? And why couldn't he tell his news without theatrics? The only announcement Bella could ever remember him making was two months ago, when he'd cheerfully informed her that he was planning to marry a woman she'd never met. She yanked out a snarl and thought darkly, *"I hope he's not planning to make these little surprises some sort of habit."*

The thought struck her that Venizia might be pregnant, but after a horrified moment she decided against it. Venizia was younger than Father, but with two grown daughters already, Bella guessed she wasn't quite young enough to conceive again. At least, she hoped not; it was hard enough to suddenly share Father with two new stepsisters, let alone with an infant brother or sister. She sighed in frustration and set the brush down firmly on the vanity. She would just have to put up with the anxiety until tonight.

"Probably the announcement is something completely unimportant," she consoled herself. Maybe Father had found a suitor for Marchetta. Goodness knew the sour girl would need any help he could give. In the short time Bella had known her older stepsister, the serious girl had shown no interest whatsoever in any of the eligible men in the village, despite being more than old enough to wed.

Bella tied her braid and examined her work in the mirror. Wearing the faded blue gown that had been her mother's and with her honey-colored hair tied back in that way, she imagined she looked like her mother's portrait, the one that Father had kept in a locket until he accidentally sold it off with the rest of the jewelry. She patted back a loose strand and smiled at her reflection. With her creamy skin and bright smile, her friends had no trouble remembering her nickname, *Bella*. The boys had teasingly called her *bella-the-beautiful* as children, but now her childhood name was used with varying degrees of shy stutters and awkward glances. *"Maybe a suitor isn't such a bad idea,"* she thought absently, her thoughts trailing back to Marchetta and Father's mysterious announcement. *"I could find a nice one for myself..."* Her thoughts trailed off as the butterflies started up again. Surely Father wouldn't arrange a match for *her* without speaking privately to her first. Would he?

A few years ago she would have laughed at the idea. Father had never pressured her, not even when their debts were at the worst and more than a few of the men in the village would have paid a good bride-price for her. But now she wasn't so sure. *"He's been sweet words and kind smiles again since the wedding,"* she thought doubtfully, *"but he still flies into a rage at the slightest request."* Several times in the past year he'd accused her of being an ungrateful daughter, a millstone around his neck. She had become accustomed to his moodiness and was hoping to ride out these dark suspicions, but what if it was too late?

Bella shook her head and put on her best smile again. Worrying wouldn't do anything but put creases in her eyes, and a quick jaunt to the village would make her feel better. She slipped her feet into her shoes and wrapped a shawl around her shoulders to protect against the damp air. As an afterthought, she grabbed her small purse, wishing she actually had coins to fill it. *"Maybe I can talk the merchants into opening an account for me while I work on improving Father's mood,"* she mused.

As she stepped out of the house into the cool morning air, she was surprised to see Father still in the yard, struggling with the saddle on his mule. "Bella!" he bellowed with his usual loud cheer. He tugged the saddle strap tighter and stepped away with a satisfied nod. "How is my lovely little princess this morning?" he asked, opening his arms for a hug.

Bella smiled guardedly and picked her way through the damp grass to hug her father. "I'm very well today, thank you," she said with more warmth than she felt. "And you, Father?"

"I couldn't be better," he said heartily. "Your mother has cooked me the most delectable breakfast and now I'm off to the village on business," he said with a conspiratorial wink.

"So I heard," Bella said guardedly, politely ignoring the reference to Venizia as her 'mother'. Nor would she challenge Father's fancy that Venizia was the one doing the cooking and not the servants she had hired when she moved in. "Perhaps I could walk with you? I'd love to keep you company," she suggested sweetly. *"Maybe we can talk on the way to the village,"* Bella thought wistfully.

"I'm in a hurry," he refused abruptly. He drew back from her and stared at her with a frown while she fidgeted uncomfortably under his gaze. "Why are *you* going into the village?" he asked suspiciously. "Shopping or suitors?"

"Neither," Bella lied, laughing as lightly as she could. She smiled reassuringly, wishing she could disappear back into the house. "I'm overdue to return a few social calls," she offered. She hoped her explanation would smooth over the tension, but he continued to frown at her.

"Take Marchetta with you," he finally said, turning away from her to fuss with the mule again. His voice had a stern note to it; his curt statement sounded more like an order than a suggestion.

"Marchetta?" she repeated in surprise. "But she doesn't ... she won't want—"

"Then stay home!" He cut her off angrily. "There's no need for you to go into town just to jabber with your friends." He climbed into the saddle with some difficulty and kicked the mule. He rode away at a light trot without glancing back at her.

Bella stared after him, feeling her throat constrict and her eyes prick with tears. *"Don't cry,"* she thought furiously. *"It ruins your complexion."* It would only make Father more upset if he saw her red-faced and puffy-eyed at tonight's dinner. Besides, she couldn't break down in front of the strangers living in her home: Venizia and Marchetta and Fiorita and the house servants whose names she couldn't even remember. She wiped her eyes on the corner of her shawl and took a few deep breaths.

"*Pull yourself together,*" she thought sternly. "*It's not the first time Father has been in a bad mood.*" She took a deep breath, and imagined counting all her fingers and toes until her heart stopped pounding so quickly. Everything was going to be fine, she reassured herself. She just needed to convince him that she wasn't his enemy, that she loved him more than anyone else ever could. How she was to accomplish this, though, she couldn't begin to imagine.

The thought struck her that she wouldn't be able to ask him for anything, not for a long time. Bella ran through her mental list of immediate needs and started to panic. She really couldn't go without her cosmetics, and certainly not if she wanted to land a suitor quickly. If she couldn't ask Father for the money, she would have to ask the village merchants to open an account for her. Her thought trailed off as a new idea popped up in its place. "*Father isn't the only one in the house who has money,*" Bella realized suddenly. The trick would be getting that money without Father finding out.

She watched the empty road for a long moment before wiping her eyes one more time and walking resolutely back into the house.

Chapter 5 - Marchetta

Marchetta counted off with increasing satisfaction the mental list of things she needed to accomplish, while she climbed the stairs with an empty laundry basket on her hip. In the weeks since they had moved in with Cienzo and his daughter, she'd managed to rearrange the almost unused kitchen to her liking and had found a cook that seemed acceptably skilled, as well as a kitchen boy for running errands and washing dishes, and a laundress who came by once a week to take away the dirty clothes and leave behind the clean ones from the previous week. In light of Mama's request that tonight's dinner be appropriate for an announcement that Cienzo was planning to make, she had asked the cook to put on a roast, and she was fairly confident that the meat would be tender by dinner-time.

"Not that the household is fussy," Marchetta admitted wryly to herself as she stepped into the second floor hallway. Mama and Fiorita would eat

whatever she served, and she doubted that Cienzo or his 'little princess' would deign to complain about anything she put in front of them. Still, she had her standards and was determined to live up to them.

She pushed open her bedroom door and was surprised to see Bella bending over her vanity table and examining with intense interest the few jars that Marchetta kept on it. "*Speak of evil*," Marchetta couldn't help but think, but she bit back the sharp questions that immediately leapt to her throat. She had promised Mama that she would try to get along with her new stepsister, but Marchetta had found it hard to make the effort. She forced herself to smile and greet her stepsister. "Bella, are you all right?"

"Oh!" Bella jumped at the question and spun around to face her. Marchetta was gratified to see that the younger girl had the good grace to act embarrassed. "Please forgive me," Bella said bashfully, "I'm out of chamomile hand cream and I was hoping to borrow some from you, only I couldn't find you." She gestured weakly to the vanity behind her.

Marchetta gave her stepsister a wary smile. "I'm sorry," she said, as politely as she could, "I'm afraid I don't have any either." There was a moment of awkward silence and, peering at the younger girl more closely, Marchetta was surprised to see her eyes were red, as though she'd been crying. "Would ... would you like me to put your hand cream on my weekly shopping list?" Marchetta offered, a little uncomfortably.

"Well ..." Bella hesitated. "Are you going into the village today? May I come with you?"

"What, now?" Marchetta was taken aback. She could count on one hand the number of times her stepsister had spoken to her away from the dining table, and she could count on *no* hands the number of times Bella had asked her for anything at all, except perhaps to pass the salt.

"We could get the shopping done," Bella offered. Her voice was a little brighter than before, almost hopeful.

Marchetta hesitated. She very much didn't want to go shopping; she'd planned to get the laundry ready for tomorrow and then to balance the financial books. She also wanted to stay close to the kitchen until she felt more assured of the new cook's skill in the kitchen. It would be very humiliating if the first 'official' family dinner was ruined on her watch, even if Cienzo would just laugh it off in that guffawing way of his.

On the other hand, as strange as it was to find her stepsister trespassing in her room and on the verge of tears, Marchetta suddenly felt a surge of pity for the younger girl. *"I suppose it's not easy suddenly to have to share your father and home with a trio of women you've never met,"* she thought. Although Bella was a very pretty girl of eighteen years, she never seemed to have any friends visit the house. If she was this hopeful at the prospect of a shopping trip, then perhaps the girl was lonely and trying to make an effort to get to know her older stepsister. Swallowing her irritation at having to change her plans, Marchetta nodded at Bella and smiled. "Let me just get my list," she said, forcing some cheer into her voice, "and I'll meet you outside."

Bella grinned in relief and rushed out of the bedroom as though afraid her stepsister might change her mind. Marchetta tromped back downstairs and patrolled the kitchen slowly, gathering up her list and shopping basket, hanging up her apron on its hook, and racking her brain to think of any instructions she might need to give the cook before she left. She couldn't think of anything, but supposed it wouldn't matter too much if she had forgotten something; the village was a short walk away and they wouldn't be gone long on a simple shopping trip.

In the front yard, she was surprised to see Bella still wearing the flimsy blue frock and matching slippers that she'd been wearing a few minutes before instead of the work gown and shoes that Marchetta had expected Bella to change into before their walk. "Are you ready?" she asked doubtfully, but Bella nodded enthusiastically and set off towards the road at a brisk pace.

They weren't far from the house when Marchetta saw that her misgivings were correct: as soon as they reached the main road, Bella had openly despaired of sullying her delicate clothes with mud, and she picked her way so slowly and carefully around the mud puddles that their pace slowed to a tortuous crawl. Marchetta struggled to hide her annoyance. If it had been Fiorita, she would have sent the younger girl home immediately to change into something more sensible, but she supposed she didn't yet have that kind of relationship with her stepsister. *"Least said, soonest mended,"* Marchetta reminded herself, but she couldn't help but enjoy the occasional fantasy of 'accidentally' stepping firmly enough into a puddle to splash her fussy stepsister.

It was mid-morning when they finally reached the village, and Marchetta had long since noticed that Bella was carrying only a small handbag and not a proper shopping basket. Marchetta put this down to the same flightiness that would cause the younger girl to wear blue silk the morning after a rainstorm had turned the world to mud, and assumed that they would share her own basket. The girls strolled quietly through the marketplace going down the first few items on Marchetta's list with some difficulty, as Marchetta was not yet used to the layout of the small village with its twisty streets and dark buildings. *"I miss the open market back home,"* she thought wistfully, remembering the sound of the sea and the deep smell of salt. She also missed shopkeepers who didn't stare at her dark skin. Her color was not unusual in the city and many of the shopkeepers were as dark as she.

She knew that Mama loved Cienzo, so she didn't begrudge Mama moving them down here to this provincial village to live with her new husband. Still, she sometimes wished that she could have stayed in their old house in the city; at twenty years old, Marchetta was perfectly competent to be mistress of her own home. Even that was not a perfect solution, though, since she knew that she would have missed Mama and Fiorita dreadfully had she stayed behind. *"If Mama had to set her heart on a man, I wish she'd found one who lived in the city instead of way out here in the middle of nowhere,"* she thought wryly. Still, maybe their new home was part of Cienzo's appeal: though Venizia tried to put a brave face on it, Marchetta was observant enough to recognize that quite a few places in her home city held painfully sweet memories for her widowed mother.

Marchetta was so lost in her thoughts that she almost missed it when Bella's hand shot quickly out and grabbed a handful of long ribbons from the dressmaker's stall and tucked them into a bolt of muslin that Marchetta had folded into her basket for purchase. As soon as the movement was done, Bella strode quickly off to another corner of the stall to gaze intently at the bolts of silk on display. Marchetta didn't know whether to believe her eyes, but when she shook out the bolt of cloth for the woman to measure and price, the ribbons lay there in the folds of the muslin, red and blue in the morning sun. *"What on earth ...? Am I supposed to buy these?"* Marchetta wondered. She looked up quizzically at Bella, but the younger girl either didn't see her or refused to meet her gaze.

She decided to err on the side of caution: silently, she drew the ribbons out of the cloth and laid them out for the shopkeeper to include in her bill, trying to ignore the curious stare she was drawing. *"Is it my skin, my accent, or my bizarre stepsister that interests you so?"* Marchetta thought, forcing herself to smile politely. Once the bill was paid, she folded the ribbons back into the muslin, and gently laid the bundle in the bottom of her basket.

As they moved from shop to shop, working their way down Marchetta's list, she watched Bella carefully from the corner of her eye. At almost a dozen stalls, Bella repeated her strange behavior of quickly grabbing an item and pushing it quietly into Marchetta's basket. *"What is she doing?"* Marchetta thought, amazed. The girl always moved before Marchetta paid, and never after, leaving Marchetta each time to quietly draw the item to the attention of the shopkeeper and pay the difference. Bella watched the transactions in silence, but with her head studiously tilted away to seem as though she wasn't looking.

"Does she think she's pulling the wool over my eyes?" Marchetta wondered. *"Does she think I just pay for whatever is in the basket whether it's on my list or not?"* Marchetta didn't know whether to be insulted by this assessment of her mental faculties or simply concerned about Bella's mental health.

What puzzled her most of all was that the items being grabbed were the most trivial of luxuries: colored ribbons, a polished hair comb, cosmetic powders and creams, and the sorts of baubles that would have caught Fiorita's eye if she had come along. The price of the additions came to a fraction of her overall list, and Marchetta would have bought them as gifts if Bella had simply asked. But if Bella didn't think she needed to bother with the niceties of asking her stepsister to pay for her things, Marchetta was going to have an increasingly hard time keeping the lid on her temper.

On the way to the final stop on her list, the apothecary's shop, she peered quizzically at the nervous, pale girl walking beside her and wondered if it was pride that caused her to behave in such an odd way. Mama had told her daughters that Cienzo had been quite poor before she married him, but she had stressed that there was no shame in that. Maybe Bella felt differently from Venizia on that matter. *"Does she feel too embarrassed to ask me to pay for her shopping?"* Marchetta felt sorry for the girl, but she wasn't going to go through this charade ever again, not even for Mama's sake. The sooner they went home, the better.

There was another customer ahead of them inside the dim apothecary shop: an attractive woman about Marchetta's age was asking the old proprietor for an elixir to cure chronic headaches. Beside her, Bella jumped and grew quite animated. "Agata!" she cried with pleasure. "How *are* you?"

The other girl squealed in obvious delight and she and Bella immediately lapsed into a friendly conversation. The old apothecary continued to putter about the store, pulling out various bottles and placing them on the mixing table for his client to consider once she was no longer occupied. Marchetta sighed and tried not to cross her arms over her chest in annoyance. She would happily have been introduced to the stunning young woman or been waited on by the apothecary, but being ignored by both was the height of vexation. *"I've waited on Fiorita enough times when she's become lost in conversation with one of her friends,"* she reminded herself, reaching for patience, but Fiorita was a good four years younger than Bella; Bella was old enough to know better.

Marchetta pushed her way around the two chattering girls and fixed her gaze on the old man. "Excuse me," she said as politely as she could, "If I could trouble you for a small vial of rat poison, I can be out of your way and you can focus on this young lady."

The shopkeeper boggled at her and eyed her suspiciously. "What do you need rat poison for, girl?" he demanded querulously.

His local accent was thick and Marchetta had to strain to understand him; she bit back a sarcastic retort that she had tired of her dreary lot in life and had decided to end it all. "To poison rats," she said acidly, biting back her opinions on her new relatives and their liberal attitude towards cleanliness in general and vermin in particular. The old man frowned at her but wandered unhurriedly into the back room. When he finally came back clutching the small vial, he suspiciously counted out her money three times before handing the bottle over to her. She checked that the stopper was secure and dropped the vial into the top of her basket before turning to Bella.

"We're going home," she said to her stepsister firmly. She felt a twinge of regret at having so abruptly inserted herself in the conversation between Bella and the lovely stranger, who would no doubt take away a lasting impression of Marchetta's inexcusable rudeness, but she was nearing the limits of her patience and just wanted to get home as quickly as possible.

Bella looked up from her animated conversation and Marchetta saw panic flash across her pale face. "Oh, already? I ... I'm not finished shopping," she said, nervously.

"Shopping?" Marchetta tried not to let her skepticism spill over into the word.

"Yes!" Bella suddenly brightened. "I need some, ah, headache medicine as well." Before Marchetta could stop her, the girl reached out and grabbed the shopping basket from Marchetta's arm. "It will just take me a moment," she gushed cheerfully, "and you can wait outside where the air isn't so stuffy! I'll even hold the shopping basket for you."

Marchetta pursed her lips and studied her stepsister. Briefly she flirted with ending the whole silly charade right there, but she decided it would be easier to just play along. "All right," she said tersely, and stepped outside into the cool air.

When Bella emerged a few minutes later, Marchetta was not surprised to see that the basket's contents were awry and Bella's small purse was suddenly bulging. *"And not with headache medicines, I'll wager,"* Marchetta thought with annoyance. Before she could say anything, Bella smiled sweetly and chirruped a sugary, "Ready to go home?" before taking off down the road without bothering to see if Marchetta was following her.

The shopping trip had taken much longer than Marchetta had planned, and it was already mid-afternoon when they arrived at the house. The journey home had been significantly more pleasant than the walk to the village had been, since Bella had lapsed into a nervous silence and was additionally burdened with the full shopping basket that she had 'offered' to carry and which Marchetta had not requested back. The mud puddles on the road had dried considerably since their morning trip, but there were still a few slick spots on the road and Bella had accidentally stepped in one and ruined a shoe. This had sent the girl into a sustained sulk, for which Marchetta was privately grateful. She wondered how Bella would replace or repair the delicate shoe, but she didn't bother to ask. *"Don't make it your problem,"* she thought tiredly.

As they rounded the bend in the road that brought the house into view, she saw Mama in the front yard, looking anxious. Marchetta felt a pang of guilt; she hadn't bothered to tell Mama she was going since she hadn't expected to be gone all day. She waved to Mama, who smiled back at her in relief. "There you girls are!" she called cheerfully. "Cienzo is home early. Dinner will be served just as soon as you two clean up and come down to the dining room."

She disappeared back into the house and Marchetta quickened her pace. "Marchetta ..." Bella said quietly, and Marchetta looked back at the girl in surprise. It was the first time she'd spoken since they left the village.

"Yes?"

Bella hesitated and for a moment Marchetta thought the girl was about to ... what? *"Thank me? Apologize?"* Marchetta wasn't sure, but then the girl seemed to shake off whatever she was feeling. Instead of apologizing, she roughly pushed the basket towards her. "Don't forget your things," she said briskly. "I didn't mind carrying them for you, but now I have to go change for dinner." She shoved the basket into Marchetta's hands and strode quickly off into the house.

Marchetta simmered with anger, and briefly considered calling a taunt to the haughty girl — *"Bella, I don't see my new hair ribbons in here. Did you drop them on the road, perhaps?"* would be a particularly nice barb to hurl at her — but she reined in her temper and hurried into the house to clean up as Mama had suggested.

Dinner was as awkward as their few shared breakfasts had led her to expect. Cienzo guffawed and hooted his way through dinner, regaling them with tales of people Marchetta didn't know while Fiorita giggled politely during his pauses and Mama smiled serenely at them both. Bella had arrived at the table extremely subdued and had spoken only a few words all evening; she had changed into a red velvet gown and had brushed her hair back and pinned it away from her face. In the candlelight, Marchetta thought the style made her look younger, more vulnerable.

As the plates were being cleared away by the kitchen servant, Cienzo struggled to his feet and eyed them all with an air of somber intensity. "My family," he said in a serious tone, "I have received word this week that one of my merchant vessels thought lost at sea last year has come in to port after all this time."

He grinned at them, but his smile faded a little as the moment passed in silence. Mama was smiling at him encouragingly, but Marchetta doubted the announcement was a surprise to her. Bella was looking at him with a surprised frown, and Fiorita was smiling her perpetual smile. As for herself, Marchetta didn't know what to make of the announcement, and imagined that her face was as blank as her understanding.

"This means," Cienzo continued, a little deflated by the lack of response from his audience, "that I will be taking a trip to recover my goods and profit from the ship. I will be gone for at least a week, during which time I want you all to be very good for your mother. When I return," his voice was building to a cheerful crescendo, "I will be bringing presents!"

At last Marchetta understood what response was expected of her and she beamed a broad smile at him. She didn't have to fake her enthusiasm: it would be lovely for the household to return to just her and Mama and Fiorita for a while. *"Although I suppose we'll still have Bella in the house,"* she realized with disappointment. *"Maybe she'll stay in her room for the entire week."* It was a possibility well worth hoping for.

"Fiorita," Cienzo said graciously, "You are the youngest, so why don't you be the first to tell me what present I should bring back for you?"

Fiorita smiled at him, but Marchetta recognized it as her reflexive, nervous smile. It was obvious that Cienzo wanted to make a pleasing gesture by bringing her back some gift, but Marchetta imagined that Fiorita was anxious about being put on the spot: what if her request was too large or too expensive?

Mama smoothly came to her rescue. "My dear, weren't you just saying to me today how you would like some fine yellow velvet for a new dress?" she prompted.

Fiorita grinned in relief and excitement. "Oh, yes, Papa," she gushed, "I would like a yellow gown very much! Something bright and festive, please, that I can wear to special occasions," she added with enthusiasm.

Cienzo grinned paternally at her. "A bolt of yellow velvet for my pretty bumblebee," he announced with mock seriousness. "I better make it two, for my chubby chipmunk," he added with an indulgent smile. Fiorita blinked, but held her smile gamely in place while Marchetta struggled not to frown. "And some yellow hair ribbons to match," he stage-whispered loudly to Fiorita with a conspiratorial wink. He turned to Marchetta and beamed his smile at her. "And what about you, Marchetta? As the oldest, you should choose next, I think."

Marchetta hesitated. What she really wanted were the necessities that hadn't been available in the local marketplace today, but she wasn't certain those were the sorts of 'presents' her stepfather had in mind. "Well," she said honestly, "I could very much use some more blank ledger books, and some ink ..." Her voice trailed off as she saw Cienzo frowning.

"That wasn't quite what I meant," he said doubtfully. "I want to get you girls something *nice*, as a gift. Not everyday things."

Marchetta tried not to sigh in frustration. *"I suppose it's useless to try to convince him that I know what I want for a gift better than he does,"* she thought with resignation. "Well, in that case," she said, trying to force a note of cheeriness into her voice, "Will you please bring me some new hairpins?" He started to frown again, and she added brazenly, "Maybe some with pearls."

His grin returned in full force and he laughed in that guffawing way of his. "Pearls for my black pearl?" he teased, and Marchetta flashed him a tight smile, but his attention had already wandered to Bella, who sat with her hands folded in her lap and her eyes fixed firmly on the table.

"And for my sweet middle child," he said graciously, "Last but not least: what can I bring back for my dear little princess?" he asked.

Bella looked up at him with a wistful expression. Marchetta wondered if she would ask for shoes to replace the ones she'd ruined on their outing, or maybe for some pocket money so that she would be able to buy her own things next time. Instead, when Bella spoke, she sounded almost worshipful. "Father," she said sweetly, "All I could ever wish for is your safe return."

She smiled sadly at Cienzo, and Marchetta was surprised to see him looking rather startled. "That's very sweet of you," he said with an embarrassed smile, "but I'm sure a young lady must want more than an old man's safe return." He laughed at his joke and then said firmly, "Come now, Bella, tell me what gifts I can bring you so that I can make you happy."

Marchetta watched Bella drop her gaze to the table as if in thought, before bringing her chin back up a moment later to level her gaze with her father's. Her eyes glistened wetly in the candlelight and she smiled that sad smile again. "In that case, Father," she said smoothly, "please will you bring me a single red rose?" She gestured to her red dress and explained, "I'll weave it through my hair when you return and we gather again for a family dinner."

Cienzo seemed stunned by her request. He stared frowningly at the girl, but she met his gaze with that steady, calm expression. "Well, Bella," he said doubtfully, "if that's really all you want ..." His voice trailed off doubtfully, before his expression lit up again and became all animated enthusiasm. "I will bring a bouquet of roses for my beautiful rose princess!"

He left his spot at the table and strode over to Bella's seat where he all but hauled her out of her chair to embrace her in a tight bear hug. Marchetta pursed her lips as she eyed the pale girl beaming triumphantly in her father's approving embrace. *"Maybe I've misjudged her,"* she mused dryly. Her little stepsister may have seemed an artless thief, but she certainly knew precisely how to steal her father's heart.

Chapter 6 - Cienzo

Cienzo kept a close eye on his cart through the open door as he sipped at his mug. The liquid in his cup — he hesitated to call it *wine* — was some foul home-brew recipe with dark flecks of floating debris that weren't at all hidden by the dim light. Still, the water from the local well had looked even dirtier, and he'd had to slake his thirst somehow.

It was odd, he reflected, how the road home always seemed so much longer, hotter, and drier than it had at the start of a journey. The trip home was additionally rather trying because he was forced to keep such a close eye on his cart whenever he wanted to stop and stretch his legs. The bulk of his goods from the ship were safely on his person in the form of solid coin, but he had brought a few luxury items back with him to trade: little necessities that would fetch a low price in a port city, but a high price in his secluded home village.

"You didn't seem to like the wine much when you passed through two weeks before, sir," the innkeeper said to him with a light, teasing grin. "And yet you still came back for more!"

Cienzo coughed a little to clear his stinging throat and smiled cheerily at the slender man. The inn was a small one, really more of a dining room to serve nightly meals for the local field hands, but it was one of the few places on his road where he could rest and shake the dust from the road out of his clothes and hair. To the innkeeper's teasing question, he fibbed with a conspiratorial grin, "I'd be considered a traitor in my home town if I preferred another village's wine to our own!"

The man returned the knowing smile politely, but looked distracted as he quietly swept the empty room. Cienzo lapsed back into his wine, wishing he wasn't so bone weary from the road, and wondering how much longer it would be until he was home.

"You're a merchant, I think?" the man asked abruptly, and Cienzo nodded.

"Yes, I'm on my way back home from a trip to the port," he confirmed. He smiled again, but a little warily. He'd been lucky so far not to have to deal with any extortion on the road, and he didn't want to press his luck now. "I haven't had the best luck on this trip," he confessed, trying to look pensive and poverty-stricken.

The innkeeper brightened at his lie. "Well, perhaps you can make a profit in our village," he said cheerfully. "We're always needing replacement field tools and sturdy clothing, and it's so hard to find an honest merchant to make the trip out here frequently." The small man looked a little bashful and confessed, "We don't have a lot of coin to trade, but we do have our crops — and even some goats!"

Cienzo couldn't stop himself from laughing at the thought. "Goats, huh? What would I do with those?" he asked with a grin. The thought of his sweetly spoiled Bella being presented a scrawny village goat sent him into a guffawing fit. *She wouldn't know whether to milk the beast or slaughter it,* he thought, chuckling heartily. Her delicate sensibilities would probably have her fainting at the thought of doing either. He jovially slapped the slender man hard on the back and hoped the innkeeper would excuse his outburst. "I'm sorry, my good man," he apologized, "but I'm afraid I can only trade for coin. My ladies eat well enough at home without me bringing back goats."

He winked good-naturedly at the man and turned back to his mug, but then stopped as an idea struck him. The thought of Bella had jogged something in his mind, and he suddenly remembered that he was still missing her present. A single rose, she'd asked for. He'd been frustrated by the unexpected amount of time and effort that the request had demanded. When he'd asked around in port, the few bouquets he found had wilted within hours of his purchase, and the little bush he'd bought in a basket had died a day later. One woman had recommend that he dry the flowers, but he must not have followed her instructions properly, because the dried flowers were wrinkled and ugly and he'd thrown them out when they started to drop their petals. He'd finally given up and put the whole silly thing out of his mind: it was sweet that his little princess hadn't wanted armfuls of clothes and jewels, but he wasn't going to spend any more time or money chasing the matter. But here, so close to home, maybe a rose might stand a chance of surviving the rest of the trip.

"However," he said to the slender man, who had returned to his silent sweeping. "There is one thing I could trade for ... does anyone in the village keep any roses?"

In the dim sunlight struggling through the cracks in the thatched roof, Cienzo could see the innkeeper's eyes swivel up to gaze suspiciously at him. "Roses?" the man asked in a peculiar voice. "Why do you ask about those?"

Cienzo shrugged. "Just something one of my ladies back home has asked for," he said simply. "Who can explain the whims of a woman, but it's always best to keep them happy, eh?" He smiled helplessly at the innkeeper and privately hoped the man wouldn't charge him too much for the knowledge. "Are there any roses growing in the village that I could take off your hands?"

The innkeeper leaned on his broom and stared out the door at Cienzo's cart for a long moment, long enough that Cienzo started to become nervous. He cleared his throat twice, and was just about to thank the man and clear out in a hurry when the man smiled warmly at him. "I can't think of any roses here in the village," he said with another bashful smile. "I'm afraid none of the women have time to tend flowers after a day in the field, and it's still too early for wild roses."

Cienzo's face fell in disappointment, but the man continued cheerily. "But if you're willing to go just a bit out of your way, you could try at the castle. The old lord planted plenty of early-bloomers around the estate before he died, and there's no one left to bother you if you take one for yourself."

"The castle is empty?" Cienzo asked in confusion. He knew of the local lord, but he'd never bothered to visit the country castle or sell his wares there. Even before he'd stopped trading for so long, it had been common knowledge that the man's lands were failing and his coffers were barren. Still, he was surprised to hear that the castle was empty now. *"Has the royal family moved to greener pastures?"* he wondered.

"Oh, yes, the old lord died from illness very recently," the innkeeper said matter-of-factly, "and his heir left soon after. The servants left with them and most of them came back to live with their families." He shook his head glumly. "But the royal family did leave behind the most lovely rose hedge ringing the estate, a beautiful foreign strain that is very hardy." He smiled cannily at Cienzo. "Just the thing for your lady, sir," he said with a wink.

Cienzo quickly calculated the remainder of the trip in his head. The castle couldn't be far from the village, and he had made good time on the road so far. A quick side trip wouldn't put him too far out of his way. It was an awful lot of trouble just to humor Bella's request, but the extra effort would be worth it if it made her happy. *"And it's been so long since she asked for something that wasn't powders and silks,"* Cienzo thought with a pang. It was no good to pine for the simple little girl his daughter used to be if he wouldn't then honor her wishes for gifts of his heart instead of his money. What was more, he'd bought the presents asked for by Marchetta and Fiorita and it seemed wrong to bring back pearls and velvets for his new daughters and not fulfill a request from his own flesh and blood.

He made up his mind; he would go. "Thank you, my good man," he said warmly to the innkeeper, and he absentmindedly tossed the man a thick coin that would cover the cost of his drink and then some before striding out of the dim cottage to his carefully-covered cart.

The distance to the castle was farther than Cienzo had guessed, but it was an easy path to follow the road to the edge of the estate. He noticed that the wagon tracks that cut into the road had been washed over with the spring rains and had not been traveled in at least a fortnight's time, which confirmed the innkeeper's story that the royal family no longer occupied the castle. The story had seemed odd to him during the telling, but the more he thought about it, the more it made sense that a young prince might move out of his family's country castle to somewhere a little more comfortable. *"Country estates are for old men,"* Cienzo thought, waxing poetic. No doubt a young prince would want to move a little closer to the city for some high living and sophisticated entertainment.

It was strange, though, that there hadn't been a steward left behind to maintain the property and ensure that the fields were worked. Either the royal family was richer than he'd thought and didn't need to bother with such things, or their lands were so poor that leaving behind a steward and a complement of field workers would have cost more in the long run than just abandoning the land outright. *"Probably the latter,"* Cienzo mused.

By noon, the sunlight was beating down on him through the forest canopy. He had just about decided to give up on the whole business when his cart crested a large hill and he blew a low whistle in astonishment. Before him stood the most beautiful gate he'd ever seen, with delicate silver bars that stretched towards the treetops and gleamed brightly in the rays of sunlight streaming through the trees. What astonished him, though, was that just through the silver bars of the gate he could see a thick green hedge, easily as tall as a man, and covered with beautiful red roses. A touch of dew still glistened wetly on a few of the petals, and for a moment all Cienzo could do was stare at the bright red blossoms.

He pulled up the reins on his mule and the tired animal was all too happy to stop its steady trudging. Cienzo hopped down from his seat and found a low hanging branch to loop the reins around. He walked slowly to the silver fence, still astonished that such a lovely and delicate piece could be left on an abandoned property, and amazed that it could shine so beautifully without anyone to maintain it. The metal couldn't be silver, Cienzo decided, it would be too expensive and impractical to maintain. *"Some new alloy from the city?"* he wondered. He didn't know much about metal-work except what he needed to know to sell jewelry, but he imagined the women back home would go wild for jewelry made out of this stuff.

Cienzo walked the length of the fence a few yards in each direction, each time coming back to the gate where he'd left his cart. Both the silver fence and the rose hedge inside its bounds stretched as far as he could see in either direction through the forest. He had hoped to reach between the bars to pluck a rose, but there was a good yard-length between fence and hedge. Cienzo looked at the gate hesitantly. He felt uncomfortable intruding on someone else's property, but would anyone ever know or care? The hedge was loaded with roses that would surely fade in a few short months; it couldn't hurt for him to take just one.

The gate was unlatched and opened inward at his touch, moving lightly over the smooth dirt road. Cienzo stepped quietly on to the estate property, unwilling to break the silence that had settled over the forest, and wincing a little when the silver gate swung closed behind him with a clang. He held his breath and waited, but when no one appeared to challenge him, he laughed at his own nerves and strode confidently over to the lovely hedge. The road cut through the hedges down into the valley below, and through the overgrown gap he could see a dingy castle. Cienzo looked long enough to see that there was no movement in the neglected fields and empty courtyards, and nodded to himself in relief when he saw nothing stir on the abandoned property.

The first rose he plucked from the hedge was truly gorgeous: a soft red bloom, perfectly shaped and completely symmetrical, with a profusion of gently opening petals clustered around the delicate center bud. He'd reached deeply into the hedge to keep the stem as long as possible, and a few sharp thorns had scratched him. With a breed like this, it was no wonder the hedge had been fenced in, if only to keep the deer out, he mused. No sense in having all the forest game bleed themselves to death trying to get at those tempting blossoms. He turned to go, clutching the rose gently to his chest, but then paused and looked back at the lovely hedge. It seemed silly to come all this way for just a single rose, and it was surely a waste to leave so many pretty flowers behind when he could just as easily take a whole bouquet home.

He laid the rose gently on the grass and walked back over to the hedge. It was the work of a few short minutes for him to collect an impressive pile of long-stemmed roses. He lay each one carefully on the grass beside the others, quietly counting as he went. After the first dozen, he hit upon the idea to pick another six for a total of eighteen beautiful roses for his eighteen-year-old Bella. Smiling at his cleverness, he reached gingerly into the hedge for another stem.

The roar only reached his ears after he'd been bowled over into the grass with a force that knocked the breath from him and left him desperately gasping for air. Cienzo scrabbled under the weight of something huge and hairy. An animal howl reached his ears and he felt something wet and sticky running down his right arm. The world above him seemed to be spinning, and in his confusion all he could make out was that he was grappling with some kind of wild animal. Panic seized him and he kicked out at the strange creature on top of him — *"Some kind of bear?"* he wondered wildly — and was rewarded with a pained howl.

Cienzo scrambled to his feet and dashed to the gate, crashing into it in his terror. Not daring to look behind him, he pushed madly at the gate, but it refused to budge. After an eternity measured in seconds, his mind supplied him with the hazy detail that the gate opened inward. Gasping with relief, he yanked on the gate, but to his horror the gate still would not move. His eyes shot down; the latch had somehow fallen into place and no matter how he tugged at it with his bare hands, it wouldn't yield to him.

A strange calm fell on Cienzo as he stood there, his hands helplessly resting on the stubborn gate latch. His eyes followed the stream of blood that poured slowly from three long gashes on his arm and was dripping into the fine detailing on the silver gate and its heavy latch. Behind him, he heard the labored breathing of an angry animal, and as Cienzo looked about him for any possible weapon or escape, he realized he was going to die. The realization stirred only a little surprise in him, which in itself was surprising; he felt suddenly light-headed. *"Am I going to faint?"* he wondered. Losing consciousness now would perhaps be a mercy. Slowly, he turned to face the beast that would kill him, and his eyes widened in renewed terror.

The beast was unlike any Cienzo had seen before. It stood on two legs, like a bear, but it was huge, and even hunched over at the shoulders it stood taller than he. One paw clutched at its stomach in a gesture that looked almost pained — *"Was that where I kicked it?"* Cienzo wondered — and the other hung at the beast's side, claws dripping with Cienzo's blood. But what was most stupefying was that somehow the beast was dressed in fine clothing as though it were a man. Cienzo stared at the creature in amazement wondering how and why someone would dress up a beast in a mockery of human fashion. *"Is it a trained bear?"* It was the only explanation his mind could supply.

"You have trespassed on my land!"

The voice was an animal roar, but the words were impossibly human. Cienzo stared at the beast in astonishment, mouth agape, certain that his mind had left him and that the words were strange fancies that his dying mind had spawned. "Wha ... I ... It ..." he stammered meaninglessly.

"You have stolen my roses!"

This time there could be no doubt that the beast had spoken; those strangely intelligent eyes bore angrily into him and the rage was clear in its guttural, howling voice. Cienzo's eyes darted towards the pile of abused roses that he had so carefully laid on the ground, now sadly trampled in the dirt. "Your ... roses?" he asked in amazement. He felt as if he were in some kind of trance, and that he might wake up at any moment and find himself back on his gently jolting cart, lost in a thick daydream.

"You will die for this, thief!"

The beast dropped the paw that had been cradling its stomach and the claws tensed in anticipation. The creature started to stalk towards Cienzo.

His dreamy stupor fell away and he felt only fear. Desperately, he clawed clumsily at the gate latch behind him, but his fingers were sticky with blood and the latch was still firmly stuck. An impulse struck him, and he flung himself on the ground before the approaching monster.

"Please, my lord," he begged the strange animal, hoping that it could understand him, praying that it would respond to flattery. "Please forgive me! I didn't realize that these roses were yours, I didn't understand what they meant to you. Please, I'll pay you for your loss — I'm a wealthy merchant and can pay you thrice what you've lost!" Cienzo realized he was babbling, but still the beast approached him with determination in its eyes. Tears welled up in his eyes and blurred his vision. Pleadingly, he moaned, "Don't take me from my daughter ... Please, sir."

A long moment passed as Cienzo cowered in the dirt and waited for his end. He felt the tears streaming down his face; dirt and sweat dripped into his eyes and stung him, but he didn't dare move to wipe them. Above him, he could hear the beast's slow, panting breaths and he could feel the heat of its body so close to him, ready to strike.

"You have ... a daughter?"

The voice this time was different: no longer full of rage, but rather something else that Cienzo couldn't identify through the strange guttural accent of the creature. *"Pity?"* Cienzo hoped. He dared to look up from where he crouched on the ground. With a vague sense of shock he registered that the beast had hooves for feet, instead of the bear paws he had expected. He craned his neck up further to see the beast's face hovering high above him, those strange black eyes fixed intently on him.

"Y-yes, my lord," Cienzo answered in astonishment. Would the beast spare him for his family? With a glimmer of hope, he gushed, "I have three daughters, my lord, very lovely and delicate girls. They would be lost in this world without their father. Please don't take me from them." He dared to smile up at the beast, and then hastily dropped his gaze back to the ground — would showing his teeth to this animal set it off in another rage?

Above him, he heard the beast snort; the sound would have seemed almost introspective in a human creature. When it spoke, however, the voice was low and threatening. "I will let you go," the beast said fiercely, "if you promise to bring back one of your daughters to be my bride."

Cienzo raised his head again to stare at the creature in astonishment. "Your ... bride?" he asked incredulously, and the beast growled so fiercely that he immediately dropped his gaze again back to the ground. "I ... I will do as you ask," he said meekly. *"Anything to leave this place,"* he thought.

"Promise!"

The voice was a howl of rage and anger. "I swear it, my lord," Cienzo vowed quickly into the dirt. "If you let me go, I will bring one of my daughters to be your bride."

He felt the beast's paw on his shoulder, and he trembled in fear, certain that its claws were about to rip him open from head to toe. Instead, the strangely hand-like paw gripped him like an iron vise and he felt himself being hauled painfully to his feet, as the beast's claws dug deeply into his shoulder. Even at his full height, his head was level only with the top of the creature's fine garments; the beast would have to stoop just to rest its chin on Cienzo's head.

The beast moved around him to stand between him and the gate. It stood there gazing solemnly at Cienzo for a long moment before lightly touching the bloodied gate latch with the tip of one claw. Before his astonished eyes, Cienzo saw the blood magically draw up into the latch and disappear. Within seconds, the gate was all gleam and polished silver again. With a soft click, the latch lifted easily under the beast's paw and the gate swung silently open.

The beast gestured to him and Cienzo stepped forward, once again feeling as though he were in a dream. At the threshold of the gate, the beast laid a hand on his shoulder, stopping him. Cienzo quivered in fear.

"Remember your promise," the beast growled. "If you do not bring a daughter to be my bride, you will die." The grip on his shoulder tightened, and Cienzo gasped in pain as he felt the claws draw fresh wells of blood. "You can't escape my magic," the beast warned. Cienzo nodded helplessly, and the creature released him. Before he could work up the courage to move away, the beast stooped to the ground and retrieved a bruised rose from the ground. The beast handed the stem to Cienzo and silently turned back to the valley, striding off in a loping gait down the road.

Cienzo moved as quickly as he could. His mule had almost broken its own neck straining at the tied halter to escape the smell of the strange beast. Cienzo leapt on to the cart seat and yanked the reins free, along with the better part of the attached branch, and the mule took off down the road at a frenzied pace.

The sun was low in the sky before the mule slowed to its usual pace, but Cienzo's heart was still pounding. The strangeness of the day remained immediate and dangerous. Bright colors still swirled before his eyes: shining silver metal, deep green leaves, and his own red blood soaked into his shirt. He looked down and saw that the bruised rose lay on the cart seat beside him, still beautiful in spite of its limp form and dirty petals.

Chapter 7 - Venizia

Venizia smiled as the strains of music floated up from the downstairs sitting room. The melody was a simple one and proceeded with a halting, uncertain gait, but she was still so proud of Fiorita for all that she had learned in the last two weeks, and was so pleased with Bella for being willing to teach the girl.

She had been worried that Bella would be unhappy in her father's absence. Indeed for the first few days, Bella had barely a presence at all in the large house: sleeping well past breakfast, dressing silently in her room, walking alone into the village for her social calls, and taking dinner privately in the sitting room while she practiced on her portative organ.[18]

Venizia had watched the girl's determined solitude with growing vexation and had wondered if she should step in and address the issue directly, but she had struggled with the question of how to approach the young woman. Each day she had resolved to let the matter wait one more day. *"More flies with honey than vinegar,"* Venizia had reminded herself, although the advice had been easier to dispense to her own daughters than to herself.

Still, she puzzled over the situation. During their whirlwind courtship in the city, Venizia had been attracted to Cienzo's fierce love for his daughter almost as much as she had been to Cienzo himself. There were many men in the city willing to marry her for the inheritance left by her late husband, but few who would have described with such ardor the vibrant daughter eager to welcome a new stepmother into her home. Venizia had seen in Cienzo a rare soul who would love her own daughters as much as she. Yet when she moved into her new home and met the anticipated Bella, she'd found the young woman to instead be surprisingly quiet, almost to the point of furtive. Only time would tell if the young woman was sullen or merely shy, but Venizia harbored a silent doubt that her husband understood his daughter and her wishes as well as he believed.

On the fifth day of Cienzo's absence, Venizia had looked up from her conversation at the dinner table with Marchetta to notice that Fiorita had slipped quietly away from the table. Her youngest daughter had crept into the sitting room and was now gazing over Bella's shoulder as the girl played a melancholy piece. Bella's eyes were closed and she swayed slightly to the music issuing forth under her fingers; Fiorita watched her wistfully with obvious fascination.

When Bella finished the piece, Fiorita broke the sudden silence with a sigh, saying, "You play so beautifully."

From the dining room, Venizia could see the pale girl start back from Fiorita's voice, her eyes opening wide in surprise at the younger girl's unexpected proximity. She took a moment to calm herself; Venizia saw Bella frown slightly as she answered with a simple, "Thank you."

If Fiorita could hear the coolness in the older girl's voice, she didn't show it; she plopped down on the seat next to Bella and sighed again with longing. "That song was *so* sad and lovely, I wanted to cry as you played it." She grinned in admiration at the older girl and volunteered, "Mama tried to teach me the harp when I was younger, but I never could get the hang of the strings. I'd give anything to be able to play the organ like you do."

Bella blinked at the younger girl, taking a moment to digest all this. When she spoke, her voice was tentative as she offered, "I could teach you a little ... if you want?"

"Oh, would you?" Fiorita squealed happily, and threw her arms in gratitude around her startled stepsister. She drew back almost immediately, beaming with delight, and asked, "Can we start now?" In her enthusiasm, Fiorita all but dragged the portative organ from Bella's lap to her own, as Bella watched her stepsister with curious astonishment.

As Bella began to explain the different organ keys in a low voice, Venizia glanced at Marchetta to see her eldest watching the scene with the same intense interest as her own. Casually, mother and daughter picked up the conversation where they had last left it, while Venizia privately counseled herself not to raise her hopes too highly. For the rest of the evening, Venizia would glance periodically into the sitting room to see the two girls huddled over the instrument as Bella patiently explained its workings to the younger girl.

From that day forward, a new pattern slowly emerged in the household. If ever Bella failed to appear to breakfast or dinner, Fiorita would cheerfully dash off to find and coax her to the table; by the end of the week, Bella was quietly sharing her meals with them without having to be asked. Evenings were spent immersed in music lessons. Afternoons saw Bella and Fiorita walking to the village together, with Fiorita cheerfully clutching the pocket money she'd begged for both of them. Venizia was only too happy to spoil the girls; she was overjoyed to see her energetic daughter drawing Bella out of her shell, and if the girl still seemed reserved around Marchetta and Venizia, her stepmother was certain that familiarity would come with time.

Venizia was brought out of her reflections by the clatter of a cart on the road, the sound drifting up from the lawn and over the strains of music coming from the downstairs sitting room. Quickly she set her book on the dressing-table and hurried to peer out the thick windowpane. Cienzo had been gone over a fortnight, well over his initial estimate of a week's journey; with relief she saw through the bubbled glass that the cart was his and the hunched figure in the cart seat was his own.

She hurried out of the bedroom, calling to the girls to come meet their father, and taking the steps two at a time in her excitement. As much as she had enjoyed the quiet time alone with her daughters again and as thrilled as she was that his absence had allowed the girls to grow closer together, she still had missed her husband and was relieved to have him home again. Having him gone for such a long time had reminded her acutely of how much she loved his infectious laugh and his hearty embrace. Venizia flung open the front door, intending to run to embrace him, but the sight of him from the open doorway rendered her motionless in shock.

Outlined in the bright sunset, Cienzo sat hunched over in his seat as though a great weight were on his shoulders. His face was covered in streaks of dirt, smudged with tears. The sleeve of his shirt was torn in deep gashes and hung down his arm in strips, and dried blood coated his arm and sleeve. Marchetta's sudden gasp in the doorway beside her brought Venizia out of her shock and she rushed forward to take the reins from her husband.

"I'm fine, I'm fine!" he snapped at her, keeping a tight grip on the reins as he guided the mule slowly into the yard. "I'm fine," he repeated again, quietly this time, and Venizia could not tell if his changed tone was meant to be an apology or if he had simply succumbed to whatever misfortune afflicted him.

Setting her mouth in a firm line, she offered him her hand, and he looked at it in incomprehension before allowing himself to be helped down from the cart. "We must get you inside," she said crisply, "that needs binding." Up close, she could see the deep gashes in his arm, still seeping lightly with wet blood.

"I'm fine," he said again, but he allowed her to guide him up the lawn and into the house.

At the threshold, he stopped to survey the three girls. Bella and Fiorita had come running at the announcement of his arrival; Fiorita still clutched the portative organ in her hands, now sadly forgotten. Bella's eyes were wide with shock and her face was such an ashen white that Venizia feared the girl would faint right there on the doorstep.

"Your gifts are in the cart," Cienzo said to the girls sadly, as he sagged against Venizia for support. "Except for yours, Bella." He stretched out his hand to the shocked girl and Venizia saw that he was clutching a wilted rose tightly in his fist. Numbly, the girl reached out to take the flower from him. Cienzo sighed deeply and said with a trace of bitterness, "That rose cost me everything." The girl stared at him blankly, and Venizia placed her arm around her shattered husband and guided him unprotesting up the stairs to their bedroom.

Once she had sat him on the edge of the bed, he lapsed into a stunned silence. Carefully, she pulled his shirt off and began to clean and bandage his wounds as best she could. She watched his face as she worked, and became more worried; outside of a few winces in pain as she probed his fresh wounds, he acted completely dazed, not at all like the husband she had known just a few weeks ago.

"Cienzo?" she ventured to ask, once his wounds were clean and bandaged as tightly as she could wrap them.

"Hmm."

She wasn't sure if it was an answer or just a response to the sound of her voice. "Cienzo, what happened? Were you attacked?" Obviously he had been, but she couldn't imagine who the culprit could be. The marks on his flesh had been animal, not man-made, so she didn't think the trouble could be bandits, but if an animal had attacked him on the road, why would it not go for that sluggish cart-mule instead of her loud husband?

She stood and paced anxiously to the opposite side of the room, turning to stare at him in worry. He sat motionless at the edge of the bed, staring down at his knees, his white chest covered with hair matted in blood and sweat, and with thick lines of black dirt coating his fingernails. Suddenly very tired, Venizia wanted nothing more than to have a good cry at this unexpected twist of events, but instead she lifted a glass of wine from her dressing-table, and brought it to Cienzo's lips.

He drained the glass automatically before dropping the wineglass. The empty wineglass rolled unbroken on the floor, and Venizia was grateful for small favors. Placing a hand on his shoulder, she said in a firm voice that she hoped would break through to him, "Cienzo, what has happened? Tell me now."

Her husband drew his head up reluctantly from his hands. His face was red and the skin around his eyes was puffed and bright with tears. "Do ... you remember ... the country castle ...?" he stuttered between sobs.

Venizia frowned, trying to remember. There was a castle some distance from the village, and not far from Cienzo's route to the city. She hadn't ever been there herself, never having felt the need to leave the comforts of the city to gawk at the antiquated wealth of an unimportant country lord. Moreover, the provincial lord was rumored to be something of a womanizer, and any desire she might have had to see the place was quenched by an unwillingness to tempt ill fate. "Did you stop there?" she asked in surprise. She had thought Cienzo had planned to come straight back home after leaving the city.

"Only ... to collect ... a rose," he sniffed.

"A—?" Venizia's voice trailed off in a question, but her memory supplied the answer faster than her mouth could react: Bella had asked for a rose as a gift. Venizia had found the request a touch sad, but she had noticed that Cienzo had been obviously pleased. Obviously he had not been able to find one in the city, which was not terribly surprising considering the earliness of the season, and had gone off his route searching for one in the wild.

"A rose!" Cienzo howled in answer to her question, and buried his face again. "My life for a rose," he mumbled piteously.

"Cienzo, stop it!" Venizia said, her rising voice sounding harsh in her ears. She felt that one or both of them was about to dissolve into hysteria. She knelt on the floor before him, and pulled his hands away from his face so that he was forced to look at her. "What happened? Tell me exactly."

He sniffed and frowned at her petulantly, but then his face crumpled into tears. The words seemed to spill from him in sniffling sobs. "The royal family is gone from the castle ... there is a powerful magician there that takes the shape of a vicious bear ... He accused me of stealing his roses and placed a curse on me. If I do not bring him one of my daughters to be his bride, I will die." His story told, he pulled his hands from her grip and slumped sideways on to the bed, sniffling with his face pressed into the quilts.

Venizia stood slowly in astonishment, walked to her dressing-table, and sank quietly on to the bench. The story her husband told was too fantastic to be true, but there were the deep furrows on his arms, now covered by her bandages. Had some fever in his brain transformed a bad encounter with a mundane animal into this tale of magic, or did those deep cuts really support his outlandish story? She stared at her husband, slumped over the bed, whimpering to himself, and she couldn't imagine that *he* at least didn't believe his own story. "What are you going to do?" she whispered to him.

Slowly he opened his eyes and stared at her in incomprehension. "What *can* I do?" he asked, helplessly.

"You'll ... you'll have to get your affairs in order," she said hesitantly, hardly believing she was having this conversation.

In a burst of energy, he sat bolt upright in bed. "What?" he demanded, dismayed, "Just like that? You're giving me up for dead?"

She blinked at him in confusion. "Cienzo, I hardly know what to think," she said slowly and carefully, unsure how to react to his changed tone. "If you are really cursed—"

"I am!" he insisted stubbornly.

"—then we can travel to the city to seek some sort of ... help ..." Venizia struggled with the concept. There were magicians aplenty in the city, even some claiming elaborate genealogical descent from obscure gods or powerful fairies, but she had always chalked the whole lot of them up as charlatans. She continued resolutely, "But we have to face the possibility that they may ... fail." The situation seemed so unreal. Occasionally a story would drift through the city of some rich family being visited by magic and disaster, but those were things that happened to other families, not her own. A chill ran through her and she wrapped her arms around herself for warmth. *"Is this happening?"* she wondered. *"Can life really change so suddenly in a single day?"* Cienzo was either cursed or mentally disturbed, and she could think of no way to help. She walked to her dressing-table and leaned against it for support. When she looked up, he was staring at her with an odd look on his face.

"There is a third option," he said. "We can give the magician the bride I promised." He tried to stare her in the eyes as he said this, but his eyes slipped down to the floor before he could finish his proposal.

Venizia stared at him in horror. "What?" she asked hoarsely, her voice barely reaching her own ears.

"Think about it," he urged. "He asked for a *bride*, not a *meal*, so we can be sure she will be safe with him. He is powerful and rich, and all he needs is a kind, sensible wife to civilize him. Fiorita or Marchetta—"

In an explosion of rage, Venizia hurled her book from the dressing-table directly at his face. With a yelp, Cienzo ducked and the book flew wide; the heavy volume smacked the far wall with force and dropped with a sickening *thunk* as loose pages fluttered and slid across the floor. Venizia realized her fists were clenched at her side as she shook with fury. Never had she thrown anything at another human being before, she realized, and never had she been so angry.

"Don't you dare," she hissed at her husband, as he stared at her in shock. "Don't you even *think* of trading my daughters to settle your debts." He opened his mouth to protest, and she cut him off with a sharp gesture. "I will kill you first," she promised coldly. "I swear it."

"So you want me to die?" he asked angrily, but with tears welling up in his eyes again.

"Yes," she spat furiously, and then truthfully and with a trace of sadness, "No." She took a few deep breaths, turning sideways so that she might gather her thoughts without looking at him, and unclenched her fists. With as much calmness as she could muster, she said firmly, "I love you, Cienzo. I do not want you to die, and I wish this had never happened. Whether you must go back to this beast-man to die, or die here in your bed, or travel the city looking for someone to remove this curse, I will be by your side the whole time."

She turned and looked straight at him, and hoped that her face and eyes conveyed all her sincerity and none of her residual anger. "But if you so much as attempt to take my daughters from my care, I will kill you myself."

He flinched at her words and sank despondently into a reclining position on the bed, his face buried in the blankets. Suddenly weary, Venizia walked as calmly as she could to the bedroom door and stepped out into the hallway. "Stay here," she said firmly to her motionless husband, and shut the door behind her.

Out in the hallway, she saw a bottle of wine and a small tray with bread and cheeses. "*Dear Marchetta*," Venizia thought, her heart heavy. She wondered fleetingly if it was right to burden her daughter with her troubles, but Marchetta would know how to counsel her. Whether or not this overwrought story about magicians was indicative of a deeper problem, Marchetta could help her figure out how best to handle it. Quietly, she stepped down the hall to her eldest daughter's door in search of a solution to her husband's madness.

Chapter 8 - Fiorita

Fiorita plunked tunelessly on the portative organ as Bella sat mutely next to her on the window seat. Her chubby fingers still had difficulty picking out precisely the correct keys, but she had been excited at the prospect of learning if it gave her something to do in this small village and a way to connect with her quiet stepsister. Mama had been, if not *distant* exactly then at least *busy* since her marriage, and Marchetta had sunk into a solitary melancholy and busied herself in the management of their new household. Now Fiorita felt more alone than ever as she found herself playing doggedly in an attempt to distract her new friend from the shock of seeing Cienzo drive up to the house covered in blood.

Bella sat clutching the strange, withered rose that Cienzo had brought her. Fiorita had suggested putting it in a glass of water, but Bella had shook her head and clutched it all the more firmly. Fiorita supposed the older girl was still in shock. She could distantly remember the news of her own father's death at sea when she was a little girl, and wondered if Bella was feeling the same falling sensation that Fiorita remembered from that day. Surreptitiously, she inched closer to the pale girl and hoped that her nearness would bring comfort.

Upstairs came the sound of a closed door, and then the sound of another door, farther down the hall, opening and shutting firmly. Fiorita shot a quick glance at Bella, but she didn't react to the noises coming from above them. Fiorita stopped her tuneless playing and immediately switched to an easy song — a scales exercise Bella had taught her — and carried on as loudly as she could, hoping to block out the disturbing sounds.

As Fiorita was finishing the scales and considering starting the song again from the beginning, she felt Bella draw in her breath sharply. Fiorita looked up to see Cienzo quietly limping down the stairs and into the drawing room where they sat.

"Father!" Bella jumped up and hurried over to him, but Cienzo waved her away in a manner that was probably meant to be kind, but which left Bella looking dejected. He sat down slowly in a delicate chair opposite their window seat, carefully moving the chair closer to be near them. Bella sank back into her seat next to Fiorita.

They sat in silence for a moment, while Fiorita shifted uncomfortably. The atmosphere was heavy and awkward, and finally she blurted out, "Are you all right, Father?" Mama had told her and Marchetta how important it was to Cienzo to be their 'father' and not 'sir' or 'stepfather', so she hoped that her earnestness would excuse her forwardness in breaking his reverie.

Cienzo looked up at them, and Fiorita tried not to frown. His face was a strange study of opposites: the sun from his trip had left his skin brown and burned, but in the light of the drawing room he looked gray, as though soot from the fireplace had seeped into the cracks of his lined face. She wondered if he was sick. Cienzo ignored her question and looked long and hard at Bella, reaching forward to clasp her free hand. "Bella, dear," he said hoarsely, "I have bad news."

Fiorita could feel Bella trembling slightly beside her. Bella cleared her throat, and tried to stay calm, but her voice shook as she asked, "What is it, Father?"

Cienzo hung his head and stared at the floor. When he spoke, Fiorita had to lean forward to hear him clearly. "Bella, I was a fool. I plucked that rose from the garden of a magician — no, it's true, only I didn't know it at the time," he hurried over the startled noise that came from her throat. "Let me finish. The man came to me in the form of a bear — that's where these cuts are from," he said, gesturing to his arms. The cuts they had seen from the road were now covered with white bandages that seeped red at his elbows. "He placed a curse on me: my life for the life of the rose. I will die soon, just as that flower wilts."

At this bizarre speech, Bella gave a start, and stared in shock at the rose she clutched in her hand. Her fist unfurled around the stem, and Fiorita saw her hold the flower delicately between forefinger and thumb, gazing at it in disbelief. Quietly, Fiorita leapt up from her seat and ran to the kitchen.

The kitchen was empty. The servants were surely in the yard unloading Cienzo's cart, and Marchetta and Mama were nowhere to be seen. A glass of water had been left on the kitchen table, and Fiorita snatched it and ran back into the drawing room at full pelt. Once there, she presented the glass to Bella. "Here. Water." Fiorita panted in relief as the rose was gently lowered into the lukewarm water. Bella clutched desperately at the glass before offering it silently to Cienzo, who sat watching them with haunted eyes.

"Thank you, daughters," he said wearily, "but I'm afraid that won't much prolong my life. I will die as that rose does, slowly sapped of life."

"Isn't there any way to break the curse?" Bella asked, her voice barely a whisper. Her eyes were filling with tears. "I can't ... lose you. Not after Mother ..." She sniffed, wiping her sleeve against her nose.

Cienzo looked at her gravely, and took her free hand in his once more. He offered his other hand to Fiorita, who grasped it a little hesitatingly as she sat on the edge of the seat next to Bella. His voice addressed them both, but Fiorita felt his eyes fixed on her as he said evenly, "There is one way to break the curse. The magician will free me if a girl will go to him in my place to be his bride."

For a moment, they were silent as the girls registered this statement; then Fiorita gasped and pulled her hand back from her stepfather in surprise. Bella sat motionless, but the blood drained from her face and she swayed slightly in her seat. Fiorita was certain that her stepsister was on the verge of fainting, and she placed her hand on the older girl's back to hold her steady. With her other hand, she fanned Bella's face awkwardly.

"Thank you ... I'm fine," Bella said after a moment, as the color slowly returned to her face. She placed her cold hands on Fiorita's own, and gently pushed the hand down to rest in Fiorita's lap. She looked sadly at Cienzo, and tears filled her eyes again. "Are you asking me to do this, Father?"

He looked uncomfortable, and once again Fiorita saw him glance at her with a curious expression. He stared at her, even as he answered Bella with a slight stammer, "Well ... I can hardly ask you — *any* of my daughters — but you asked what could be done ..." his voice trailed off.

Fiorita felt the older girl squeeze her hand, and she squeezed back, unsure what else to say or do. Bella was staring at Cienzo, her cheeks reddening in emotion. When she spoke, Fiorita was surprised to hear Bella's voice was low and angry. "How can you ask me to do this? How can you ask me to marry this dangerous man?" Her face flushed brighter, and her grip on Fiorita's hand tightened. Fiorita squirmed. *"Where is Mama?"* she wondered. *"Where is Marchetta?"* Gently, she tugged at Bella's fingers, wondering if she could disentangle herself in order to go and find them.

Cienzo shifted his gaze from Fiorita to Bella. Color rose to his face as he snapped back at her, "You are my daughter. I've taken care of you all my life, and you owe me for that care," he said hotly. "When your mother died, I shielded you from the worst of it. I never sold you to pay my debts."

"But now you'll sell me to save your life?" Bella cried angrily. She glared at him, but could not sustain the emotion and crumpled into tears, her face buried in her free hand.

"Bella ..." Fiorita mumbled softly, hoping her voice would soothe her stepsister. She wanted to hug her, but couldn't reach around her while her hand was twisted in Bella's. She wanted to tell her that she didn't need to cry, but she couldn't find the right words to say. "Bella—" she tried again, but Cienzo spoke over her.

"I only picked the rose for you," he said pleadingly. He spread his hands in a gesture of defeat; Fiorita stared at him in shock as Bella sobbed desolately beside her. "I'll die for you, Bella," he offered quietly, "but you can save me if you want."

The pale girl cried quietly for a few moments longer as Fiorita quietly shifted her weight from side to side in a mounting panic. This shouldn't be happening, and yet clearly it was; she glanced at Cienzo and his intense gaze frightened her. *Should I call for Mama?* Fiorita wondered, but she couldn't imagine how Mama could make this horror all better. *Would she ask me to give my life for Cienzo?* The thought seemed impossible, but then she had never imagined that her stepfather would make such a terrible request of Bella, either.

Slowly, Bella straightened up and with her free hand brushed the tears from her face and eyes. Her hand moved deliberately, first one side of her red face was swept with her palm, then the other. She looked down at her other hand, her fingers laced so tightly with Fiorita's that the younger girl's hand had lost all feeling. Gently, Bella pulled her fingers away, leaving Fiorita to rub the circulation back into her numb fingers and to stare with intense concern at the older girl's downturned face. Fiorita craned her neck to catch Bella's eyes with her own, but the older girl turned and shrugged so that her hair fell between them, cutting her off. Bella turned her head up to look at her father, seated only a foot away, staring intensely at them.

"Fine," she said, her voice barely above a whisper. "I'll do it."

"No, Bella!" Fiorita grabbed at her stepsister's arm. "Please don't do this!" Her voice choked, and she felt tears coming.

"Come, Bella," Cienzo said solemnly, standing and reaching out a hand to the girl. "We must go, the rose won't last much longer." He half-helped, half-pulled the silent girl to her feet with one hand. With his other hand, he reached out to brush Fiorita from her hold on the girl's arm.

Fiorita yelped. She had imagined a full scream coming from her mouth but somehow her body had not drawn in enough breath, and the sound was a high squeaky thing that barely reached her own ears. She shrank back from her stepfather's touch, scrambling to the far end of the window seat and jumping to her feet. "Let her go," she cried angrily. He ignored her, leading Bella towards the door. The girl walked slowly, her face tilted forward and her eyes on the ground, as though she had only enough strength to watch where she stepped.

Fiorita felt her breath coming in quick, panicky gasps. She drew in breath to scream, but her throat felt constricted and dry. She considered leaping on Cienzo and pounding his back with her fists, but Cienzo was older and bigger, and she was frightened to touch him. Would he drag *her* off to marry this strange magician? She couldn't leave Bella ... she shouldn't ... but after a moment's helpless indecision, she turned on her heel and ran up the stairs moaning a low guttural call for help.

As she ran, she watched through her tears as Bella stepped out of the dark house and into the bright rays of the sunset, her father's arm gripped firmly around her shoulders.

Chapter 9 - Bella

Bella squinted into the setting sun as her father led her out of the house. She felt disconnected from reality, and stared blankly at the ground, watching her feet move towards her father's cart. The servants were unloading the goods and tending to the mule; from a distance she heard her father's voice waving them away, and felt his trembling arm guiding her into the cart. Then he was climbing into the seat beside her and shouting for the mule to start the journey, and they were off.

It occurred to her as they rattled down the dirt road that this might be the last time she would see her home again. The realization didn't immediately bother her, and Bella wondered if her lack of reaction was normal. She felt she ought to look back one last time at the retreating house; she was born there, after all, as was her own mother. Bella turned her head to her home, and through her wet eyes the house seemed more vivid than ever before. The green grasses in the yard swayed in the evening breeze and the sun rebounded from the windows with blinding force.

As she watched the house, she saw her stepmother and stepsisters spill out of the house on to the front steps. At this distance, she could see Venizia cast up a hand to shield her eyes from the bright sunset, but she could not read the woman's facial expression as she ran uselessly after the cart. She heard Venizia shout, her voice panicked and angry, but Cienzo merely tightened his grip on the rein and urged the mule on faster. Bella thought she could hear Fiorita crying, but couldn't be certain she hadn't imagined it.

Looking back at them, Bella realized that waving goodbye to her sisters might be the most polite thing to do. She raised her hand and waved slowly, and hoped they would see the smile she forced to her face. "*I won't be able to finish teaching Fiorita the organ,*" Bella thought sadly. And now she would never have the chance to thank Marchetta. Bella suddenly realized that all her belongings — her dresses, her hair ornaments, her childhood toys — had been left at the house. Her mother's old clothes, except the favorite blue gown she now wore, were lost to her. She felt a stab of dizziness and gripped the side of the cart for support.

Father must have noticed the movement, for he shifted the reins to a single hand and reached over with his free hand to pat her knee reassuringly. Bella looked up at him, and the mixture of sadness and determination on his face threatened to send her into tears again.

Her whispered voice struggled to rise over the clatter of the cart on the dirt road. "Father, are you really doing this?" He frowned at her, and she thought he looked almost frustrated. "*What more does he want from me?*" she thought, her heart sinking within her chest.

"Bella ..." he said quietly, and then he turned his attention back to the road. "These things have a way of working out, you'll see," he said briskly. "You hear these rumors all the time: a lonely magician in a desolate castle, seeking a bride. You're so lovely that he's sure to be kind to you, and he will give you a life of security and luxury." He patted her knee. "It will be a blessing in disguise, mark my words."

He hesitated for a long moment, and then added with a sideways glance at her, "I ... I didn't think *you* would volunteer."

Bella stared at him in astonishment, but he kept his eyes firmly on the road and refused to meet her gaze. Emotions churned within her — sadness, that he hadn't believed she would love him enough to save him; anger, that he wouldn't now apologize for misjudging her — but more than anything else she simply felt tired and drained. *"I wish Mother was here,"* she thought, and then lapsed into dull silence, lulled by the rhythm of the cart.

The stars were out and the moon was high in the sky when they reached the end of the road. The heavy fatigue that had allowed Bella to doze on the road fled from her, and she sat up straight in her seat, rubbing the sleep from her eyes, and staring at the sight that greeted her eyes.

A delicate silver gate towered over them and shimmered ethereally in the moonlight that streamed through the forest around them. Behind the gate was a tall hedge, a vivid green-gray mass of thorns and thick branches in the moonlight, but covered with the brightest, reddest rose blooms she had ever seen. Each rose was at full bloom, even at this late hour, and each shimmered wetly with dew where the moonbeams struck it, though the rest of the forest was quite dry.

Bella shivered as the night seemed to close in around her. The hedge was lovely, but its radiance was unnatural. The gate was beautiful, but it gleamed like a silver cage waiting to trap her. *"Is it there to keep people out, or in?"* she thought grimly.

Cienzo climbed down from the cart seat and tied the reins to a nearby tree. The mule seemed skittish, despite being dead tired on its feet. Bella spared a moment of sympathy for the creature before Father was there at her side, reaching up for her hand so that he might help her down. The numbness that had accompanied her for most of the trip was gone; she trembled in her seat and stared down at him in shock.

"Father ..." she pleaded, but she couldn't think of any words to follow it. *"Please don't ask me to do this? Please love me enough to take me home? Please don't make me have to ask you this — that if I have to ask, I already know the answer?"* She didn't have the courage to speak. Better to go to her death as a willing sacrifice, Bella thought sadly, than as an unloved bargaining chip. Bitterly, she placed her hand in her father's and allowed herself to be helped down from the cart.

"Bella ..." Cienzo said, almost tentatively, and she looked at him expectantly.

"Yes, Father?"

"Try ... not to look frightened," he said, his eyes sliding away from hers. "You don't want to ... create the wrong impression."

She stared at him in disbelief. "Of course not, Father," she said sharply. Seized with a strong desire to be as far from him as possible, she stepped towards the gate, placed her hand tentatively on the silver bars, and pushed slightly. The gate opened inwardly, moving on silent hinges, and she walked apprehensively inside. Her heart beat furiously inside her chest and she could hear Father walking behind her. Bella almost felt impatient to get whatever this was over with — let the worst happen now so that she could stop dreading it.

"Hello?" The voice that came behind her was her father's, but was so soft she could barely hear it. "Sir ... my lord?" There was no answer, save for a chill breeze that fluttered the rose petals on either side of them.

"Down there?" Bella asked quietly, lifting her hand to point down the hill into a valley that showed through a gap in the hedges. The gap was barely wide enough for a cart to pass through, but through it she could see moonlight streaming into the valley and striking the gray stone walls of a castle that was larger than any building Bella had seen before.

"I think so." Cienzo sounded uncertain. "I hadn't expected ... I thought he would meet us at the gate ..." His voice trailed off in confusion.

"Forwards, backwards, or neither?" Bella thought, blinking back her tears. Father wouldn't let her go back, and while staying in the cold night air was more appealing than continuing onward, it would only prolong her suffering. She sighed, and began the walk down the dirt road towards the imposing castle that sat dark and cold under the moonlight. Father shuffled quietly behind her, but whether he came to comfort her or because he dared not stay alone, she couldn't bear to guess.

As they entered the courtyard, the silence was disturbed by the loud creak of hinges as the giant castle doors swung slowly open. Jarred from her unhappy thoughts, Bella's gaze shot to the open doors and she stumbled in mid-step, barely righting herself from sprawling. No torches shone within the castle, and the door was so heavily shaded by an overhang that it was impossible to see anything beyond the dark threshold. For a long moment, Bella stood still in the courtyard and waited, trembling anxiously.

Something slid slowly into the splash of moonlight that seeped around the edges of the entrance overhang. Bella stared at the strange object, its edges blurred by the pale white light, and then felt her skin crawl as she realized that the object was a hoof attached to a hairy goat's leg. "What—?" she asked under her breath, and then gasped as the leg moved forward and the rest of the beast emerged into the cold night light.

Behind her, she heard her father suck in his breath in recognition. Bella wanted to turn on her father in anger, but dared not take her eyes from the apparition before her. Cienzo had told her that the magician took the form of the bear, and Bella had tried to prepare herself by imagining every festival bear she had seen as a child, but this abomination was anything *but* a bear.

The creature stood on two legs and was shaped astonishingly like a man, but was impossibly tall; Bella was certain her head wouldn't come up to its chest. Its arms were long and lanky, and were jointed as deeply as its tottering goat-like legs. The creature's hands hung loose at its sides, and Bella shuddered to see that each finger ended in a long claw that glistened sharply in the moonlight. Worst of all was the face, not like a bear at all, but instead a strange mishmash of animals: a lion's snout, a boar's tusks, a buck's ears, and above it all two pitch-black eyes that glittered like dark jewels in the pale light. The creature looked terrifying, wild, and completely unnatural.

Most jarring of all, the creature was dressed as a man. A white tunic hung loosely over the beast's form, the torn sleeves stopping short at the elbow and the shirt hem inadequate to reach all the way down the tall, elongated body. Similar shortcomings were evident in the creature's leg coverings;

fabric flapped loosely at its thin, hairy knees. Even from a distance, and in the moonlight, Bella could see that the creature's clothing had once been especially fine, and it seemed obscene that such expensive garments be wasted in dressing this bizarre animal.

She heard her father clear his throat nervously, breaking the silence. He made no move forward, and no attempt to stand between her and the strange beast, but simply ventured pleadingly, "My lord? I have returned with my daughter."

The creature did not even glance at him; its large black eyes stared eagerly at her. "I see that." Its voice was low, the sound of gravel grinding underfoot, and though Bella had known it would speak, still she jumped in surprise to hear anything come from that strange mass of small, sharp teeth and large boar tusks. "Have you come to save your father, maiden?"

Bella swallowed deeply and tried to find her own voice. Her mouth felt dry and she felt herself shaking in the cold night air. If only those strange inhuman eyes were not staring so hungrily at her! She gulped a breath of air and said as bravely as she could: "Yes."

"You are a very loving girl," the beast said gravely.

Bella inclined her head automatically at the familiar compliment. "It's my name," she said, nervously, "I'm called Bella."

The beast seemed puzzled for a moment, but simply said, "Of course you are," in that same grave tone. At the beast's confusion, Bella realized belatedly that he had not said she was a *lovely* girl, the complement she was most accustomed to. *"Not the most auspicious start,"* she thought to herself, her inner voice mimicking the creature's formal tones. She stifled a nervous giggle and wondered if she was on the verge of hysteria and whether or not she should leap over the edge and be done with it.

"Bella is a very good girl," Cienzo offered, his voice high and tight with fear. "She'll make a very good wife, and you'll have no occasion to ... well, ah ... *complain*." His voice trailed off quietly, and Bella wondered if he'd meant to say 'devour her' or something equally more candid.

The beast shambled slowly across the courtyard toward her, and Bella had to fight a powerful urge to run in the opposite direction. Warily, she eyed those long legs and lanky arms, and imagined that the beast would be able to outrun even the fastest human. Trembling, she held perfectly still, her eyes fixed on its face; the creature stopped a few feet from her and extended one of those long arms. She stared at the hairy arm, unsure what was expected of her. *"Should I offer a compliment?"* she wondered.

"Will you take my hand as my bride?"

The question was solemn and serious; this strange creature was not jesting with her. She had assumed that 'bride' was a euphemism for being the creature's dinner, and what it could actually mean now, Bella could hardly imagine. Wives cooked and cleaned and shopped and managed the household servants and they bore children ... Bella's thoughts trailed off as she felt a blush rise to her cheeks. She couldn't do any of these things for this beast, and she didn't even want to *try*.

The beast was still looking at her intently, its hand outstretched towards her. She glanced back at her father, but Cienzo just nodded anxiously at her, urging her forward. *"I don't have a choice,"* Bella realized with fear. She didn't want to become a bride, with whatever that might entail, to this frightening creature, but neither did she want to be devoured in a rage if she refused.

"I ... do," she said, hesitating over the words. *"What is the correct way to wed an abomination?"* she thought mournfully, but she stepped forward and gingerly placed her hand on the extended palm. Long furry fingers curled over her hand, completely engulfing it, but the touch was gentle and it obviously took care not to scratch her with those sharp nails. Bella tried not to shudder at the strange touch. Its hand was warm and the coarse hair was not too different from a hunting hound they'd had when she was a child, but the sensation felt very different coming from this human-shaped beast.

"Congratulations!" Cienzo bellowed in relief behind them. His loud voice broke through the quiet night and sent a shiver down Bella's spine. He started to babble in a nervous frenzy, "You two will be very happy together, we need to have some kind of party to celebrate, maybe a banquet—"

"Get out."

The beast's voice was changed in that moment: the polite gravity drained from its voice and in its place was a low, animal growl. Bella would have pulled away in fear, but her hand was still encased completely in its own; the slightest sudden movement and she might lacerate her hand on those claws.

"My lord ...?" Cienzo pleaded, stumbling a few steps backward.

"Get out. Go home. Don't come back."

Over her shoulder, Bella watched her father intently in the cold light. He drew a breath as if to say something, but a long look at the beast's face and he deflated. Shoulders hunched, he nodded in defeat and turned to go. "The gate ... my lord?"

The beast waved at him dismissively with its free hand. "It will open at your touch," the creature growled airily. "Come, Bella." Gently but firmly, it led her towards the open castle doors. Bella cast one last look behind her at her father's back as he began to trudge up the slope of the valley walls before she turned to stumble uncertainly after her new husband.

At the castle entrance, she balked a little. The beast noticed her gait slow and it turned to face her. Up close, the creature was even more frightening, and she flinched as those wide black eyes locked on to hers. Sensing her fear, it uncurled its hand from hers and she saw the beast's ears twitch with some animal emotion. Slowly, she drew her hand back, and wrapped her arms tightly across her chest, trying to draw warmth and comfort from the gesture.

"Bella," it said tentatively, "You don't need to be afraid of me. I won't hurt you."

She blinked up at the beast, and felt tears pricking at her eyes. *"Don't cry now!"* she thought fiercely, biting her lip hard, praying she wouldn't break down. "It's not that," she said quietly, hoping she would not offend the strange beast. "I just ..."

"Yes?" The voice was almost tender, its neck craning forward as it stared intently at her.

Bella glanced away from that frightening face, into the dark void of the castle that she was expected to enter. She shivered, and said uncertainly, "I can't see in the dark."

She looked back up at its face and suddenly stepped back in fear; the beast's mouth was wide open, with sharp animal teeth gleaming hungrily. "I'm sorry, my dear, I've become used to seeing in the dark," it said between strange choking sounds, and Bella realizing with astonishment that it was laughing. *That's a smile!* she thought, faint with relief that those teeth weren't about to tear into her.

The beast stepped quickly inside the castle without another word, and Bella was left standing on the doorstep wondering if she was to follow. She couldn't bear to enter that dark void without a light; her mind flinched from imagining what horrors she might trip over in the castle of a beast. Within the darkness, she heard the soft whoosh of a flame, and there stood the beast, a lit candle in one hand and grinning the same toothy smile. The beast came outside to join her, shielding the candle from the cool wind with its free hand, and offered the light to her.

"Will this help?" the beast asked hopefully.

"Thank you," she said, as politely as she could. She took the candle carefully by the base and cupped her hand around the warm flame. "You're very kind," she offered cautiously. The beast smiled at her again — *Those teeth are sharp as needles,"* she thought anxiously — and motioned for her to follow into the castle.

"Come," it said, and she saw no way to politely refuse. With trepidation, she followed into the castle, careful to stay close as the creature led her through wide halls and narrow turns. Everywhere they walked, the castle was silent, and Bella wondered if they were the only living things on the entire estate. She held her candle carefully as she walked, but through the dim light she discerned no grim horrors; the castle seemed rather like what she would have expected from her childhood imaginings: lots of rich tapestries, though a bit more dusty than she would have thought.

"Where are we going, my lord?" she asked cautiously as they rounded another corner and Bella was certain she was hopelessly lost.

"To bed, of course," the beast said absently. "I was asleep when you arrived. You must be tired, it's well past midnight." There followed a strange noise, a series of low moans and bones cracking gently, and Bella realized the huge creature was yawning with fatigue. Quickly she averted her eyes to a nearby tapestry; she didn't care to see any more of the beast's teeth.

"To bed?" she asked with what she hoped sounded like casual curiosity, but her voice cracked with apprehension.

"Oh, yes, you'll like the bedroom. The fireplace keeps it quite warm during these chilly spring nights, and it's very cool in the summer." The voice was proud, the proprietary manner of an owner showing off his treasured estate. Through the dim light, she saw its head crane back to glance at her, and she forced herself to smile and nod encouragingly.

"I ... is that so ...?" she stammered politely. She wasn't sure what more to say, but she was saved as they rounded a corner.

"Ah, here we are." The beast stooped down and touched a door latch. "Ladies first," it said, backing away carefully in the narrow hallway and holding open the door for her.

Bella felt an icy fear. *"How can I go in there?"* she thought with panic, but slowly she stepped into the room. With a smile plastered on to her face, she turned in a circle and pretended to survey the room with pleasure. Behind her, the beast stooped low to walk through the doorway and straightened again once inside the room, smiling at her all the while.

"It's lovely," Bella said, and it wasn't a lie. The room was larger than the drawing room in her home. A big fireplace was cut into the wall and glowed with red embers, filling the room with a comforting warmth. The walls, as far as she could see in the dim light, were covered with beautiful tapestries, some depicting fantastical scenes and others splashed with stunning patterns of colors and shapes. Dominating the far wall, however, was a single enormous bed, its sheets and quilts very recently ruffled by their previous occupant.

"It's very comfortable," the beast assured her, watching her gaze intently. "I hope you'll sleep very well."

She looked up at the beast, and could feel the tears coming now, despite the danger. *"I'd rather be eaten now than ..."*

The beast craned its head at her, and those long ears suddenly twitched.

"Bella?" it said, the gravelly voice thick with concern. "Bella? Why are you crying, dear?"

The room swam before her eyes. "I can't ... I can't!" she cried.

"Bella?" It stepped quickly towards her, arms outstretched; a sharp scream ripped from her throat as she scrambled backwards out of reach. In the corner of the far wall, she trembled fearfully, and watched her dropped candle sputter on the stone floor.

The beast stood frozen in the center of the room, staring down at the floor. Its face was twisted with emotion and its hands were clenched tightly, but as she studied the creature fearfully, the thought struck her that it looked more sad than angry.

"Bella," it said, and the voice was so soft she strained to hear it. "I am not going to hurt you. I promise you that." The beast's body stayed motionless, but those eyes moved up to hers. She blinked slowly and thought that the eyes seemed full of remorse. *"I've hurt ... its feelings,"* she thought with astonishment.

"I ... I'm sorry." She wasn't sure what she was apologizing for, but it seemed like a good place to start. "I ... I can't ... I can't be your ... wife." She gestured helplessly at the bed, before quickly pulling her hands back to wrap around herself again.

The beast stared at her in incomprehension for a moment, and then buried its face in those hands. *"Is it crying?"* Bella marveled but, when it spoke a moment later, the voice was more embarrassed than sorrowful. "Bella, I'm so sorry. I wasn't clear." Hands lowered from its face, the beast looked at her with clear eyes and a hint of that strange smile, almost sympathetic. "I don't expect you to do anything but sleep here at night and keep me company with your conversation during the day. I'm really not going to hurt you — I won't even touch you, Bella."

She looked at the beast warily. "Promise?" she asked, and immediately regretted it. *"You're not supposed to argue,"* she chastised herself angrily.

"I promise," it said solemnly. The creature cast a long look at the rumpled bed, and finally offered, "I'll even sleep on the floor tonight, if it will make you feel safer."

Bella stared at the beast, unsure of what to do with this offer. "You would?"

"Yes. But I would prefer not to," it said, curling up one lip in an almost human expression of distaste at the cold floor.

In her nervousness she laughed, and then immediately clapped a hand over her mouth. The beast watched her quietly; after a long moment's thought, she said with a sigh, "No, it's all right. I don't ... mind." She couldn't stop it from entering the bed if it took a mind to, and it was better to keep the creature happy, no matter what promises were claimed.

She flashed what she hoped was a convincing smile, and carefully climbed into the large bed, settling herself down on the edge, as far from the center as possible. The beast watched her the whole time, its ears twitching gently. *"Is it distress that makes them do that?"* she wondered curiously. Once she was settled, it stepped forward slowly and gently placed a hoof on the still-guttering candle. The light extinguished quickly, leaving only the glow from the fireplace to light the dark room.

Slowly, the beast shuffled to the far side of the bed and carefully climbed in. Bella could hear breathing, thick and heavy to suit the huge frame that barely fit the length of the bed. She kept her own breathing steady, wondering if she could trick it into thinking she was already asleep. *"I won't sleep a wink tonight,"* she promised herself fearfully.

Beside her, the beast sighed contentedly. "Good night, Bella," it murmured into the darkness.

She struggled within herself: to keep up the pretense of sleep or risk being considered impolite? "Good night ... my lord," she finally murmured uncertainly.

Beside her, the beast yawned again, its jaw popping and snapping loudly with the strain. "Oh," it said sleepily. "You can call me Ezio."

In the darkness, she blinked in surprise. *"It has a name?"* she thought. Quietly, she repeated, "Good night ... Ezio," but there was no response except a deep, rhythmic snore. And though she did not intend to sleep, she could feel the exhaustion of the day wash over her and her eyes began to droop against her best efforts.

Chapter 10 - Ezio

It was still dark when Ezio awoke from a nightmare, not that "dark" had meant much to him in the weeks since his grotesque transformation. Even the slightest source of light, such as the warm red embers that still glowed on the hearth, was enough to light the room clearly for him. He lay motionless and allowed his eyes to dart about the room, struggling to keep his breathing calm.

He was usually a heavy sleeper, but he'd slept badly with the girl lying in bed next to him. He'd been tormented by a vivid dream in which he turned to embrace her, only to find that he had accidentally shredded her to pieces with his sharp claws. The bed linens had been doused with warm blood, and his ears were still ringing with the dream-howl that had erupted from his throat at the sight of the body. Now that he was awake and his rapid heartbeat was slowing to normal, he could hear the girl snoring softly beside him and he knew that she was safe.

Ezio turned his head slightly to stare at the girl. She was astonishingly lovely, with honey-blonde hair that spread over her pillow like a curtain and skin the color of cream. With her eyes closed and her deep breathing, she looked innocent and vulnerable, though the effect was spoiled somewhat by her soft, rhythmic snores. In the dark, Ezio frowned. Though he had tumbled a few maidservants in the past, the trysts had been quick and clandestine; Ezio had never actually *slept* with a lover in the same bed. He hadn't mentally prepared for the idea that his wife might snore, and he wasn't pleased that the girl was exhibiting such a trait. Still, he supposed it was a small price for the return of his true form. If it bothered him in the future, Ezio reflected, he could always adopt his father's custom of separate bedrooms, but for now the shared bed was a necessity: he needed the girl to see that he could be trusted with her safety.

The sun would be up soon, but Ezio suspected that after the strain of her journey the night before, the girl might sleep for most of the morning. He stifled a sigh. There was no telling how long it would take before the girl fell in love with him, and it was best to get started soon. For the moment, though, it was probably best to let her sleep rather than shake her awake and risk frightening her. Still, Ezio felt too restless to stay in bed any longer; he was awake now and wanted to make the most of the day. He decided he would visit Guerrino. Ezio hadn't seen the old man since he had woken Ezio a few hours before to report that the girl and her father had arrived at the gate.

Slowly, so as not to disturb the sleeping girl, Ezio sat up in bed and maneuvered his body so that his feet touched the floor. He stood quietly and took a step away from the bed, but immediately realized that he had a problem: every step he took with his hard hooves on the stone floor, no matter how gingerly he moved, resulted in a loud *clop* that was deafening in the silent room. After the first few steps, each more careful than the last, Ezio stopped to think. A glance back at the bed told him that the girl was still sleeping as deeply as before. He tried sliding his hooves across the floor, but the scraping sound was even more jarring than the distinct *clop* of individual steps. He gritted his sharp teeth — earning himself a light cut on his lip in the process — and stepped as quietly as he could out of the bedroom, closing the door gently behind him.

Once out in the hall, Ezio could move more freely. He breathed a quiet thanks, as he had every morning for the past fortnight, that his ancestral home had been built with extremely high ceilings. The vaulted ceilings had always seemed a design flaw in the past, making the castle uncomfortably breezy and cold, but the payoff was that he could navigate the hallways easily and could even climb the narrow steps of Guerrino's tower without too much stooping.

The door to Guerrino's room was closed, and Ezio pounded excitedly on the wooden frame. After a long wait, he heard the bolt open on the other side, and the door opened. Guerrino stood on the other side of the door, dressed for bed and blinking sleepily at the prince. Ezio ducked his head and shouldered his way through the narrow door as Guerrino stepped back to accommodate the prince's tall frame.

"Have you seen her?" Ezio asked the old man in triumph.

"Is she gone? Is something wrong?" Guerrino looked immediately alert, his voice tinged with concern.

Ezio laughed. "No, everything is perfect," he said. "I just meant: have you taken a good look at her yet?"

The older man frowned. "No," he said, shaking his head, "I woke when they touched the gate last night. I waited to see from my window that they were coming down the road, and then I woke you. After I returned to my room, I didn't look out again for fear they might see me."

Ezio regarded the older man curiously. "Why wouldn't you want them to see you?" he asked.

Guerrino sighed and sat down on the edge of the bed, rubbing the sleep out of his eyes and yawning. "Your Highness," he said in the dry, condescending tone that Ezio was learning to despise, "The girl is here to fall in love with an occupant of the castle. I think our odds will be better if she has only one candidate to choose from, rather than two."

Ezio stared at Guerrino, wondering if the dour old man was making a joke. Guerrino did not smile, but Ezio laughed anyway at the absurdity of the suggestion. "Stay in your tower then, sir," the prince joked, "for I couldn't bear to lose my pretty new bride." He strode the length of the room to the window, too excited to stand still, and stared out at the slowly fading stars. "She's beautiful, Guerrino," he said quietly, almost reverently. "The fairy sent the most beautiful girl possible to redeem me."

"Your Highness, I would imagine the girl's countenance to be little more than a happy coincidence," Guerrino said cautiously. "Visitations from *fata* are exceedingly rare, and they very rarely remain to intervene directly once a curse has been laid."

The skepticism in Guerrino's voice irritated Ezio. He turned away from the window and fixed his advisor with a harsh stare. "You don't *know* that she didn't pick Bella for me," he argued. "She's everything I need, and that can't be simple coincidence." He started to clumsily tick off a list with his sharp claws. "She's beautiful. Her father is rich, he said so himself. Her dowry is probably richer than Adelina's. And," he finished triumphantly, "it's just a matter of time before she loves me and breaks the curse."

Guerrino frowned, but instead of the argument Ezio was expecting, the older man simply yawned and said, "As you say, Your Highness. Where is the girl now?"

"I left her asleep in the bedroom. She was exhausted after last night."

Guerrino's eyes widened. He opened his mouth to speak, but for once seemed at a loss for words. Finally he stammered, "You do not mean ..."

"No." Ezio wrinkled his nose at the suggestion. "She thought the same thing," he said with a frown. "But the only important thing right now is breaking the curse. Anything else will wait."

The old man looked relieved, and lapsed into his chiding tone. "Then why is she in your bedroom, Your Highness? The girl must have been scared to death to be brought there. Bad enough that you sent her father away."

"He was only upsetting her," Ezio shot back. "And her being frightened was a good thing! She has to learn that she can trust me. If she doesn't trust me, she'll never love me."

Ezio turned back to the window in frustration, annoyed at having to defend his own actions. *"What does Guerrino know about love, anyway?"*

he thought angrily. Ezio couldn't recall the man ever having a woman, not even in the prince's childhood.

For several long moments, the only sounds in the room were Ezio's heavy breathing and Guerrino's own soft wheeze. Ezio eyed the bright pinks and golds that were starting to gently streak up through the spring sky. If everything were as it should have been, he would have been helping Flavio to saddle the horses for a brisk morning ride, or maybe an early hunt. Instead, his horses were long gone from the stables, and he was trapped in a castle with a third-rate warlock who gave himself airs and a beautiful, but utterly low-born merchant's daughter. *"Maybe she's secretly a princess,"* Ezio hoped. It was a comforting thought, at any rate.

Behind him, the old man cleared his throat with a few thick coughs. "Dawn's coming up," he said. "You shouldn't leave her alone for too long. Is she terribly slender?"

This last question caught the prince off-guard and Ezio turned to stare at him. "What?" he asked, completely puzzled. "I suppose she is rather slender, why?"

Guerrino stood to join the prince at the window, peering out into the dim morning light. "I'm concerned about the fence," the old man mused quietly. "I put the bars as close together as I could, but I think a child or a very slender adult could squeeze through the bars with enough effort."

Ezio stared out the window at the gleaming silver fence that Guerrino had painstakingly erected in the days following his curse. The roses were the key to his restoration, Guerrino had explained, and their protection was paramount. From that first morning, Ezio had acutely felt each nibble as the wild does ventured out of the forest to break their fast at the magical hedge, and as each rose died, he could feel a piece of his humanity slipping away.

Those first few days had been the worst, with little sleep and even less time to mourn what he had lost. Guerrino had drawn runes on the tower floor and chanted in strange languages from dawn until dusk, while Ezio patrolled the perimeter of the estate for hours with only quick snatches of sleep each night. The silver gate had grown slowly out of the ground, inch by inch, until finally it was too tall for any man or beast to climb over. A solid wall would have been better, but Guerrino barely had the strength to complete the delicate fence; Ezio did not think the old man would have survived a more ambitious attempt. To drive away the smaller animals, the warlock had used a dose of Ezio's urine to lay a spell on and around the thick thorn hedge: now the sharp scent of a predator permanently drove away the foxes and hares from the bright blossoms.

Almost two weeks after the night of the curse, the fence was complete and Ezio's humanity was safe from the nibbles and pickings of both man and beast. The only way in or out of the estate was through the gate, which was lined with so many enchantments that a single human touch would alert Guerrino to a stranger's presence. Then the two men had rested, and waited.

"It's good that the merchant came when he did," Ezio reflected. *"Any earlier and the fence would have been too short to trap him."* It was just one more piece of evidence that the girl was a blessing sent specifically to him. "You're worried she'll escape," Ezio said flatly.

"It had crossed my mind," the older man said dryly.

Ezio considered this for a moment. "Can you add new bars to fill in the gaps?"

"No. I'd have to take the fence down and start from the beginning, and ..." Guerrino didn't need to finish the sentence. The first effort had been exhausting, and he was still not quite recovered; Ezio doubted he could manage a second attempt.

"Could you cast another spell?" Ezio asked doubtfully. "Like the urine? Something to keep her inside and away from the fence?"

Guerrino looked thoughtful. "We keep the rabbits away from the hedge with the *smell* of wolves," he said slowly, "maybe we can keep the girl away from the gate with the *sound* of them."

"Can you do that?" Ezio asked curiously.

"It shouldn't be too hard." Guerrino had stepped over to his work table, his hands flipping gently through the thin pages of his grimoire. "A few howls at night ... some growls and a few shadows when she walks near the fence ... If she gets too bold, I can even conjure a convincing construct. It won't smell like the real thing, and wouldn't fool another animal, but it can bite and a human won't be able to tell the difference."

"Perfect," Ezio agreed, relieved that they had a solution.

"Your best bet is still to keep an eye on her at all times," Guerrino cautioned.

"I will," the prince promised. "I was going to take her on a tour of the castle today anyway, let her see her new home as a princess."

Guerrino frowned. "You're not thinking of telling her who you really are?"

There was that condescending tone again, and Ezio frowned, trying to work out what the objection could possibly be. He gave up, and tried to shrug off the question. "Why wouldn't I?"

The old man fixed him with a weary scowl. "Your Highness," he said, "The girl is here to fall in love with *you*, not your title. If you tell her you're an enchanted prince, will she even have a chance to fall in love with *you*, or will she fall in love with the *prince*?"

Ezio stared at Guerrino as his words sank in. "That's very cynical, isn't it?" he asked icily.

"It doesn't hurt to be careful," the old man said with a shrug, turning his back on the prince and returning to his magic book. Ezio had the distinct impression that he was being dismissed.

"This curse can't be lifted too soon," the prince thought. Once things went back to normal, his first order of business would be to find a nice country cottage for his advisor to retire to, the farther away the better.

Ezio crept quietly back to his bedroom, but when he opened the door and stepped inside, the sound of his hooves seemed to wake the young girl. Her saw her eyes open, slowly and sleepily at first, and then widen in confusion and shock as she registered her surroundings. She looked up at him in the doorway of the bedroom, and an expression of sudden, undisguised horror flitted over her face. Immediately, the girl realized her mistake: her face reflexively pulled back into a winsome smile that failed to reach her eyes, and she ran a hand nervously through her tangled hair.

Were it not for the frightened girl in his bed, the day would feel like any other: the morning sunlight shone brightly through the window slits and spilled on to the stone floor in bright patterns. The juxtaposition of her terror with the mundane details of the morning filled Ezio with nervous energy, and he couldn't help but laugh at how absurd the situation was. He tilted his head back as the strange cacophony of animal noises that was his laughter flowed from him, and he only hoped the sound wouldn't scare her too much.

"Good morning, darling," he said cheerily to the poor girl when his laughter subsided. He gave her what he hoped was a rueful smile. "I'm afraid *I* don't improve much in the morning light, but *you* are even more beautiful now than you were in last night's moonlight." He was gratified to see the girl's wide, nervous smile ease into a smaller, but more genuine, crooked grin at this compliment.

"Thank you ... my lord," she stammered quietly, still tightly clutching the sheet in her fists as though it were the anchor to her sanity.

"I'm just Ezio," he said simply, remembering Guerrino's advice. He pushed the thought of the old man from his mind and smiled more warmly. "And you are Bella?" She nodded. "It suits you," he said, bowing his head a little as if he were meeting her for the first time.

The girl blinked at him before smiling again. "Thank you." Her voice was warm, but cautious. Ezio supposed that the radiant girl was used to such compliments when she gave her name.

"You must be hungry," he said gently. "You travelled a long way last night, I know. I'll step out in the hallway so that you can take a few minutes to wake up, and when you're ready, we'll go eat breakfast together."

The girl nodded vigorously and her hand ran nervously through her hair again. Ezio gestured to a corner of the room where a small side chamber led off into shadows. When his mother had been alive, she had decorated the chamber as a dressing-room and it had never been renovated into anything else after her death. "You can use anything you like in there," he offered. "I think there are several brushes on the vanity table." With that, he backed out of the doorway and closed the door behind him.

Chapter 11 - Bella

Bella stared at the closed door where the beast had stood a moment before. The shock of seeing the hideous creature in the morning light was fading, and her mind was seized with a heavy drowsiness. Yesterday's events — her father's announcement and their arrival at the castle — seemed like a hazy dream, and yet here she was in this stone room. Slowly she unclenched the sheet from her fists and rubbed her fingers gingerly around her sleep-crusted eyes, hoping to clear her sight and her mind at the same time.

Light streamed down through the high windows of the bedroom. It registered in her mind that she had not woken gradually with the morning, but rather at an unfamiliar noise — she had woken when the beast opened the bedroom door, she realized. She glanced down at the bed and took in the mussed sheets beside her that still radiated a faint warmth and were covered with a fine layer of animal hair. *"He slept here last night ... but woke before I did?"* Bella wondered. Maybe he had gone for a walk while she still slept. *"He was awake, while I was asleep,"* she realized. And he hadn't touched her. He had remained true to his word.

The relief she felt in the wake of this realization was enormous. Whatever else might happen to her in this strange castle, it seemed that the beast was not interested in hurting her, or at least not yet. She swung her legs over the side of the bed, and realized that she was wearing the same clothes and shoes as the night before; she felt grimy and her scalp was starting to itch. She stepped into the side chamber the beast had indicated and smiled in delight at the bright little room. A fine vanity table dominated the small room at the far wall and the rich dark wood of the table was lit brightly from the side by a beautiful stained-glass window.

Gingerly, Bella ran her fingers over the items on the vanity, scarcely daring to breathe. A variety of brushes and combs glinted up at her in the light. Each brush was inlaid with patterns of tiny gems, and the combs were tipped with precious metals. The smallest comb had six teeth, each as long as her tiniest finger, and was made entirely of pure silver. Bella carefully picked up the glittering comb and ran it gently through her hair, marveling at the novelty of the sensation. *"I'm using money to dress my hair,"* Bella thought, suppressing a giggle. The slender comb wasn't worth much, she knew — she had seen Marchetta spend a comparable lump of silver coins on their monthly grocery expenses — yet the novelty of distilling that money into a single hair-comb seemed absurdly excessive, even for someone who lived in a castle.

"A castle ..." Bella's mind jumped at the thought and she looked around her, feeling as though she was registering her surroundings for the first time. She wondered where she was in relation to her home. Bella had lived her entire life in the village and had only traveled with Father once to the city on one of his business trips, long ago when she was a little girl. She didn't know of any castles near their home, and had been too grief-stricken on the ride yesterday to notice which roads they had taken. *"East or west or north or south?"* she thought in singsong, feeling a rising sense of panic, but it was no use — the last time she remembered the sun, it was shining

on her home as she waved goodbye to her stepmother and stepsisters. After that she remembered only gathering darkness.

Realizing that the beast was waiting on her, Bella shook herself from her reverie. She brushed her hands over her dress and fluffed out her skirt to shake off the dust from the road. Steadying herself with one hand on the vanity, she pulled off one shoe and then the other, scraping them carefully against the stone wall to dislodge the dried mud and then slipping them back on to her feet. Unable to think of anything else to do to freshen up, she turned to go, but hesitated. The small silver comb lay on the vanity table, winking at her in the light.

Her fingers itched to touch it again, to feel the steady reassuring weight in her hand. *"This is stupid,"* Bella admonished herself harshly. *"If the beast finds out ..."* It was a thought she didn't want to finish. Yet still the comb beckoned to her, glinting and glittering in the sun. She felt a part of her ache for the comb; she had nothing else except the clothes she wore. And the comb could be so useful. If she got beyond the outside gate, if she were in a position to barter a ride ... She stared hard at the glinting ornament, before reaching slowly out to stroke the comb once before deftly tucking it up the long, tight sleeve of her dress. Before she could change her mind, she marched purposefully from the chamber and through the door out of the bedroom.

The beast was waiting for her patiently in the hallway, standing well away from the door so that she could slip out of the room without touching him. He flashed those sharp teeth at her in the manner she was coming to recognize as a smile and bowed his head slightly.

"Hungry?" he asked. Bella nodded her head cautiously, and he smiled again. "Follow me, then," he said cheerfully, and he walked down the hall with such long strides that Bella stumbled to keep up.

As they walked, she studied him from behind with intense curiosity. The beast looked less inhuman from behind. He was still unnaturally tall, with grotesquely thin arms and legs, and strange hooves for feet, but his lumbering gait and the swinging arms at his side seemed more human than animal. She could not decide if his clothes lent him an air of civilization or parody. The too-short cloth sleeves and pants made him look like an adult in children's clothing, and the tears and stains in the clothes made the creature seem dangerous. Still, she decided the clothing gave him a certain dignity. *"Without the clothes, he'd seem more monstrous,"* she decided.

After several twists and turns, the hallway spilled out into a large kitchen, cold and unused, but with an open door set in the far wall that looked out on to a bright and cheerful orchard. The beast headed straight for the door, but paused mid-stride and looked back at her with an almost sheepish smile on his face.

"You don't mind eating in the garden, do you?" he asked, a little nervously.

"Not at all," Bella reassured him. "It's such a pretty day," she added soothingly. She would have agreed just to mollify him, but it was true: the breeze was cool but pleasant and the light clouds that drifted in front of the still-rising sun would provide a nice shade to sit in.

"Oh, good," the beast said cheerfully, leading her out into the bright garden. "One less plate to dirty," he said. His tone was light, but Bella tried not to stare at his long claws while wondering how such a creature might go about the washing-up.

When she stepped into the garden, Bella gasped. She stood just outside the castle, and turned slowly in place, taking in the whole of the garden. The orchard sprawled in all directions, and Bella could identify a dozen different fruits and vegetables on the trellised vines, bushes, and trees before her. The leaves were impossibly bright with reds and golds, the fruits looked succulent and juicy, and the scent was so overpowering that her stomach grumbled loudly in anticipation.

The beast stood under a nearby fig tree, shafts of sunlight sprinkling through the trees on to his dark brown fur, watching her with an expression of open pride. "See anything you like, Bella?" he asked grandly, his gesture taking in the sweep of the garden.

"It's beautiful," she breathed, and he smiled at the praise. "But ..." she reached out to touch the closest trellis, her fingers brushing gently over the fat ripe grapes. She looked up at him, her face clouded with confusion. "It's too early for these to be ripe," she said, puzzled.

He laughed his barking laugh, pulled down a couple of figs and tossed one to her. She caught the fruit reflexively, and he bit into his own with relish. "It's magic," he said simply.

With a startled cry, Bella dropped the fig and backed away from it. *Is that why he looks the way he does?"* The thought flashed across her mind, but she could find no words to politely frame the question. Her face betrayed her thoughts, and the beast's face suddenly turned serious.

"Ah, no, not *that* kind of magic," he said, shifting his weight from leg to leg uncomfortably. "Not the sort of magic that would, ah, change the eater in any way." He nodded to her reassuringly as she stretched out her hand again, tentatively, to touch a cluster of grapes.

"This is what you eat every day?" Bella asked, still unsure of the unnaturally bright fruit under her fingertips.

"Not every day," he said with a shrug. "Sometimes I have a hare for dinner."

Bella stared at him warily, her thoughts running over those sharp teeth that protruded through his gentle smiles. Suddenly a little ill, she dropped her eyes away from his face and back to the grapes under her hand. *"Better this than raw meat,"* she thought with a gulp, and she plucked a single grape and gently bit into the skin.

The juice that flooded into her mouth was sweet and clean and good; if there was dark magic in the fruit, she couldn't taste it. Delicately, she sucked the juice and flesh of the grape before quietly dropping the seed on the ground. The beast nodded encouragingly as he watched her eat. "Tastes good, doesn't it?" he asked, and she nodded. "Come on," he said, waving her further into the garden, "I'll pick the higher ones for you and we can eat on the benches."

Bella followed him meekly through the garden as he happily picked fruits and gently lay them in the little hammock she made by holding the edges of her skirt out. Her blue dress was quickly stained with the juices of the freshly picked fruits and this was a detail the beast noticed with chagrin. Between mouthfuls of blackberries, he said apologetically, "We'll have to get you some more dresses. I think there are some left in the guest bedrooms."

"Left by whom?" Bella wondered, but she didn't feel comfortable asking him any questions just yet. It was enough to know that he planned to keep her alive long enough to clothe her properly.

As they sat on the bench eating their breakfast, Bella decided she couldn't be silent any longer without appearing rude to her host. *"But how to start a conversation with him?"* she fretted. The beast had been jovial enough but his remarks had been limited so far to the goodness of the fruit, the prettiness of the weather, and other such safe topics. Bella decided that it would be safest to start with flattery.

"Your orchard is so beautiful," she volunteered.

The beast paused between mouthfuls of fruit. His teeth and tusks were stained purple with blackberry juice, which looked to Bella uncomfortably like blood at such a close distance on the garden bench. The effect was somewhat softened by the tiny fig seeds that dotted the fur around his mouth. "Thank you," he said proudly. "I've always—" he stopped abruptly and looked uncomfortable. "That is to say ... I'm quite fond of it," he finished in a more subdued tone.

Bella was puzzled by his mood swing, but decided to press on. "You must be a very skilled magician, to make the fruits ripen so early," she gushed.

Now the beast looked positively glum. "Oh," was all he said. Then, "It isn't very important."

"Have I upset him?" Bella wondered, worried. Maybe she wasn't supposed to talk about magic ... and yet he'd been so proud of the garden just moments before. Perplexed, she reached into her lap for a golden pear, when the silver comb, now glistening with a slight sheen of sweat and oil, suddenly slid out from inside her sleeve and fell to the ground.

Bella froze in place on the bench, her eyes glued on the glittering comb lying in the dark earth at her feet. She could tell by the beast's held breath that he had seen the comb fall, that he was watching her now. *"Act naturally,"* she thought, fighting back her rising panic. There was nothing more natural in the world than borrowing a comb from one's host.

Aware that she mustn't make any sudden movements, Bella stooped down and picked the comb up from the ground. Casually, she brushed the dirt from the comb and ran the silver teeth through her hair twice, making a show of patting her hair down from the wind. After restyling her hair, she slipped the comb back into her sleeve, careful that her movements were open and clear to the beast. Only then did she look up and smile at him.

His expression was guarded, but not angry. She dipped her head in a gesture of acknowledgment and grinned nervously. "I hope you don't mind me using your combs, my lord," she said with as much sweetness as she could force into her voice. "My hair is such a fright if I don't maintain it constantly throughout the day." She tilted her head and tried to look bashful.

He stared at her for a long moment, his eerie black eyes a mask that she couldn't penetrate. After a moment, he reached forward to cover her hand with his, but stopped and dropped his hand on to the cool stone bench instead. He sighed heavily. "Bella, you are my wife now," he said, and she was relieved to hear no anger in his voice, just a calm forcefulness. "Everything I own is yours: this castle and everything in it." He held her eyes with his own. "Do you understand?"

Bella nodded nervously. She felt she should thank him, or say something to express the gratitude that this sentiment ought to engender, but all she could think at that moment was that she didn't *want* the castle. Or anything in it. She smiled reflexively, hoping her thoughts wouldn't show on her face, and he continued intently. "There's just two things I need you to promise. Can you do that for me?"

"Yes, my lord," she replied automatically, and he smiled ruefully.

"Well, make that three things," he said, and his ears twitched lightly in the breeze. "First, I beg that you call me 'Ezio'. I'm no one's lord, and especially not your own. I'm just Ezio, your handsome husband." He smiled at his joke, but Bella thought the expression looked forced. "Second, I need you never to touch the roses that ring the estate."

She stared at him blankly, not understanding what he meant. "The roses?" she asked.

"Remember your father picked a rose from my hedges?" he prompted. She looked away, not wanting to speak of Father, but nodded for him to continue. "Those roses are worth more than life to me," he said earnestly. "All my plants are," he said, gesturing to the fruits and vegetables around them, "but these are for eating, and my roses are only for looking. You must never touch them, never pick them. Do you understand?"

She nodded again, before clearing her throat. "Yes ... Ezio," she said hesitantly.

He rewarded her with a smile. "And the last thing: I want you to take great care around the gate. It was built to keep the wolves off the estate, but sometimes they try to burrow under."

Bella stared at him. "Wolves?" she said, unsure whether to believe him. Father had never mentioned wolves along his trade routes, but she still didn't know if they were anywhere *near* his trade routes.

"Yes," the beast affirmed, holding her gaze steadily and frowning with concern. "They moved down into the forest with the winter, and I built the gate to keep them out."

"So ..." Bella hesitated. She didn't know how to ask without sounding rude. He nodded kindly for her to continue. "I'm ... not ... a prisoner here?" she asked quietly, her eyes downcast.

"Oh, Bella." His deep sigh sounded sad. She glanced up at him, hoping her expression was appropriately meek. "You're my wife, Bella," he said tenderly. "This is our home, but of course you're not a prisoner here. If there's anywhere you want to visit, all you have to do is ask." His smile was wide, but his eyes stared at her with an intense expectancy that made her uncomfortable. "Would you like to visit your father?"

Bella was startled by the offer and glanced down at the ground, trying to collect her thoughts. *"Is he seriously offering?"* she wondered. And did she even *want* to see Father again after he'd been so willing to leave her? She shrugged, and tried to look non-committal. "You're so kind to offer, but I don't think I need to visit just yet," she said shyly. "He probably hasn't even returned home from last night."

Bella hoped her statement would prompt the beast to say that they were actually quite close to her village, but the only response was a relieved smile. "I'm glad you're happy here," he said earnestly. "I only want you to be safe. Please promise me you won't go near the gate?"

Her mouth felt dry; she swallowed and said quietly, "I promise."

The beast looked satisfied. He gathered up several figs and pears into his arms and rose from the bench. "Thank you, sweetheart," he said. "I'm afraid I have to leave you for a few hours — I have to check on the roses and make sure that nothing has been digging under the gate. Will you be okay if I leave you to explore your new home until dinner?"

Bella was surprised. She hadn't expected to be left alone, and wasn't sure how to feel about the suggestion. The castle was so quiet that she felt nervous at the idea of exploring alone, but the beast made her feel uncomfortable, and not just because he looked so frightening. He wanted something from her, but she couldn't guess what. *"It was easier when I thought he wanted to eat me,"* she thought anxiously. The flippant thought made her want to laugh, but instead she smiled and nodded. "I'll be fine," she assured him.

"Wonderful!" He headed for the kitchen entrance, still carrying his armful of fruits — *"Is he taking them to eat later?"* Bella wondered — but paused and looked back at her. "And Bella, remember that anything you find in the castle to your liking — combs, clothes, whatever — it's all yours to use however you wish." He flashed her another smile and ducked back into the castle, leaving Bella in the bright orchard with the warm morning sun streaming down through the trees.

Bella sat still, savoring the silence and collecting her thoughts. The cool stone bench seemed to steady her, and she could hear the chirping and squawking of birds as they hopped about in the branches above her. *"It feels unreal,"* she mused. *"Will I wake up and find this was all a nightmare?"* Her stomach growled lightly, and she ate several more grapes and the remaining figs, grateful that she was alone and could spit the seeds in the dirt without an audience.

There was a well in the garden, and Bella pulled up a small bucket of water to rinse her face and hands. The cool water cleared her head. She looked back at the kitchen entrance. *"Do I just wander around?"* she wondered. The thought occurred to her that she might be here for a long time — *"A lifetime?"* — and she pushed the thought aside as more than she could deal with at the moment. Squaring her shoulders, she marched inside the castle, picked a hallway at random, and set off walking down the cool corridors.

Where the garden had been vibrant and alive, Bella was disappointed to find that the castle seemed dead and in disrepair. Several rooms were poorly furnished and in a haphazard design — beds with no bedding, and vanities with no chairs — almost as though a thief had come in the night and swept away half the furnishings. The rooms were dusty and unused, and several doors, including one that Bella thought might lead to one of the castle towers, were boarded up tight and wouldn't budge when she tried to open them.

She did find some treasures in her explorations. A few drab dresses were tucked away at the bottom of a heavy chest in what seemed to be the servants' quarters for the castle. The dresses had been heavily used and mended, but they were clean and Bella was relieved to find something to wear besides her own increasingly dirty dress. *"At least I won't have to go naked on laundry day,"* she thought with a giggle. In a room that contained a lavish stained-glass window, two velvet gowns of a deep purple and a rich red had been tossed under the bed. By lying on her stomach on the floor, Bella was able to drag them out for inspection. Both dresses were torn at the hem, and the velvet was exceedingly crumpled, but she imagined she could fix the damage if she could find a needle.

In addition to the dresses, she found a small silver spoon lying under a wardrobe, an emerald hair ornament fashioned to look like a butterfly that she found hiding behind a shabby travel trunk, and several beeswax candles scattered about the castle. Bella carried the dresses back to the beast's bedroom and laid them out on the bed, put the hair ornament in her hair, and tucked the silver spoon carefully behind the vanity. The candles she lay on the floor near the cooled fireplace, with a sense of accomplishment.

It was mid-afternoon when Bella came to a large set of heavy wooden double doors. She placed her palms on the doors and pushed, and the doors swung open with a light creaking into a dark, cool room. The air smelled close and musty, and as Bella stepped slowly inside the dark chamber, she could feel that the room was quite spacious. *"What is this?"* she wondered, moving quietly forward with her hands outstretched to keep from bumping into anything. *"It's not a bedroom, it's too big."* She was a little frightened in the dark, but as her eyes adjusted she could see a small sliver of light on the far wall. Carefully, she picked her way to the light and reached out to feel heavy curtains; these she pulled back and the afternoon light streamed into the room.

It was a library, the largest Bella had ever seen. Far larger than her father's library at home, and filled with floor-to-ceiling wooden shelves that held hundreds of books. A low table squatted on one side of the room, and a gilt-backed couch sat opposite on the other side; Bella had walked between them to reach the curtain. She walked slowly around the edges of the large room, staring at the book titles, not daring to touch anything.

On her second pass through the room, she stopped at a shelf and stared hard at the books in confusion. *"Something is wrong here,"* she thought, but she couldn't quite work out what had made her stop. Then she realized: the rest of the shelves had a thick coating of dust covering the dark wood, but *this* shelf had streaks in the dust, as though the books had been taken out and read recently before being returned to their places.

"Can the beast read?" It didn't seem possible, with those long claws. Bella imagined he'd rip to shreds any book he touched. She glanced behind her, but nothing in the castle stirred except her. Carefully, she pulled books from the shelf — five large volumes — and carried them over to the low table. Bella ran her fingers over the titles of the books, straining to read the ornate writing, her lips mouthing the sounds as she went.

A True Account of Dealing with Fata.
Mischievous Folletti and Their Curses. [19]
The Treasures and Vengeance of Monachicchi. [20]
Benevolent Creatures of Home and Hearth.
Driving Away Mazapegol Without Causing Offense. [21]

Bella had never heard the titles before, but she knew the words well enough. *"Fairies?"* Nervously she looked again towards the open library doors, but she was alone. *"Who is reading about fairies?"* She stepped over to the window and peered out the thick glass. In the distance she could see the rose hedge, the roses staring at her like bright red eyes. The beast moved slowly along the perimeter of the hedge, inspecting each flower and watering the hedge from a large bucket he carried. Bella had seen him periodically throughout the day from the castle windows; his patrol was painstakingly methodical as he examined each rose, pulled weeds, and refilled his bucket from the well over and over again.

She frowned as she watched him, and looked back at the table that held the strange books. Bella felt certain that there was some piece of logic that would make her life suddenly make sense again. *"A deserted castle,"* she ticked off in her mind. *"A magic garden. A magic rose hedge?"* The roses were as bright as the fruit trees in the orchard. *"A magic gate?"* The silver that gleamed at her in the afternoon sun couldn't actually be silver. Not even newly-polished silver shone with such intensity. *"And the beast is the magician?"*

That was what Father had told her, but why had the beast been so uncomfortable when she praised him that morning? He didn't seem naturally humble; on the contrary, everything he had shown her so far had been shown with deep pride. He had been proud of his ownership of the garden, but was *not* proud of the magic that made it noteworthy. And the night before, he had been proud of the bedroom, almost as if ... *"Almost as if he was born here,"* Bella realized.

None of it made any sense to Bella. If the beast was a magician, why wouldn't he take on a human form? There had been moments at breakfast when he had clearly wanted to touch her — to stroke her hand or touch her hair — but he had held back, apparently fearful of hurting her. *"Why would he shy away from discussing his powers, when he is otherwise so interested in impressing me?"*

A movement outside the window caught the corner of her eye: the beast was walking back to the castle, but was not looking in her direction. Quickly, Bella returned the books to their shelf before closing the curtain and picking her way out of the dark room. She closed the doors behind her, and bit her lip in thought. It would be best, she decided, not to bring up the subject of magic unless he first broached it himself.

As she walked back to the bedroom, the beast joined her in one of the intersecting hallways of the castle. He stepped out of the hallway expectantly, and Bella wondered if he had been waiting for her. *"How much do those ears hear?"* she wondered, casting a thoughtful look at the long doe ears that gently twitched atop his head.

"Are you hungry for dinner, my dear?" the beast asked courteously.

"Yes, please," Bella answered truthfully. She had been so caught up in her exploring that she had not returned to the orchard after breakfast.

"Then may I escort you?" The beast stooped and offered his elbow in an exaggerated gesture of courtesy. Bella stared at him, a little unsure, before carefully sliding her arm through his. The beast grinned at her and with slow steps to keep pace with her own short stride, he led her out once again to the garden.

Bella watched the beast from the corner of her eye as they walked. Her arm was so much shorter than his that her hand fell to rest on the sleeve of his shirt. The material was soft and rich, but she was distracted by the strange feel of his arm underneath the shirt — the squishy sensation of fur and the uncomfortable feeling of hard bone. The slow pace and stooped posture seemed to pain him, but his expression was satisfied, and almost triumphant.

The garden was bathed in the orange light of sunset, and the juicy pear the beast picked for her glowed golden in the light. The breeze was cool and clean, and full of the smells of wildflowers and orchard fruits. As Bella settled herself quietly on to the stone bench they had used at breakfast, she felt tears sting the back of her eyes. *"It's so beautiful here,"* she thought sadly. *"I could be happy if only ..."* She wasn't sure how to finish the thought. If only everything were different, perhaps, but it was hard for her to imagine what that scenario might look like.

"Bella?" The beast was watching her intently as he popped blackberries into his mouth one by one.

"Yes, Ezio?" she asked, clearing her throat and blinking back her tears.

"Did you have a nice day today?" He ducked his head in embarrassment and seemed aware of the strangeness of the question, but still he held her gaze expectantly.

Once again, Bella felt as though something was expected of her. She wished she could just ask outright what it was. She worked up her polite smile, the cheerful one that she used to put on when telling Father about her day, and gushed, "Oh, yes. The castle is so beautiful, and there's so much to explore." As she expected, his face lit up with the pride she had noticed before. *"At least I know how to flatter him,"* she thought with wry resignation.

The conversation lapsed into a familiar pattern, one that she had perfected with Father long ago. Every little discovery of her day was woven into an epic tale of delight: The work dresses that would be perfect for laundry day! The velvet evening dresses that would look beautiful once she found some thread! The emerald butterfly that still perched in her hair and was the finest thing she'd ever seen! She told her stories with animation and affected pleasure, but did not mention the library, nor the silver spoon that now lay safely behind the vanity table.

The beast listened with obvious attention and smiled obligingly at her animated facial expressions, but Bella felt his mind was elsewhere. When she had run out of ways to make her day seem exciting and interesting, she lapsed into a silence that he didn't immediately break. The sun was well below the horizon, and Bella could already see the moon and a few bright stars shining in the deepening blue sky. Beside her, the beast frowned, then cleared his throat with a strange barking sound, and then frowned again.

"Bella?" he said earnestly, and she gave him her brightest smile, hoping to soften his suddenly serious mood. "Bella," he tried again. His hand reached out in the increasingly familiar gesture of trying to touch her and yet unable to do so. "Bella, I love you."

The words hung heavily in the air as Bella stared at him, smile frozen in place. He looked at her expectantly, his face a mask of emotions she couldn't identify.

He wanted her to say it back to him, she could tell from the way he held his breath waiting for her response. Bella felt frustration rising inside her; a full day had not passed since she'd been dragged here and abandoned by her father. She quickly pushed the frustration down before it could show on her face.

"He's already my husband," she realized with resignation. *"What's one more concession?"* She smiled sweetly and imagined she was someone else when she said, "I love you, too, Ezio."

The beaming smile of pure pleasure that he bestowed upon her was painful for her to accept. *"Now I know what he wants from me,"* she thought sadly, *"but how long can I keep lying to him?"*

Chapter 12 - Fiorita

Fiorita was sitting on the front porch, just as she had every day for the last week. Ever since Cienzo had taken Bella away, she had spent her days waiting for her stepsister to return. Though Mama and Marchetta had been uncomfortably silent on the issue, Fiorita had to believe Bella was coming back. The alternative was too awful to consider.

In the mornings, she would watch Mama and Cienzo go into the village — Mama on foot and Cienzo on his gray mule — and in the evenings she would see Mama come home, bone weary but her eyes flashing with anger. Fiorita did not know when Cienzo came home; the only time she ever saw him was when he left at dawn.

She was dangling her legs over the side of the porch and wondering if she should practice the organ so she would have something to show Bella when she came home, when a boy turned off the road and walked towards her. He was a skinny boy, probably two years older than her, with the slightest hint of a mustache on his upper lip. Fiorita smiled at him, but tried not to look too eager; none of the young people in the village had responded very enthusiastically to her attempts to be friendly.

The boy stopped a few paces in front of her and fidgeted uncertainly. "Hello," Fiorita prompted kindly.

"I'm here with a message from my papa, the butcher," he blurted out. He was starting at her with open curiosity.

She wasn't sure how to respond. "Well, Mama isn't here, and my sister..." Her voice trailed off. Marchetta was weeding the back garden, and would be cooking dinner later. Since the servants quit, the morning after Bella's abrupt disappearance, Marchetta had been so constantly busy that Fiorita hated to interrupt her. "I can take the message for you," she offered.

The boy shifted his weight from foot to foot, considering her offer. "All right," he said, a little sullenly. "Papa says that if you don't pay your meat bill this week, he's going to lodge a complaint with the village council."

"Oh." Fiorita wasn't sure what else to say. "Um, thank you," she added, unsure of the etiquette the situation demanded.

The boy was still staring at her and she shifted uncomfortably, feeling the planks of the wooden porch digging into her legs. "Is there anything else?" she asked.

"How did you get so big?" he asked bluntly.

Fiorita felt the heat rise to her cheeks. "I'm not big," she said defensively. She could feel herself clenching and unclenching a fold of her skirt anxiously. She tried to redirect the question. "I'm not nearly as tall as you," she said, hoping the boy wouldn't press the issue.

"Not as tall as me, but twice as wide," the boy insisted stubbornly. He dug a toe petulantly into the lawn. "Is it because you're rich?" he asked. "Papa says rich people eat twice as much." His tone was aggressive, but his face was curious, and almost hungry.

Fiorita felt herself growing angry, and tears pricked at the sides of her eyes. "I just am the way I am," she mumbled, staring hard at the ground and blinking rapidly. *"I won't cry in front of him,"* she thought, furious with herself.

The boy stared at her a few minutes longer, then shrugged his shoulders and walked off down the road toward the village, slouching his shoulders and kicking clumps of dirt as he went.

She waited until he was out of sight before rising to her feet and shaking the splinters out of her skirt. She didn't want to leave the porch, but she didn't want to stay either. *"Maybe Marchetta needs help in the garden,"* she hoped.

Marchetta was in the yard behind the house, kneeling in the dark earth digging weeds out with her long, slender fingers. Fiorita knew her sister hated gardening, yet she thought Marchetta looked beautiful in her dirt-stained apron and with her wide-brimmed straw hat covering her long braids.

"Can I help?" Fiorita said, walking over to kneel beside her sister on the ground.

"You can take those to the stable," Marchetta said, gesturing at the pile of weeds beside her. "And then—" She stopped as she glanced up and saw her sister's face. "Oh, sweets," she said gently. "You've been crying. Is it Bella?"

"No," Fiorita shook her head and then immediately felt guilty. She *should* be crying over Bella, and not because some stranger had been rude to her. She tried to shrug. "A boy from the village came by and hurt my feelings a little, that's all," she said trying to sound indifferent.

"What, just now?" Marchetta asked, confused. Fiorita nodded. "Who was he?" Marchetta was frowning deeply. "What did he do?"

Fiorita kept her eyes on the ground, and stroked one of the herb leaves with her thumb. "He said he was the butcher's son," she said with another shrug. "He said his father wanted our bill paid by the end of the week or he'd complain to the council."

Marchetta scowled deeply. "That swine," she muttered angrily. "I offered to pay him yesterday when I bought the meat and he refused to take my money, said he knew we were good for it." She glared at the garden and then stood up, brushing the dirt from her dress. "He's just trying to cause trouble for Mama, but there's no help for it," she said briskly. "We're just going to have to go pay him."

"Now?" Fiorita asked in surprise. "But he said by the end of the week."

"That may be, but if he's set on causing trouble, he could complain today. We'll go into the village and get it taken care of now," she said firmly. Marchetta gathered up her basket and headed into the house.

Fiorita stood slowly and followed her. "Can I stay here? I don't want to go." She thought of the rude boy staring at her and didn't think she could face him again without crying. Ever since they had moved to the village, she had felt like an outcast; her skin, her size, her accent all marked her as different from the others in the village. Marchetta had managed her weekly shopping visits just fine, but for Fiorita it had become more than she could bear, especially now that her only friend was missing.

Marchetta stopped inside the kitchen and looked back at her. Her expression softened; she put her basket down and walked over to embrace Fiorita. "I know, sweets," she said gently, "but you can't stay here alone."

It felt comforting in her sister's embrace, but Fiorita frowned and pushed gently away. "Marchetta," she said seriously, "what's going on? Ever since Cienzo took Bella away, you hover over me like a hawk, and Mama goes into the village every day for hours and comes home exhausted. And you don't talk about Bella at all. I keep waiting for her to come home and she never does!" She saw Marchetta catch her breath and hesitate. "Please! Tell me," Fiorita urged.

Marchetta turned from her and fiddled with untying her apron strings and hanging the garment up by the kitchen door. When she finally spoke, she sounded tired and drained. "Mama is trying to register a complaint with the village council against Cienzo," she said. "She wants to organize a search party to bring back ... Bella."

"She was going to say 'the body'," Fiorita realized as ice crept down her spine. "You don't think Bella is coming back on her own then?" she asked quietly.

Her older sister hesitated. "If she's hurt or injured," she said gently, "she may not be able to come home on her own."

Fiorita felt her throat constrict. "When is the search party going out?"

"That's the problem," Marchetta said, her face settling into a scowl. "It isn't yet. The council is divided on whether to believe Mama or Cienzo. He's telling them that he found Bella a rich suitor on his last trip to the port and that she's happily married and living like a princess." Fiorita thought her sister looked angry enough to spit. "It's come down to a question of who to believe. The younger men on the council are champing at the bit to ride out and rescue her, and the older men on the council are backing Cienzo against his foreign wife."

Fiorita sat down heavily at the kitchen table, unsure if her legs would support her. She felt sick; so that was why Mama had been so tired. Fiorita couldn't imagine going before a group of strangers every day for a week and trying to convince them to do something to help Bella. "Can't we ... can't we go look for her ourselves?" she asked.

"If Mama can't convince the council to act soon, we will," Marchetta said with a heavy sigh. "But it's a long shot — there's a lot of ground out there to cover."

Fiorita frowned, trying to work out the puzzle. "Well," she said slowly, "what if we started with the magician?"

Marchetta looked confused. "What magician?"

"Cienzo said he was taking Bella to a magician, remember?" Fiorita said. "He must live somewhere, and there must be people in the same area that will know he's a magician, right? Maybe we could ask around and find him."

Marchetta rubbed her eyes tiredly. "Fiorita," she said, her voice tinged with exasperation, "there isn't any magician."

"But Cienzo said—"

"Cienzo is sick!" Her voice hung in the air, hoarse with frustration. Fiorita bit her lip and looked away; when she looked back, Marchetta was pressing one hand tiredly to her forehead. "I'm sorry, Fiorita," she said, "you don't deserve to be shouted at." She dropped her hand from her forehead and reached across the table to squeeze Fiorita's hand gently. "Cienzo is ... very ill. Mama made a mistake when she married him, a mistake leaving him alone that day — she didn't realize he was so ill, didn't realize he could do such a thing." Her voice cracked a little with emotion. "There's not a magician, there never was. Cienzo took Bella out into the country and ... hurt her. Or left her there. We're not sure. But magicians don't grow magical roses to capture brides from passing merchants. Cienzo is confused, and that's why Mama has been locking the house up so tight at night. He's been sleeping in the stable."

Fiorita stared at her in astonishment. "I didn't know," was all she could mumble.

"I know. Mama boards up the house after your bedtime, and that's why I can't leave you during the day." She stood up briskly. "And that's why I need you to come with me."

Fiorita didn't move. "Where is Cienzo now?" she asked.

Marchetta frowned. "He's in the village with Mama," she said, "Arguing before the council. Again."

"Then he can't come back while you're gone?"

"No, but—"

"Then I'm going to stay here," Fiorita decided.

"Fiorita," Marchetta said coaxingly, "please don't be stubborn. Get your walking shoes and come into the village with me. You don't need to see that boy—"

"No!" Fiorita stood up, frustrated and angry. "I'm staying for Bella! She was my friend and I'm going to wait here for her. When she comes back, someone will need to be here to let her in." She rushed out of the kitchen and up the stairs to her room, slamming the door behind her. She could hear Marchetta call her from the kitchen, but she ignored her and settled down in her seat by the window to wait.

A few minutes passed before she saw Marchetta slowing walking the path from the house to the village road. Her sister looked up at Fiorita's window, but Fiorita could not make out her expression clearly through the thick glass. She saw Marchetta wave to let her know she was leaving, and

Fiorita waved back.

"Marchetta thinks that Bella is dead," Fiorita realized sadly. And that meant Mama thought so as well. Marchetta had said that if Mama could convince the council to act soon, they would leave to look for Bella, but what did that really mean? *"We'll go back to the city,"* she guessed. They would look for Bella along the way, but if they really thought Bella was gone, they wouldn't waste much time on the road. They'd be too focused on getting safely home.

The thought of going home without Bella churned her stomach. Marchetta had said there was no magician, but Fiorita couldn't give up the one thing they had to go on. It was no wonder that Mama and Marchetta were discouraged, if they thought the magician was nothing more than fantasy. It suddenly struck her that perhaps *she* could search for Bella. She hadn't thought to do so before because she'd believed that Cienzo would bring Bella back. But if he wasn't going to and if Mama was stuck dealing with the village council, she might be the only one who would try. *"But where do I start?"* she wondered.

Marchetta was right: there was a lot of ground out there to cover. Cienzo had left in the evening and had not returned until well after sunrise the next morning. And they had left by cart, which was faster than walking. Still, she had to start somewhere. *"Half the time would have been the drive back, wouldn't it?"* she thought, trying to imagine Cienzo's route. *"He must have gone by road, because he wouldn't leave the cart by itself."*

She was peering through the window at the point where she had last seen Bella and grappling with the choice of leaving now or talking to Marchetta first, when she noticed a man standing silently on the road and staring at the house. Though Fiorita could not see his face clearly through the window, something about the man seemed familiar. After a moment, she realized it was his tunic that jogged her memory.

He had passed by the house several times that week, always walking slowly and with one eye trained on the house. Fiorita had seen him from her vantage point on the porch and couldn't help but notice that his rich green tunic contrasted sharply with the workday browns that the other villagers wore. When he caught her watching him, he had smiled; a little nervously, perhaps, but that was more kindness than the villagers showed her. She had the impression that he looked at her a little sadly. *"Maybe he's heard gossip about us,"* Fiorita thought.

Feeling bold, Fiorita dashed down the stairs and out of the house, hoping to reach the road before he moved on. Maybe he would travel with her part of the way down the road to ... well, until she found Bella or gave up, she supposed. It would be nicer to have a companion on the road instead of traveling alone.

He was still standing there when she burst out of the house and called out, "Hello!" He looked startled and Fiorita thought he might hurry off; plaintively she called "Oh, no, please wait!" The man hesitated, but to her relief he stayed where he was.

It took her only a moment to run across the field to the road, but once there she doubled over, slightly gasping for breath. "Excuse me ..." she said politely between breaths, "but I didn't want ... you to leave without ... me saying 'hello'." She sucked in a lungful of air and felt herself regaining her wind. "I hope you won't mind me asking, but if you're going down the road, can I walk with you — oh!"

This last part was uttered as she looked up and realized that the man had a horse with him, a beautiful brown stallion tied to a nearby copse of trees. The trees had shielded the animal from her eyes until she drew close. *"If he's wealthy enough to own a horse like that, he must be from the city,"* Fiorita realized with surprise.

Like most men, this one was taller than her but shorter than Marchetta. He had dark hair and a light olive complexion that contrasted pleasantly with his rich clothing. He was watching her warily, as though afraid she might hurt him. Fiorita felt silly, bursting out of the house and frightening him like she had. "I'm so sorry," she said, a little shyly. "I was going to ask if you were walking down the road and if you would mind my company, but I see you aren't walking at all," she smiled and nodded at the horse, which was quietly munching on a dandelion. "Please have a good day," she said cheerfully, and with a parting nod to the gentleman, she headed resolutely down the road.

Fiorita was surprised to hear the man untie his horse and follow her on foot down the road. He caught up with her quickly, and fell in beside her; his long strides slowed to match her pace and his horse walked patiently beside him. Fiorita cleared her throat nervously and glanced sideways at the man, who was watching her closely. "You really don't have to walk with me," she assured him. *"Maybe this isn't such a good idea,"* she thought nervously. She could feel her heart pounding in her chest and wondered if she oughtn't turn around and run home.

"Oh no," the man said solemnly. "I wasn't raised to let a lovely lady walk alone without an escort." She shot him a worried glance, sure that he was mocking her — or worse, threatening her — but the smile he flashed was so warm and friendly that she couldn't help but smile in return. "Besides," he said, and his voice warmed with the smile, "Charger likes to rest. He's such a lazy thing." He shook his head with exaggerated sorrow, and Fiorita laughed out loud at the sight.

"Charger? Is that your horse?" she asked, gazing admiringly at the animal on the other side of the man. Since moving from her home in the city, she rarely had an occasion to see horses, and this one was particularly beautiful with its glossy dark coat and deep black eyes.

"A very ill-fitting name, I assure you," the man said. "I'd offer to let you pet him, but he bites."

Fiorita glanced from the beast's dark eyes to the man's laughing ones, and couldn't decide if he was teasing or not. "And what's *your* name?" she asked, again feeling quite shy.

"Flavio," he said. He worked a bow fluidly into his walk without altering his gait. "It is equally ill-fitting, I'm afraid. My good mother named me for my head of golden hair that turned brown almost before I began to walk." He flashed that bright teasing smile at her again.

She gave him a shy smile in return. "I'm Fiorita," she volunteered, realizing that etiquette would prevent the man from asking her directly. She felt she should say something else, but it had been such a long time since she had spoken with anyone other than Mama and Marchetta that she wasn't sure where to start.

"A lovely name," Flavio said smoothly, but for the first time in the short conversation he seemed otherwise lost for words.

They walked in silence for a few moments while Fiorita fretted. The man seemed nice enough, but her plan of accompanying him as far as his destination and then continuing on alone had somehow changed into his apparent intention of following her aimlessly wherever she went. She couldn't imagine that he was motivated by courtesy alone. She was considering turning back home — *"Better safe than sorry,"* she thought — when he cleared his throat and said, "This road, I think, leads away from the village?"

"Yes, I believe so," Fiorita said carefully.

"May I ask ..." He hesitated nervously, "May I ask why a young lady is walking to the countryside without an escort?"

Fiorita stared straight ahead, unsure how to answer. *"I could say I'm visiting a friend,"* she thought, *"Or gathering herbs."* Neither of those answers were true, and she hated to lie without a good reason. The man must have some idea of who they were; there would be gossip about the missing girl, spread by the council families and the servants who had left. She looked at him directly and said, "I'm looking for my sister, Bella."

If possible, the man looked even more uncomfortable. "I had wondered if that might be the case," he said, his tone apologetic. "I've heard rumors that she ... has gone missing recently?"

"Is that why you've been watching our house?" Fiorita asked. She tried to keep her tone curious, not aggressive, but the man flinched.

"I'm afraid so," he said, and one end of his mouth quirked up in a self-conscious smile. "I've been staying with a friend ... well, let's say a 'fellow soldier', in your village."

Fiorita shot another glance at the man, but could see no weapons on his slender frame. *"Not like any soldier I've seen,"* she thought, remembering the burly port guards of her home city. The man was watching her carefully, waiting for a response; she nodded for him to continue.

"I heard an unfortunate story about your sister. Bella, was it?" She nodded again. "I've been trying to figure out what I should do about it, actually." Flavio glanced away from her, looking intensely uncomfortable.

"Why should it concern you?" Fiorita asked in slight astonishment. What possible connection could this man have to her stepsister?

When he answered her, his voice was slow and serious. "They say in town that your father took your sister away and she hasn't been seen since. They say that your mother accuses him of insane ravings about a castle and a bear-man and a magician and a forced marriage." He coughed and looked apologetically at Fiorita. "They say that your father killed your sister in the forest."

Fiorita felt tears prick her eyes. "That's what they say," she whispered hoarsely. She stared at her feet, concentrating on putting one foot in front of the other. "So why do you care so much?" she asked, trying not to sound bitter.

Flavio was silent for a long moment before Fiorita realized that he was no longer beside her. She stopped walking and blinked back the tears that had blinded her. When she looked back, he stood in the middle of the road, head hung down, horse waiting patiently beside him. "What if it's true?" he asked, not meeting her eyes. "What if there really is a castle and a bear-man?"

Fiorita stared at him. The thought struck her that he knew something of her sister. All other considerations — that he might be lying, that he might be a lunatic — fled from her mind in the face of the hope that seized her. "Do you know where my sister is?" she asked, her voice tight. "Do you know who has her?"

The words seemed to spill from his lips. "My brother, my *half*-brother is a prince. Three weeks ago, a fairy invaded the castle and turned him into ... a monster. I don't know how else to describe it." He hung his head again, unable to hold her gaze. "I fled the castle ... everyone did. I was Captain of the Guard and this ... this was the seal of my post." He held out his hand and Fiorita saw a beautifully wrought brooch, finely worked with a royal coat of arms in bright gold.

"Your brother ..." her voice caught in her throat, "did he *eat* my sister?"

"No!" Flavio shook his head violently, and then flushed red at his outburst. "I don't think so. I think he's just ... lonely with everyone gone."

Her mind was racing. "This means that Cienzo was telling the truth," she said, working out the details. "He really *did* take Bella away to be a bear-man's bride." She looked up at Flavio suddenly. "You can tell everyone!" she realized. "You can support Mama before the council, and tell them where he took Bella, and they'll have to listen and help her!"

He shook his head. "I can't," he said miserably. "They'd never believe me, but even if they did ... Don't you see?" he pleaded. "They'd organize a mob. People would get hurt. My brother ... would die." He shook his head again and looked on the verge of tears. "I don't want your sister to suffer," he confessed, "but I can't let my brother die, either. And it's my fault for leaving him in the first place."

Fiorita studied Flavio for a long moment in silence. *"What if it were Marchetta?"* she thought, but she couldn't imagine what she would do in his place. She couldn't just leave Bella alone, though. She knew that much for certain.

She walked over to Flavio, and gently pried the reins from his loose grasp. She tilted her head and looked up into his downcast eyes. Firmly, she said, "Take me to her."

Chapter 13 - Ezio

Ezio repositioned his body so he could watch Bella out of the corner of his eye while inspecting the roses. In the week since she arrived at the castle, the two had fallen into a routine. They would have breakfast together in the orchard, and then Ezio would spend the day tending the hedges while Bella explored the inside of the castle or strolled the grounds with a picnic basket and a book. In the evenings, Ezio would prompt her to tell him about her day, and when the sun set, they would head off to bed and sleep.

Overall, he was satisfied with the routine. Bella seemed more comfortable with him each passing day, and she fell asleep easily at night, curled safely into herself on her side of the bed. Ezio was especially pleased at how docile and eager to please she was; every night he would tell her he loved her, and every night she dutifully responded in kind. *"It's just a matter of time before she really means it,"* Ezio thought.

As he watched the girl surreptitiously from the hedgerow, Ezio reflected that he preferred the days when Bella stayed indoors. Today she had spread a tattered tablecloth by the side of the road and was lounging on it while mouthing the words to a book she had brought from the castle library. Her reading spot was halfway between the castle and the hedge, well out of the shadows of each, but Ezio was acutely aware of how close the girl was to the gate. He felt a surge of frustration; he needed to examine the hedge thoroughly every day, but it was hard to concentrate when he had to keep checking on the girl. Both the roses *and* the girl were his remaining links to humanity and it wouldn't help to save the one and lose the other.

He tried to turn his attention to the task at hand. Most of the bright blossoms looked healthy, but a worrying few were wilting slowly. Ezio knew nothing about gardening, but Guerrino had advised him that water would help, and possibly some judicious trimming of the thorny branches. Ezio held his breath with every cut and fervently hoped that he was doing the job right. The water was easier, if heavier work, and he spent hours lugging buckets from the well and wetting the ground around the enormous hedge. The work was discouraging; Ezio never saw any new buds growing to replace the dying ones.

He cast a glance back at Bella as he moved down the hedgerow. He wouldn't be able to walk much farther before the castle would block her from his field of vision, and he was uncomfortable letting the girl out of his sight. Ezio wondered if he should ask her to walk with him, but he was trying to keep her as far from the cursed roses as possible. She had accepted his command to stay away from the hedge, and he didn't want to accidentally encourage difficult questions.

As he watched the girl, he saw her demeanor suddenly change. She sat up stiffly on her picnic blanket, staring intently at the gate, her face a mask of astonishment. Instinctively, Ezio whipped his head back to the hedge and cupped his hand around a nearby rose. From the corner of his eye, he saw Bella turn to glance at him before returning her attention back to the gate.

She made a quick motion with her hand, palm held up and out. Ezio's mind raced, weighing possibilities. Was she signaling a friend? Was it her father? Should he go over there? He saw the air shimmer beside him and turned to see the outline of Guerrino standing there. In full sunlight, the shape and outline of the invisible magician looked like a thick bubble of water, through which could be seen the castle yard on the other side.

"Who is it?" Ezio asked anxiously under his breath.

"A stranger at the gate." Guerrino's voice flowed quietly from the glassy outline. "A woman, I think, but I couldn't see more than that at this distance."

"Is the gate closed?"

"It is," Guerrino confirmed, "but I still think she could squeeze out. Should I bring out the wolf?" he asked tensely.

Ezio closed his eyes and tried to shake his thoughts into coherence. He couldn't let Bella escape; he didn't have enough time to start over. He risked a quick glance back at her. The girl was hunched over her book, shoulders tensed and eyes glued unmoving to the page. *"She's waiting for me to move around the side of the castle,"* he realized angrily. If he hadn't seen her initial reaction, if Guerrino hadn't laced the gate with spells, she might have gotten away without his noticing. *"I should lock her in Guerrino's tower,"* he thought with frustration.

"The wolf, Your Highness?" Guerrino prompted, breaking into his thoughts.

Ezio hesitated. As much as he needed to get rid of this threat, at the same time he wished he could see what Bella would do. *"I know so little about her,"* he realized doubtfully. "Can you make *me* invisible?" he whispered to Guerrino.

The glassy outline was silent for a long moment, before the hesitant reply, "Yes."

"Follow me, then." Ezio carefully stalked the perimeter of the hedge. As he disappeared behind the castle, he imagined he could feel Bella's eyes on him. "Hurry," he urged. The magician started to mumble softly, and Ezio felt a strange tingling sensation as his body slowly faded out around him. As the color washed from his body and disappeared completely, Guerrino's own form filled in slowly, like a painting being brought into existence under an artist's brush.

"I can't hold the spell over both of us at once," Guerrino warned. "Whatever you're going to do, do it quickly. This has all been for nothing if the girl gets away."

Ezio peeked around the edge of the castle. Bella had stood up and was walking towards the gate with a show of nonchalance, stopping every few steps to pick a wildflower by the side of the road. Quietly, Ezio stepped forward on the spongy grass, grateful for the muffle of his hooves. He followed at a distance, mindful of the limits of the spell. Bella disappeared through the wide gap in the hedge. *"She's almost at the gate,"* Ezio thought, feeling his heart pound anxiously, and he increased his pace. Within moments, he was at the edge of the hedge, peering around the corner.

He had been expecting the girl's father, but the sight that caught the prince's eye surprised him. A young girl stood on the other side of the gate, weeping softly and embracing Bella through the slender silver bars. The girl was shorter than Bella, deeply plump, and had warm, dark skin. Bella embraced the girl fervently, and Ezio strained to hear what his bride was saying through her soft choked sobs.

"Are *you* all right, Fiorita? And Marchetta and Venizia?"

Ezio frowned, wondering who they could be. *"Relatives?"* he hazarded doubtfully, but then remembered, *"The merchant said he had daughters."* They must be sisters, then. He studied the plump black girl again and amended himself: *"Stepsisters, at any rate."*

"We're fine," the young girl was saying, between tears. She released her grip on Bella and wiped her wet face with the back of her hand, a gesture that struck Ezio as touchingly child-like. She smiled bravely and said, "We're all fine. Are you *sure* you're all right, Bella?"

"Yes," Bella responded instantly, but Ezio was frustrated to hear the sadness in her voice. *"Am I just a hardship to her?"* he thought, but was mollified to hear her say, "Ezio has been nothing but kind to me."

"Ezio?" Fiorita asked with a frown. She glanced behind her, and Ezio was astonished to suddenly recognize Flavio hanging back against the tree-line of the forest, blending into the deep shadows and looking exceedingly nervous.

What was Flavio doing here? Ezio could hardly imagine. *"Kidnapping my bride in revenge? Or just hiring out to the girl's family?"* He felt his blood boil; it was bad enough that Flavio fled with the rest of the ingrates, but to make his living from Ezio's misfortune was truly low.

"That's the prince, the beast-man?" Fiorita asked Bella, after receiving an anxious nod from Flavio.

Ezio held his breath. *"No no no no."* The word was pounding in his brain. *"I should have charged the gate when I had the chance,"* he thought, but it was too late. His bride was nodding slowly.

"Y-yes," she said hesitantly. "Yes, Ezio is my ... well, I'm not sure." She shook her head. "My beast, my prince, my husband." She laughed, her voice high and strained. "All three, I suppose. He says he loves me." A little fearfully, she glanced back over her shoulder, and Ezio cringed as her eyes swept over the area where he stood. The spell held, though, for he did not see recognition in her eyes.

"She didn't see me," Ezio thought with relief.

"Bella," Fiorita begged. "Please, can you come home? Everything is so wrong without you."

Bella seemed unable to meet the girl's gaze; she stared intently at the ground, and asked in a whisper, "Does Father want me to come home?" Ezio watched the other girl hesitate for a moment too long, and he felt an unexpected sympathy for Bella when she squared her shoulders and said calmly, "I see."

"It's not like that," Fiorita insisted, but her voice held a note of doubt. "It's more ... complicated than that. Cienzo has told everyone that you've married a rich man, which I suppose is true, but Mama has told everyone that he's abandoned you in the country or left you with a monster, and the village is choosing sides."

She glanced back at Flavio, who was still peering nervously at the castle. "That man, Flavio," Fiorita whispered and Ezio had to strain forward to hear. "He's afraid there will be blood if Mama convinces enough of the villagers. Please, Bella, you have to come back."

Bella looked so dejected that Ezio thought she might cry. He held his breath and waited for her to suggest a way to get through the fence. *"Tunneling under or squeezing through?"* he thought. Either way, he needed to be ready to step in. Instead, she said finally, "I ... I can't leave, Fiorita."

Ezio's heart swelled with relief, but it quickly died when Bella half-heartedly tugged on the gate latch and said, "It won't open for me, you see?"

Tears welled up in Fiorita's eyes. "But we rode all this way to get you."

"I know," Bella said. She placed her hand on the girl's cheek. "I know, and thank you. You don't know what this means to me." She smiled and said, "I'll come home to visit as soon as I can. Don't worry; he said I could. Until then, please give Venizia and Marchetta my love, all right?" She reached through the bars and embraced the girl again before kissing her once on the cheek and turning away.

Ezio strode quickly back to the castle's edge, looking anxiously for Guerrino and sighing in relief when he saw the old man staring at him from the deep shadow of a stone overhang. "Well?" Guerrino said tersely when Ezio joined him, panting from the exertion of his walk.

"She's ... staying," Ezio said. Guerrino nodded and began his quiet mumbling to reverse the spell. Ezio watched with detached interest as color slowly seeped into his body and drained out of Guerrino's own. "She told them the gate wouldn't open for her. She never suggested squeezing through."

The outline that barely glimmered in the dark shadows nodded approvingly. "It's lucky she hasn't thought of any alternatives," Guerrino said. "I'll be in my tower, watching to make sure they leave. Who were they?" he asked as an afterthought.

Ezio hesitated, still breathing deeply. "Her sister, I think," he said, "and ... and my brother." He could feel Guerrino's hard eyes on him, but the shape merely nodded and walked away, shimmering briefly as he passed from shadow into light.

Ezio stared after the retreating magician, feeling drained. It suddenly struck him that he was lonely. *"Should I have let them come in?"* he wondered, but then dismissed the notion. He'd had a hard enough time competing against Flavio's charm when he was a prince. Now that he was ... what he was, a girl like Bella would never look at him again if she had his handsome half-brother to focus on instead. Better for Flavio to go back to wherever he came from.

He started his circuit around the hedge again, lost in his own melancholy thoughts. When he rounded the other side of the castle, he saw Bella had resumed sitting on her cloth by the road. She was facing the castle now, instead of the gate, and as she stared at the book that lay in her lap, Ezio could see her eyes weren't moving over the page. *"She looks so miserable."*

The sun was starting to set for the evening and bright orange streaks were spreading through the sky. Usually, the girl would have taken this as a sign to pack up her basket and head into the castle, but Ezio could see no signal that Bella was ready to go inside. She seemed lost in her thoughts, and Ezio felt a pang. *"She hasn't complained once since she got here,"* he realized. Maybe it wasn't fair for him to expect so much of her so soon, nor to blame her for wanting to leave.

A thought occurred to him, and he quietly made his way along the hedge back behind the castle. The stable entrance was cold and dusty, but the door opened easily and he slipped inside. He headed quickly to the kitchen and grabbed up a basket and stepped out into the orchard. He moved methodically down the rows of trees and vines, pulling down the produce that Guerrino's magic kept perpetually ripe and juicy. *"I need more pears,"* Ezio thought, surveying his half-full basket. Bella was particularly fond of pears.

Once his basket was full, he held it carefully in the flat of his palms and strode out to the front road where Bella was still sitting. He saw her glance up and jump guiltily to her feet; as she shoved her book in her basket and started to fold up her seating cloth, he called to her.

"Oh, no, please don't get up!" If possible, she looked even more startled.

He tried to temper his voice into a more casual tone. "You looked so peaceful sitting there, I thought we might have dinner out here."

Bella hesitated, but nodded and smoothed down the corner of the cloth. When he reached her, she gently took the basket from his hands and lowered herself into a sitting position on the cloth. He knelt carefully beside her and pulled a fig from the basket, nodding for her to start eating.

"Thank you," she said, as polite as always.

"You're welcome, Bella," he said, hoping that his smile was reassuring to her.

They ate in silence, with none of the cheerful chatter that Ezio had come to expect from her. She seemed distant and sad, and Ezio alternated between feeling sorry for the girl and sorry for himself. Nothing was the way he wanted it to be. Instead of living his life and planning his future, he was stuck in a body repellent to him, wooing a melancholy merchant's daughter. He hadn't asked for the *fata* to curse him; he hadn't asked for any of this. He looked at the girl, still lost in her own thoughts; *"She hasn't exactly asked for any of this either,"* he thought wryly.

"Bella," he ventured, breaking the silence, "Are you ... happy here?"

She looked up sharply, and he thought he saw worry on her face before her features resolved into a mask of polite cheerfulness. "Yes, thank you," she said brightly. "The castle is so lovely, and you've been so kind." She smiled at him, a smile so wide that Ezio imagined her teeth must ache.

"Bella ..." he said, and his voice trailed off. *"How can I break through to her?"* he thought with frustration. "Bella, that's very kind of you to say, thank you. But I know that you must have left things behind when you came here to live with me." He hesitated, looking for the right words. "You must have had friends, and ... and your father said you had sisters?" He saw her eyes widen, and he realized she was thinking of Fiorita's visit. He plunged on awkwardly. "I just mean ... it would be perfectly natural for you to miss them." Ezio wondered if he'd made matters worse.

She was quiet for a moment, staring down at her hands as they played nervously with a peach pit. When she spoke, her voice was so low that Ezio had to strain to hear her. "You *have* been very kind," she said, "but you're right that I left my stepmother and stepsisters when I came here. I ... I miss them. And I worry that they don't know whether I'm safe or not." She looked up nervously at this last part, and Ezio tried to smile reassuringly.

"And your father?" he prompted, hoping to keep the girl talking.

"Yes. I miss him too. I think." Her eyes were filling with tears, but she managed a smile. "It's complicated, I suppose," she said with a weak laugh.

Ezio stared at her in the gathering dusk that still seemed as bright as day to his changed eyes. What plans had this girl made before she'd given them up to save her father's life? Had she had a lover she was planning to marry, or was she considering a profession? From the way she repaired the gowns she'd found in the castle, Ezio knew she was handy with a needle and thread, but beyond that he knew almost nothing about her. When he turned back into a human and regained his titles and lands, he could give her a comfortable life, one where her hands need never be dirtied with common chores. Work was done by the servants who lived on his lands; his bride's life would be a comparatively easy one. *"But she doesn't know that,"* Ezio realized.

She was still looking down at her peach pit. "Your father should be very grateful for what you did for him," Ezio offered awkwardly. She looked up at him warily, and he stumbled a little. "I mean ... it can't have been easy to give up your freedom in order to save him."

"I'm sure he would have done the same for me," she said, but her eyes slid away from his. "He's always told me how much he loves me," she said quietly.

"My father ... I never really felt like he appreciated me," Ezio said quietly. She looked up at him, and he was surprised to find himself saying, "I never felt like I was enough for him. Even though I was his only legitimate son, it seemed like he cared more for my half-brother than he did for me." He blinked at her, wondering why he was saying all this. *"She must think I sound like a spoiled child,"* he thought with chagrin.

"Where is your father now?" she asked, curiosity winning over her politeness.

"He died. Not too long ago," Ezio said. His voice sounded flat in his

ears and he wondered if he should feel some emotion beyond numbness at his father's passing.

"I'm very sorry to hear that."

"Thank you," he whispered. He laid his hand carefully on the blanket beside her own; it was the closest he could come to touching her. His eyes met hers, and he felt less alone. "You're here now," he said warmly. "That's all I need. Bella ..." he hesitated, surprised by the strength of emotion that swept through him. He felt like crying, or maybe laughing, or possibly both. "Bella, I love you."

Once again, that sweetly sad smile stole over her face. And just as she had said every night for the past week, she said, "I love you too, Ezio."

Ezio felt his heart sink. It was the right thing to say: she was, as always, willing to say what she thought he needed to hear. She wanted to please him, and he knew that was a first, crucial step. But, even so, he felt a sudden pang of sadness at her docile answer. *"I meant it this time,"* he realized sorrowfully.

Chapter 14 - Bella

Bella opened her eyes to the warm morning sunlight and stretched sleepily in bed. She was alone in bed, which was not unusual. In the days since she'd come to live in the castle, Ezio had rarely been in the room when she woke. At first his absence had been a welcome relief, but now that she no longer feared him, it was merely curious. *"He's probably checking his roses again,"* Bella thought. His obsession with the hedge still baffled her, but she supposed it represented a feast for his eyes in the same way that the magic orchard provided feasts for his stomach.

Thinking of the hedge reminded her of the strange events from yesterday, how Fiorita had suddenly pitched up at the front gate with a stranger and horse in tow. Bella had longed for news of her family, but Fiorita's tale had not brought her any comfort: Father and Venizia at odds, and Father insisting that Bella had married well to a rich suitor. Bella frowned and picked at a piece of lint from her pillow. *"Does he believe that?"* she thought.

For that matter, was it true? She'd searched the house from room to room, and had found no treasures beyond a few pieces of silverware and three gold coins tucked in the back of a cupboard. Her prince-husband, if indeed that was what he was, was not hiding any riches unless they were in the boarded-up towers. *"At least I won't go hungry here,"* she thought with a smile, thinking of the magical orchard.

She hadn't told Ezio about Fiorita's visit, and that fact made her uneasy. The beast, *her beast* — as she was beginning to think of him — had never hurt her, had never even raised his voice to her, and it seemed somehow wrong to deceive him about the visit. Yet she still remembered the bloody cuts on Father's arms that so closely corresponded to Ezio's sharp claws, and though she had worked up the courage last night to admit to being homesick, she still couldn't justify exposing Fiorita to danger.

"Not that she isn't already in danger," Bella thought with a deep frown. It wasn't wise for Fiorita to be riding all over the countryside with a strange man as her escort. She hadn't had the time to ask Fiorita if the man was safe to travel with, but she fervently hoped that he was someone she knew and trusted from her home city. She wouldn't quite put it past Fiorita's trusting nature to run off with any stranger who was willing to listen to her tale.

Bella sat up in bed and ran her fingers through the tangles in her hair. *"There's nothing I can do about it now,"* she thought guiltily. She just hoped that Fiorita was safer on the outside of the gate with her male companion than she might have been on the inside of the gate with Bella's beast-husband.

She frowned at her fingers and wiped them on her dress; after ten days at the castle, her hair was grimy and her clothes weren't much better. *"I wonder if I can get Ezio to help me draw a bath after breakfast?"* she thought. The sun was starting to stream steadily through the bedroom windows, but Ezio hadn't returned from wherever he went in the mornings. That was strange.

When her stomach started to lightly grumble she decided to look for Ezio in the garden. She hopped up and pulled on her shoes, and then hesitated at the door. Her hair was not properly brushed and she was wearing the same clothes as yesterday, but after a moment she shrugged and threw open the bedroom door.

"If he notices at all, he'll just say I look better than he does," she thought with a smile. Whatever had afflicted her prince with the form he now wore, it had also left him with a sense of humor about his frightening looks. *"It would be easier to be despondent,"* she reflected, but then shied away from the thought. She was pleased he hadn't hurt her, and she appreciated his kindness, but she still wasn't sure she wanted to stay any longer than absolutely necessary.

The orchard was as bright and lovely as it was every morning, but Bella noticed a dark bank of clouds far off in the sky that heralded rain. Soon the mild weather would pass, and she wondered how storms would affect life at the castle. *"Will the roof hold up?"* she thought, peering up at the castle behind her. She vaguely remembered Father having their own house re-roofed after a bad storm a few years back, and now she wished she could remember the details more clearly. There was just so much she didn't know. *"I'll have to ask Ezio when I find him,"* she decided.

"Ezio?" She called his name quietly as she walked between the orchard rows, unwilling to disturb the silence of the wind-rustled trees by raising her voice. The emptiness of the castle still unnerved her enough that she sometimes had the superstitious feeling she was being watched. "Ezio?" she asked again, her voice barely a whisper in the wind.

Relief washed over her when she rounded the corner of a row of fig trees and saw him sitting quietly on one of the stone benches that decorated the orchard. He sat perfectly still, his fur gently ruffled by the wind.

"There you are," she said brightly, walking cautiously toward him and seating herself on the bench next to him. She saw that he had a basket of fruits already at his feet and she bent to grab a pear and bite casually into it. "I've been looking for you."

He looked up at her and smiled, but his movements were slow. "I'm sorry," he said. "I was deep in thought and lost track of the time."

"He seems so sad," Bella realized with surprise. *"Is it because of last night?"* In her short time with Ezio, she'd seen his moods flow from humorous to

whimsical to serious, but before yesterday all his moods had seemed focused on her, never on himself. Now he was acting painfully introspective, and she wondered if he was still thinking of his father.

Force of habit prompted her to try to lift his dark mood. *"But what can I say?"* she thought helplessly. She snatched at the first thing she could think of. Cheerily she patted his shirt sleeve and said, "I know you have to check the hedge later, but do you think you could help me with something today?" She grinned at him.

He looked as surprised as she had hoped; rarely had she asked anything of him. "What do you want?" he asked in that same flat voice, but Bella was certain she could hear a note of curiosity underneath it.

Bella looked down shyly and felt a blush color her cheeks. "I was hoping you could help me drag one of the baths out to the well," she explained. "I need to do some washing, and it would be nice to have a bath while the weather is warm." She nodded at the dark clouds building on the horizon. Bella took a deep breath, and steeled her courage before playfully poking Ezio in the ribs and teasing, "You could use a bath too, you know."

He stared at her for a long moment, and Bella felt the blood drain from her face. *"Did I go too far?"* she thought anxiously, but then his feline lips parted in a wide grin. "Are you suggesting," he said, in a falsely hurt tone, "that your humble beast smells like anything other than a bed of roses?"

"More like a wet dog," she countered with a wrinkled nose, but her hand stroked his arm reassuringly so that he would know she wasn't serious. She plucked at his sleeve and stood up. "Will you come help me now?" she asked.

He rose slowly, glancing back at the basket at his feet. "You haven't had any breakfast," he protested, but she smiled and pulled him after her.

Bella remembered the thick wooden washing tub that she had found four days earlier in the servants' quarters. It was far too heavy for her to move, but Ezio managed to turn the heavy tub on its side and roll it through the empty stables to the well. With each bounce, dust flew from the wooden slats, and what remained behind was whipped away by the wind as soon as it was dragged out into the sunlight.

Bella prattled cheerfully as they worked. Ezio drew the water while Bella soaked and washed all her dresses save the one she had on. She was careful to keep the conversation light; she told him of the village she grew up in and some stories of her friends, and Ezio listened with obvious pleasure, interrupting frequently to clarify some point or detail in his mind.

Once her dresses were cleaned and hung carefully over a few thick tree branches to dry, she turned to Ezio. "Do *you* have any clothes that we can wash?" she asked, a little embarrassed. She'd only ever seen her beast-husband in the same torn and ragged clothing.

He looked equally uncomfortable as he gently pawed at a trailing ragged edge on one sleeve. "No, I'm afraid all I have are these," he said. Bella thought he looked as though he wanted to say more, but he offered no further explanation.

"Well, that's all right," she said cheerfully. "You'll just have to, ah, wash everything all together." She felt herself blush, and saw Ezio watching her with interest. "We don't want you to catch cold," she said hurriedly, "so I'll get a fire started in the yard." That, at least, she could do; she'd helped Father burn scrub in the yard enough times that she could light and tend a fire without difficulty. She hurried off, wishing that her cheeks weren't burning so brightly.

She hadn't planned it, but the fire turned out to be a good excuse to walk the perimeter of the property between the silver fence and the rose hedge. Bella walked slowly, gathering branches that had fallen from the forest trees over on to the castle property. All the while, she scanned the forest nervously, searching for any sign of Fiorita and cringing a little at the occasional wolf howl that issued from deep within the forest. *"I hope she's all right,"* Bella fretted, biting her lip and feeling guilty all over again. When she had a large pile of wood and dried leaves, she carried them carefully back to the castle yard.

The fire itself turned out to be easier than she had expected. A large fire pit had already been dug out back behind the stables. The grass had been cultivated away from the pit, but a few weeds were starting to poke through the dry ground; Bella pulled them carefully before starting her small fire.

While she worked, she couldn't help but glance back at the wooden tub and its occupant. Ezio washed with his back to her, his features obscured by the wooden walls of the tub and the distance between them. *"What would it be like,"* she wondered, *"to wake up with a different body from the one you'd always had?"* She turned her attention back to her fire and fed the small flames a few more dried twigs.

A thought struck her, and after checking to make sure the fire was contained, she ran quickly back inside the castle. She grabbed a sheet from their bed and hurried outside, holding the sheet awkwardly in front of her. "Ezio?" she called out, turning her head away as she walked towards the tub, "Ezio, I'm bringing you a sheet."

She stumbled a little on the lawn before the tub came into her field of view and she stopped, staring intently at the ground and holding the sheet out expectantly. She heard the beast rise from the tub with a great deal of splashing and shaking — *"He really does smell like a wet dog,"* she realized with a startled giggle — and the sheet was taken gently from her hands.

"Thank you," he said warmly, and though she closed her eyes politely, she could not help but peek out a moment later. Ezio stood with his back to her as he carefully wrapped the sheet around himself. His shoulders and back were covered in the same coarse animal hair that coated his limbs and face. *"If he was once human, he's not anymore,"* she thought. *"Not underneath his clothes, anyway."* Bella was surprised that the realization was tinged with disappointment. A part of her had hoped for a hint that the beast was once human, that he might perhaps be able to turn back.

"The fire is over there," she blurted out, pointing and squinting her eyes against thoughts she wasn't ready to work out.

"Thank you again," Ezio said, and Bella opened her eyes to see the smile she heard in his voice. He had wrapped himself quite neatly in the sheet and was bowing teasingly before her. "Let me draw fresh water for you first, though," he said.

He was better than his word. After dumping out the dirty bathwater, Ezio rinsed the tub twice and filled it with clean water. Then he carefully carried stones that had warmed near her small fire and dropped them into the water to take the edge off the cold. Lastly, he stepped into the orchard to change back into his nearly-dried clothes before draping the sheet into a curtain to shield her. "I feel like a princess," she teased, and he grinned at her.

"Now you'll know I'm not watching while I tend my roses," he said.

"Thank you," she said gratefully, and he grinned again before heading off towards the castle gate.

Bella sank into the bath with a sigh, feeling as though all her worries were drawn out into the lukewarm water. She crouched low in the tub, dipping her hair and scrubbing furiously. Once the grime had worked out of her hair, she leaned her head back against the edge of the tub and stared lazily up at the afternoon sun.

It was odd, she reflected, how life could turn out so differently from what was expected. When Father had married Venizia, Bella had looked forward to having servants tend the household again; she had been more than ready to relinquish the laundry and cleaning duties. And yet working with Ezio had been rewarding, almost fun. She was proud at how she'd been able to coax him from his melancholy, and she had felt free to talk to him in a way that she never before would have with her friends and family.

"Maybe it's because I'm not trying to impress him," she thought solemnly. Somewhere during their work that morning, she had stopped watching every word. Absorbed in her work, she'd spoken freely without worrying about putting herself in the best light or ensuring that he was perfectly entertained and completely happy. Instead, she'd just talked, and Ezio had listened as though she were the most interesting person for miles, which she supposed she might well be. It was nice.

Bella shook her head slowly to settle her thoughts and splashed water on her face. *"You're supposed to be thinking about getting out of here,"* she chided, but she frowned and stared at the wavy reflection of her face in the water. Did she want to go home? She wasn't sure. She missed her stepmother and stepsisters, and she needed to see Father, if only for one last time. As angry as she was with him, she didn't want their final farewell to be that frightening and confusing night when she was first brought here.

And yet, a part of her was starting to see some value in staying. Bella had always known she would marry, so she had kept her dreams deliberately vague; there was no sense in wishing for a life your husband wouldn't let you live. Here, trapped in this castle, she felt a paradoxical sense of freedom: within the limitations of her confinement, she could live however she liked. Food was abundant, the library was full of more books than she could read in a lifetime, and the company was pleasant and eager to please. Here she was loved, here she was wanted. *"There are worse ways to live,"* Bella mused, thinking of some of the wives back home.

The sun was setting fast when Bella stepped out of the tub and into her clean clothes. They had dried stiffly in the sun, but soon warmed with her body heat. She stared appreciatively at the orange and pink streaks that shot through the blue sky. *"It's not like I have to make my mind up right away,"* she thought, in answer to an unspoken question.

"Bella!" The voice carried down the valley. "Bella, are you decent? Is the fire still going? I've got dinner for us!" She pulled down the sheet curtain to see Ezio striding down the road, a dead hare dangling from his raised fist.

"I ... What is *that*?" she called to him, not sure whether to believe her eyes.

"It's a hare that I caught," he said proudly, veering towards the fire and motioning eagerly for her to follow. Involuntarily she made a face, and Ezio burst out his barking laugh. "Oh, please don't frown so," he teased. "I caught it in a trap and broke its neck; I didn't use my teeth. See?" he held the hare out for her to inspect. "I wouldn't get blood on my only clothes," he said with mock solemnity.

Bella peered nervously at the hare, but saw that he was right. She looked up at him in alarm. "How ... do we get the meat out?" she asked uncertainly. She'd never butchered a hare before, though she'd cooked a few whole for Father and herself.

"That's easy enough," Ezio said, but his pride was tinged with a touch of embarrassment. He brandished his paw carefully and said, "These claws aren't just for show, you know." His ears twitched lightly and Bella stared at him in shock before giggling nervously.

"I suppose they aren't," she agreed, and together they knelt by the fire. Bella fed the flame more wood as she watched Ezio expertly skin and cut the hare flesh with small, precise movements of his claws. He dipped his fingers in a small bucket of water that Bella fetched for him, and carefully threaded thick strips of meat on to long sticks to suspend over the fire. As the fat on the meat crackled and spit, Bella felt her stomach growl with anticipation.

"You've done this before," she said with open admiration.

"I used to be quite the hunter," Ezio said proudly, before suddenly cutting himself off and falling silent.

Bella had seen him do this before, and now the pieces fell into place. *"He doesn't like to talk about when he was human,"* she realized. She supposed she might not either, in his position. She pushed the thought aside, determined not to lapse into unhappiness. "I'm impressed," she assured him. "Between the well and the orchard and your hunting skills, I'm well provided for here." She smiled warmly at him as his head swung up to meet her gaze.

His eyes held steady for a moment before sliding away from her own and focusing on the flickering fire. In the waning daylight, he looked positively morose. "Not well enough," he said quietly, and Bella leaned forward to hear. He tried to smile ironically, but the effort didn't reach his eyes. "I don't even have a second set of clothing here."

She stared at him, weighing her options. "Ezio?" He looked up at her. "You said I was free to visit my family if I liked?"

His eyes widened, and she saw his ears spasm violently. "Do you want to leave me?" he asked, and his voice held a rising note of panic.

"I've really upset him," Bella thought. She leaned forward and placed her hand gently over his. "Ezio," she said evenly, "I do not want to leave you." She put as much force into the words as she dared, hoping to reassure him. "I want to visit my family." She hesitated, looking for the right words, feeling his dark eyes watching every expression that crossed her face.

"My father, when he brought me here, was in ... a hurry." She spoke slowly, picking her words carefully. "My stepmother and sisters ... I didn't have a chance to say goodbye. I think they are worried about me, and I want a chance to reassure them that I'm happy here." Bella paused, but he was still staring silently at her, offering nothing. She continued doggedly on; "If I go for a visit, I can demand my dowry from my father and bring back some necessities for us." She smiled cheerily at him. "And then you *can* have a second set of clothing. I'll sew it for you myself," she finished.

She held her breath and waited. Torn between keeping eye contact with him to prove she was sincere, and looking away to give him space to think, she settled on focusing on the roasting meat and gingerly turning it over the flames. Her ears strained so hard to hear Ezio's breathing — *"Too fast? Too slow?"* — that she jumped when he spoke.

"Bella ..." She looked up to see his eyes gazing sadly at her. "Of course you can go." He looked down at the ground, his face as downcast as Bella had ever seen.

"Thank you, Ezio," she said meekly, and knelt to sit next to him. She felt giddy with relief; *"It really is going to be just fine,"* she thought. She leaned her head against his shoulder, and breathed deeply the smoke and scent of cooking meat. "I'll walk to the village tomorrow," she murmured happily. "Just as soon as you tell me the way. I won't be gone more than a week at the most, you'll see."

Ezio nodded, but said nothing; Bella decided not to push the issue any further. They ate in silence, the warm meat filling her stomach and adding to the sense of well-being that permeated through her. As the sun dipped below the horizon and the embers slowly smothered in ash, she snuggled closer to him, basking in his warmth. *"Maybe someday he'll tell me how we can change him back,"* she daydreamed. *"Although I don't mind if he stays this way forever."* She sighed contentedly, and allowed herself a quiet giggle at the thought that her companionable beast was a better husband than any man in her home village.

"Bella?" he said quietly.

"Yes, Ezio?"

"It's time to go in to bed, I think," he said softly.

Bella realized she had been nodding off. "All right, Ezio," she said sleepily, and as he gathered up the bedsheet and her dresses from the trees and carried them inside, she was happy enough to follow him through the winding corridors of the dark castle.

Once in bed, she began to shiver. Now that they were away from the warm fire, her wet hair suddenly seemed especially cold and damp.

"Do you want me to light a fire?" Ezio asked, lying still in the bed next to her.

"No ... here ..." Blinking back sleep, she gently gripped his arm and pulled it out from his side. Carefully avoiding his claws, she lay down next to him with her head pressed into his shoulder and her face nuzzled into the warmth of his side. "Good night," she mumbled into his chest.

She could feel his heart beating wildly and she sensed that he was holding his breath as though he were afraid to move. "Good night, Bella," he said. He hesitated, and then asked, "Are you sure you're comfortable?"

"Yes, thank you," she murmured. It occurred to her that during dinner Ezio had broken his nightly tradition: he hadn't announced that he loved her. *"Does he feel bad always being the first one to say it?"* Bella wondered blearily.

Turning her head slightly so that he would be able to hear her, she said, "I love you, Ezio." Then she cuddled her head back into the safety of his warmth and closed her eyes.

Chapter 15 - Ezio

Ezio lay perfectly still, hardly daring to breathe for fear of disturbing the sleeping girl. He felt her warm breath stir over him as she snored quietly. His shoulder ached slightly from the weight of her head, but he was too shocked to mind the pain.

"She loves me!" She had said so unbidden, without his usual prompting. She loved him, and she had touched him without fear, and now everything was going to be all right. Ezio closed his eyes and waited for the transformation to take him, imagining the look on Bella's face when she would see him as a human for the first time.

He felt the seconds tick by slowly, and with every minute that passed, he was acutely aware of nothing happening. He opened his eyes, but every detail of the room was still unnaturally bright to his animal eyes; he had not turned back.

"Maybe I need to fall asleep first?" Ezio wondered. His anxiety was

building, and he felt his stomach clench painfully. He shut his eyes tight and hoped fervently for sleep, but his mind could not stop racing. Bella's snores seemed to pound at his brain. *"Just relax. Be calm,"* he counseled himself, but Ezio knew that he was nowhere near sleep.

The uncomfortable tingling in his shoulder was starting to spread through his arm and down his side. He shifted his arm carefully and was able to draw his arm out from under her head. A soft squeal of displeasure escaped her lips as his sleeve caught and pulled sharply on her hair, but after a quick adjustment the girl lapsed back into sleep and Ezio was free.

He sat up slowly in bed and swung his legs over the side. *"Now what?"* He couldn't sleep, and he couldn't bear to contemplate why he hadn't changed back into the form he so desperately craved. The girl was shivering slightly in the bed beside him, and Ezio realized that the air had become much cooler in advance of the coming storm.

Instinctively he reached out a hand to stroke her wet head, but as always he paused just before contact; it would be too easy to hurt her accidentally with his claws. *"At least she was impressed at the way I filleted the hare,"* he thought sadly. The alternative — that she would be frightened and horrified — had been enough motivation to restrict his diet to the orchard since she arrived, but he had decided to take the risk when he had glimpsed her in the bath and realized how slender she had become. *"She isn't accustomed to this life,"* he thought, but became more despondent as he realized that neither was he.

Ezio decided that he would build a fire; if he could not warm the girl with his hands, then he could at least make the room more comfortable for her. He stepped carefully across the room, grateful again that Bella could sleep through his loud footsteps. Kneeling by the fireplace, he carefully set and lit the flame, mindful of his own fur and the danger it represented. *"If I burned all my hair off, would I be a man again?"* he thought with a smile, but once the flame was lit and he knelt back to bask in its warmth, he felt his spirits sink again.

Why hadn't he changed back? Bella had announced her love for him. Even in her sleep, she had spoken with a strength and determination that had never before accompanied her declarations of love. He believed her, and he believed that *she* believed it as well. Wasn't that enough? Was there some rule of magic he didn't understand, some trick or final condition that needed to be fulfilled? Did he need to fall asleep, or be woken with a kiss? Did he have to walk through fire or pass through a hedge of thorns?

His musings triggered a distressing realization: the hedge of roses would soon be nothing *but* a hedge of thorns. When he had left Bella to her bath, he had been disheartened to see that a fair number of the roses were wilting or withered, significantly more than the amount he had come to expect per day. He didn't know if his own tardiness had caused the roses to sicken, or if the heavy weather was to blame, or if the culprit was merely the inexorable passage of time, but one thing was clear: he only had a few more weeks before his fate was sealed. *"And now Bella wants to go back to her village."*

Ezio rocked back and forth on his slender legs, feeling the anxiety course through his veins and through his stomach. He'd had to tell her she could go. If he had denied her the right to say a proper farewell to her family, she would have been lost to him forever. He knew that, and should have known since she first asked if she were his prisoner. Her love for him was utterly dependent on her perception of her own freedom.

He blinked slowly at the flames that danced in the fireplace as a thought worked through his mind. *"Her love for me ... depends on her freedom?"* He glanced back at the sleeping girl. She was so lovely in sleep, even as she snored softly into the pillows. The light from the fire flickered over her pale face, etching her delicate features into deep shadows. She looked fragile, yet Ezio knew she was strong to have adjusted so well to this situation.

The *fata* had said he needed to find a love who would sacrifice everything. If Bella loved him, but only as long as she were not his prisoner, would that be enough to break the spell and return him to his human form? Ezio stared for a long time at his hands, furry and gnarled in the dwindling firelight.

"I have to talk to Guerrino," he decided, and with a heavy heart he pulled himself to his feet and slipped out the bedroom door.

Chapter 16 - Guerrino

Guerrino leaned against the stone frame of his tower window as he watched the stars. The constellations in the sky were lately his silent companions, and he was faintly sad to see the spring patterns slowly giving way to their summer cousins. Since the girl's arrival, he had become nocturnal in his habits, renewing his spells on the orchard and fence at night and sleeping through the day. Time was starting to weigh heavily on him, and he felt increasingly restless and confined.

"Who'd have thought I could be lonely?" he thought wryly. His one source of conversation — his mornings with the prince — was rapidly becoming something to dread. He had nothing left to say to the young man except his repeated assurances that everything was going as well as could be expected. When the prince had failed to knock on his door this morning, Guerrino had been almost as pleased as he was surprised. He only hoped that the prince's uncharacteristic absence didn't bode ill for their futures. *"Maybe he*

doesn't need my encouragement anymore," Guerrino thought, but he wasn't hopeful.

His own assessment of their situation wasn't rosy. He had known it would be easy to obtain a woman: once the fence was in place, it was only a matter of time before a woman could be coaxed into the trap. But he wasn't certain that a woman could be persuaded to fall in love with her captor, at least not the kind of love the *fata* would demand. Curses were shaped by more than mere words; if the woman didn't love the prince in precisely the manner envisioned by the caster, then the condition would not be fulfilled.

The prince seemed convinced that the girl they had was perfect for the situation and was encouraged by her compliance, but Guerrino wasn't so sure. Once or twice he had followed the girl invisibly through the castle corridors, watching her burrow under beds and dig out cutlery from behind dusty cabinets. He thought he recognized in her a survival instinct that mirrored his own, an almost feral sense of self-interest that precluded genuine, sacrificial love. *"Or perhaps I'm so desperate for companionship that I'm imagining a connection with the girl,"* he thought wearily.

It was time to think about leaving. During his nightly inspections of the fence, Guerrino had noted the roses dying at an alarming rate; he guessed the prince only had a month or two left. He couldn't plan to stay that long if the girl wasn't going to break the spell. He was as ready now as he'd ever be, and delay at this point would just worsen his situation. The spells on the gate and the garden were a constant drain on him, and the supplies that they had brought up from the castle pantry for him to live on would not last forever.

Guerrino mentally sized up the remainder of his supply of dried meats, hard cheeses, and preserved vegetables, trying to calculate how much he could carry away with him. *"I'll set aside a full pack now,"* he decided, *"and at the very latest I'll leave when that's all I have left."* He felt a twinge of guilt for abandoning his former student, but he'd done enough for the boy to pay his debts. He would feel foolish if he left and the girl ended up breaking the curse and bestowing Ezio with riches after all, but in the unlikely event of that happening, he could always come back and lay a claim on the prince for the aid he rendered in securing the girl. *"He'll be happy enough to pay me to go away,"* he thought. Ezio wouldn't want him around as a reminder of his embarrassment, and Guerrino would be only too happy to be bought off.

His thoughts were interrupted by the muffled pounding that signaled the prince's arrival at his tower door. Guerrino sighed. *"It was too much to hope to go a full day in peace,"* he thought sourly. "I'm coming," he hissed softly, but the prince continued to beat urgently on the door until Guerrino pulled it open. "Come in," Guerrino said wryly, but Ezio was already striding in with the same unconscious arrogance that he always carried with him.

"Is something wrong?" Guerrino asked, eyeing the prince cautiously. The young man looked haggard; his ears drooped low and he kept rubbing his palms together in a nervous motion.

"She loves me!" Ezio blurted out, but his voice sounded miserable. "She loves me, but I haven't changed back yet!"

"Then she doesn't love you, Your Highness," Guerrino said patiently, fighting the urge to press his fingers to his throbbing temples. *"Best to be encouraging,"* he thought. The faster he could calm the prince down, the faster the young man would go back to bed. "But it's very promising that she says so. It's just a matter of time now." He tried to smile reassuringly.

"No, you don't understand." He was pacing anxiously in front of Guerrino's work table. "She loves me, I'm certain of it. I just don't think it's enough. Can you open this?"

Guerrino narrowed his eyes at the young man; his clawed hands were poised in mid-air as though to touch Guerrino's grimoire. Cautiously, he walked over to the table, speaking casually as he moved closer to the prince than he would have liked. "If you are thinking that we should try another candidate, we could perhaps use her to bring back Flavio. If romantic love isn't working, perhaps brotherly love—"

"No, no," Ezio cut him off impatiently. "I need to see the curse." Guerrino hesitated, and then gently turned to the relevant page. The prince stared at the words for a moment before sighing and slouching to Guerrino's bed to sit dejectedly with his head on his hands.

Guerrino glanced down at his own handwriting in the grimoire, wondering what track the prince seemed to be on. His mouth moved as his eyes followed the words:

You shall take a form as beastly without as you are within.

You must find that love which is willing to sacrifice everything.

Without such love made manifest before the estate-roses die, a beast you shall remain.

"How important is the wording of the curse?" Ezio asked, staring intently at him.

Guerrino hesitated. "The wording is the verbalization of the caster's intent." He watched the prince wrinkle his nose in concentration. "It's not enough to satisfy the letter of the curse if the intent is not fulfilled," he explained, fighting the instinct to back away from those bared teeth.

"I think ..." The prince spoke slowly, working out his thoughts as he talked. "I think the problem is that she loves me, but she doesn't love me enough. I think she has to love me enough to 'sacrifice everything'." His shoulders slumped. "But I don't know what that means, exactly. Her dreams? Her family? Her life? She's already *done* that."

"She did that for her *father*," Guerrino corrected, his eyes narrowing in thought. "She loved *him* enough to sacrifice everything. But perhaps she doesn't love *you* enough for that." He shrugged and tried to look unconcerned. "Still, we know she's capable of that sort of love, so it's just a matter of time."

Ezio looked down at the floor. "We don't *have* time," he moaned miserably. "More roses are dying every day, and now she's planning to leave for a week to see her family."

"What?" Guerrino asked. He blinked incredulously at the young man. "And you told her she could go?"

"Well, I could hardly say 'no', could I?" the prince shot back angrily. "That will make her fall in love with me, won't it? 'I'm sorry, dear, but you're a prisoner here and forbidden to leave.' I'm sure she'll unreservedly fall for me then." The prince actually snapped his sharp teeth angrily on the last line.

"Couldn't you have—" Guerrino bit back the rest of his response. There was no point in arguing or telling him that he should have invented some excuse; it was too late now. *"It's not my problem,"* he thought fiercely, but he knew he was lying to himself. If the girl left, he wouldn't have a clean hope of escaping while the prince was distracted.

Guerrino walked to the tower window and stuck his head out into the thick night air. He could sense the energy of the storm gathering. He felt trapped, claustrophobic. He wanted to climb out the window and scale the tower bare-handed; he wanted to rush past the monstrous beast that blocked his way to the door and fly from his tower. *"I want an end to all this,"* he thought with a shiver.

"You're sure she loves you?" he asked sharply, not looking back at the prince.

"I know it."

"Fine." Guerrino strode over to his workbench and started pulling herbal components from their bottles. He felt energized by the decision, and buoyed by his conviction that one way or another he would soon be free of both curse and castle.

"What will we do?" The beast was at his shoulder, watching his movements with those bright black eyes.

"It's simple, Your Highness," Guerrino said coldly. "She was willing to give her life to save her father from a beast. Now we'll see if she's willing to do the same for you."

Chapter 17 - Bella

"You're *sure* you'll remember the way?" Ezio was staring at her with such sad eyes that Bella wrapped her arms around his bony form.

"You worry too much," she said sweetly, trying to inject as much lightness as she could into her tone. *"I hate to see him so miserable,"* she thought. Bella hoped that her light, happy tone would erase some of Ezio's obvious anxiety. "You've told me three times now, and I'm sure I won't get lost once I'm on the main road." She stroked his arm gently, hoping her touch would reassure him. "I'll only be gone a few days, long enough to pick up a few things and say goodbye to everyone. Come here."

She tugged on his arm, and he bent down uncertainly until his face was just level with hers. She stood on tiptoe and carefully kissed his feline nose. When she pulled away, she was surprised to see that his black eyes were wet with tears. "Please don't worry," she said quietly, cupping her hand to his neck. She gathered up her skirt in one hand and turned towards the gate, signaling that she was ready to leave.

"Bella ..." Ezio's voice trailed off, and she glanced back at him. He looked unsure of himself.

"Yes?"

"No ... nothing," he shook his head and stepped forward. When he touched the gate latch with his claw, it gave an audible click and the latch came open easily in his hand. Ezio opened the gate wide and Bella stepped through with one last smile before heading resolutely down the road.

Once in the forest, and now that she no longer needed to be brave for Ezio's sake, she felt less confident. The wind was chilly and whipped at her hair. Ezio had tried half-heartedly to convince her to stay until the coming storm passed, but she was anxious to get on the road. The prospect of traveling in bad weather frightened her, but she hoped that the rain would keep the roads empty of troublemakers. She clutched at her sleeve where she had tucked a silver spoon and three gold coins, and mentally rehearsed her strategy. If she saw anyone threatening on the road, she would throw the money as a distraction and run in the opposite direction.

Despite the chill wind, Bella was happy to be on the road. For many days, she'd been convinced that she might never leave the castle, and now that she was free she felt an elation of spirit that lightened her every step. She walked quickly, wondering if she could reach home by nightfall and anxiously making lists of things she wanted to do and say. *"I need to thank Venizia,"* she thought firmly, *"And I want to apologize to Marchetta."* Most of all, she wanted to see Fiorita again, and to reassure herself that the girl had arrived home safely. *"I'll never forgive myself if she didn't,"* Bella thought, quickening her step.

What she was less certain of was her feelings towards Father. Whenever she allowed herself to think of their last day together, she found herself more and more angry, and this reaction made her feel guilty. *"I didn't have to offer my freedom for his life,"* she reminded herself, but a part of her always countered rebelliously, *"But he didn't have to ask me to, either."* She was glad that Father hadn't died, but sad that he had been able to give her up so easily. *"Would I have done the same?"* She wasn't sure of the answer.

The wind had picked up and was whipping her hair sharply across her face when she heard the first scream. It reverberated through the forest, high and painful and completely inhuman. She jerked her head back to stare fearfully down the road behind her; the howl had come from the castle, she was certain. The trees around her shook loudly in the wind, and above the noise she heard a cacophony of sharp, angry barks and a thick, wolfish howl. Another inhuman howl of pain and outrage ripped through the wind, and she knew the voice was Ezio's.

Bella caught her breath, and she felt her stomach churn sharply. She hesitated for a moment, her mind frozen with fear and confusion, but one thought won out over the clamor in her mind: *"Ezio is hurt!"* She dug her heel into the dirt road and ran back towards the castle, pushing her hair away from her eyes and blinking back the sting of the wind in her eyes.

Howls and screams reverberated through the forest around her, mixed with the sounds of the worsening storm. Rounding the top of the hill, she saw the silver gate before her, as closed to her as it had ever been. Panting, she skidded to a halt in front of the gate. She picked frantically at the latch with numb fingers, but the gate remained stubbornly closed.

Another howl, sharp with pain, ripped through the air, and Bella stared helplessly about her. *"I have to get inside the gate!"* she thought, her panic rising. She placed her hands on the slender silver bars and pulled in frustration, but the metal refused to bend even a little to the pressure.

Inspiration struck her. Turning sideways, she slid a leg between the bars and solemnly gauged the tightness of the fit. *"It'll be close,"* she thought anxiously, but then a low moan of pain carried on the wind, and she knew she had no time to waste. Sucking in her breath as tightly as she could, she pressed her way through the bars, wincing at the pain as she squeezed through to the other side.

Once inside the castle property, she was suddenly gripped with indecision. The howls were Ezio's, and she knew that he needed help, but where was he? *"He'd be checking the roses,"* she thought frantically, *"but which side?"* Would she find him on the inner circuit of the castle, or in the outer space between the hedges and the gate? *"He always does the castle side first,"* she remembered, and set off at a breakneck run alongside the hedge, calling his name as she ran.

"Ezio! Ezio, where are you?"

A low growl and a deep moan brought her to a halt by the hedge. Looking around, she could see nothing, but when she turned to her left, she could see movement distantly through the sparse hedge branches. *"He's on the other side!"* she realized, peering anxiously through the gaps in the thorny hedge.

Her eyes widened with fear as the scene resolved before her eyes. Ezio lay stretched out on the grass, unmoving. His hair and clothing were matted in dark, wet blood, and Bella felt her stomach churn at the scent of it. The biggest wolf she had ever seen stood over him; its muzzle was red with blood and he chewed fiercely at a deep wound in Ezio's shoulder. For a moment, she was certain that Ezio was dead and the thought left her numb, but then she heard a low moan escape from his lips and relief washed over her.

"I've got to scare that wolf away," she realized, *"and then ..."* She wasn't sure. *"He's losing so much blood ... and I don't know if I'll be able to drag him ..."* She felt paralyzed with indecision, but through the turmoil of thoughts, one thing was certain: she could not stand by and watch him die.

"You! Wolf! Go away!" Her shouts sounded soft in the roar of the wind, and the animal only paused to give her a single moment's glance before continuing to worry at Ezio's bleeding shoulder. Bella clapped her hands helplessly, feeling foolish, and cast about her looking for some kind of weapon. Several fallen tree branches lay scattered on the ground, knocked there by the force of the wind. She grabbed up a thick branch and turned back to the hedge but then hesitated.

She needed to get to the other side of the hedge, but the only gap in the hedge was at the gated entrance to the valley. She could run there and back in a few minutes, but she was already trembling with the stress and exertion. Beyond physical considerations were her emotional ones: she blinked back tears as she gazed at Ezio's motionless form and realized that she couldn't leave him, even temporarily. *"If I leave, he'll die."* A superstition, she knew, but a powerful one. Her hands tightened around her makeshift club, and the rough bark cut into her palms. She hesitated, rocked lightly on the balls of her feet, and then held her breath and plunged into the hedge.

The shock of pain took her breath away. In a single moment, she was surrounded by a tight web of hard branches studded with sharp thorns. Her hair yanked painfully away from her scalp, and the hem of her dress caught and pulled in a dozen different directions. Bella clenched her eyes shut, terrified that a sharp thorn might land in one of her eyes, and pushed blindly forward. *"It's not a wide hedge,"* she reminded herself, gritting her teeth. *"If I can just keep moving, I'll get through in a moment."*

Thorns scratched at her arms and legs sharply enough to draw blood. The pain was intense as hairs tore away from her head, but still she pressed on. She felt the branches pulling her back, but she pushed forward and held her club tightly against the grasping net of the surrounding hedge. After a short eternity of pain and doubt, Bella's groping hand reached empty air. Eagerly, she pressed her face through the last of the hedge and into the cool air just as the storm clouds burst.

Chapter 18 - Ezio

Ezio watched through half-closed eyes as Bella emerged struggling from the hedge. He had been shocked to see her plunge into the thick cluster of branches, and now he winced in sympathy as he saw the deep cuts on her hands and face that bled thin rivulets. His own badly-bitten shoulder ached deeply; when Guerrino had explained his plan, Ezio had not fully appreciated how much it would hurt. *"I just hope the wound doesn't carry over to my human body,"* he thought fretfully. It would be a dark irony to finally regain his human form just to bleed to death in the rain that sluiced around him.

Above him, the wolf that Guerrino had fashioned from dried herbs and strange ritual magic, and which he was now animating from the comfort of his tower, growled long and low at the girl as she fought to break free of the clutching thorns. Ezio heard the rip and tear of cloth, and then she stood before him, her wounds seeping and the bottom half of her skirt hanging in uneven tatters around her calves.

"Bella," he whispered, unsure if she could hear him over the roar of the rain. "You came back." His heart swelled with gratitude that he knew was not counterfeit. He had known completely that her love was true, and now she was here to prove it to the *fata*.

"You! You, wolf! Go!" she shouted over the wind. Her wet hair was plastered to her scalp, and Ezio was concerned to see her wobble unsteadily on her feet. *"She hasn't lost too much blood, has she?"* he wondered uncertainly. She was carrying a tree branch loosely in one hand, and now her grip tightened and she raised the club slowly with both hands. "Get out of here!" she insisted.

The wolf paced the ground angrily, head lowered and eyes raised to her face. Its slick coat glistened in the rain, and Ezio watched with fascination as the animal bared its sharp, bloodied teeth at the girl. A low growl vibrated from its throat and the creature released three short, sharp warning barks. Guerrino had warned him that he could not perfectly replicate a wolf's body language in a way that would fool another animal, but the message intended for the human girl was clear: it wasn't going to abandon its meal without a fight.

Bella took a step forward, and then another, edging closer to Ezio. The wolf gave another low warning growl, and the girl screamed her own wordless defiance; Ezio was surprised to feel the anger in her shrill cry wash over him. "I'm not scared of you!" she shouted at the animal. She swung the branch in front of her, once and then twice, the brandish a warning to her opponent. Her eyes blazed with fury. "Get away!" she screamed, her words whipping away with the wind.

When the wolf lunged, Ezio caught his breath in shock. The animal moved with astonishing speed, striking out at the girl. He saw her swing the branch; a wet *thunk* and a strangled yelp of pain from the wolf told him that her aim had struck true. A corresponding shout of pain echoed faintly through the thick storm from the direction of the castle. *"Was that Guerrino?"* The thought flashed through his mind in shock, but before it could register, he heard the low warning growl again behind him.

Ezio squinted through the sheets of rain and saw that the wolf was lamed in one leg, but hadn't given up the fight. The animal stood on three legs, its forepaw bleeding profusely and held tight to its chest. The creature's eyes were dark and murderous. Ezio stared in surprise at the bright blood that spilled over the rain-slick fur, far too much for a lamed wolf and yet more than enough for the wounded man controlling the creature. Ezio's eyes flicked back to Bella; numbly, he registered the frail sway of her body as she stubbornly gripped the heavy club that was sinking under its own weight.

"Bella—!" The scream registered in his mind, but never reached his lips. The enraged magical construct leapt forward and Ezio heard through the rain the startled gasp of pain and fear that ripped from the girl's lungs as she fell backward under the weight of the wolf.

"No!" He jumped to his feet, and the world swam sickeningly around him; he had forgotten his own blood loss. Dimly, he saw the wolf tear furiously at his bride's throat, and he stumbled forward drunkenly. "No!" he cried again, and the wolf pulled away from the girl to stare in his direction. For a moment their eyes locked, and Ezio imagined he saw something human in the creature's eyes. *"Regret?"* His clouded mind registered the emotion as if in a dream. Then the wolf leapt to its three unwounded feet and hurled itself through the bars of the silver fence and into the dark forest beyond.

Ezio stumbled forward, falling to his knees beside the wounded girl. "Bella, Bella," he crooned uselessly. His claws slashed across his chest as he pulled his shirt away from his body and pressed it frantically to her torn and bleeding neck. The shirt immediately bloomed red with blood, and Ezio knew that the wound was too deep and too wide to staunch. He felt tears sting his eyes as he cradled the young woman to his chest.

"Ezio?" The voice was so faint that he worried he had imagined it.

"Yes! Yes, Bella?" He cupped his hand behind the girl's head and leaned her back gently. His face hovered over hers, trying to provide relief from the thickly pouring rain.

"Are you all right?" she asked weakly. He nodded helplessly, his throat too constricted with sorrow to speak. She smiled at him, the same beautiful smile she had used not an hour before to reassure him that she would be with him again soon. "I'm glad," she said softly. "You've ... been ... so kind ..." Her voice trailed off slowly.

Ezio choked back a sob as the girl's eyes closed. "No, no," he murmured into her hair. His murmur grew into a wail. "No, no, no, no!" He lay her gently back onto the cold ground and stared in horror at his own blood-drenched hands. *"She's dead,"* he thought numbly. *"She died for me."*

Blinking back tears, he threw back his head and howled miserably into the storm.

Chapter 19 - Marchetta

It was gray morning when the cart pulled tentatively over the hill and Marchetta received her first sight of the castle.

"See? There it is!" Fiorita's arm shot out to point at the building that dominated the little valley. Tendrils of mist — the aftermath of yesterday's drenching downpour — curled over the valley and gave the castle a sinister, ugly look.

Marchetta pursed her lips and glanced over at Cienzo. The man seemed on the verge of a breakdown; the slight trembling that had shook his frame since Venizia had told him that he was coming on this trip had escalated into violent shaking.

"Is this it?" Venizia asked him sternly. "Is this where you left her?" He nodded nervously, but a look of puzzlement crossed his face. "What is it?" she asked sharply, glancing warily at the forest that hemmed in around them.

"The gate ..." His voice trailed off, and Marchetta squinted at the black fence that ringed the property. On second inspection, she realized that the fence was actually a dull silver that disappeared in the gray morning under a thick coating of black tarnish. She exchanged a quick glance with Mama, before guiding the mule to a stop before the gate. Marchetta handed the reins to Venizia and hopped out of the cart.

"No—!" Cienzo cried out, his voice a high squeak of panic as she reached out to unlatch the gate. Marchetta glanced back at him and then tentatively brushed her fingers against the gate latch. To her astonishment, the entire gate dissolved into dust at her touch. Marchetta leapt backward from the swirling black dust that settled slowly into the wet ground.

"What is this?" she asked, her voice sharp with tension. Cienzo shrugged and looked miserable. Cautiously, she grabbed the side of the cart and swung herself back into her seat, and Mama cracked the reins gently to urge the nervous mule forward.

Marchetta shivered as they passed where the gate had been. Looking to her left and her right, she could still see the fence on either side, somehow intact even after a large section had vanished into dust. From this angle, the remaining bars of the fence seemed semi-transparent, as though ready to puff into dust at the first stiff breeze.

Vigorously, she rubbed the sleeves of her gown; the chill in the air and the stillness of the valley were starting to get to her. *"Poor Bella,"* she thought. Marchetta couldn't imagine abandoning anyone to this gloomy valley. And now, after the incident with the gate, she could no longer hold to the belief that all the magic in Cienzo's and Fiorita's stories was nothing more than flights of fancy.

Not that she had disbelieved her sister for a moment on the more mundane aspects of her story. When Fiorita had come riding up to the front porch with a strange man in tow — and *after* Venizia and Marchetta had nearly collapsed in relief to see that Cienzo had not spirited away another girl after all — Marchetta had believed her sister immediately when she swore she had seen Bella.

Convincing Mama had taken longer. Marchetta could see that she was anxious at the thought of taking her daughters into a situation that she considered dangerous. Marchetta had argued that they could take Cienzo as ballast in case Bella's captor turned violent and Venizia had considered this for a long moment before setting her mouth grimly and nodding.

Marchetta had been less inclined to take along the young man that Fiorita had picked up on the road, but he had solved the problem by begging off the expedition. Fiorita had been disappointed, but not even her disapproving frown could persuade him; he had kissed her hand and told her that he was at her service for anything else she might require of him, before slinking guiltily out the door. *"Good riddance to bad rubbish,"* was Marchetta's opinion, but she knew better than to voice this to her little sister.

A dip in the road shook the cart and Marchetta grabbed at the side for support. Her eyes were drawn back to the mass of thorns and broken branches that ringed the estate behind them. Here and there, bright red roses shone through the fog, but even from a distance they seemed limp and dying. She nearly leapt from the cart in surprise when Fiorita suddenly yelled beside her. "Look!" Fiorita was pointing frantically at the dilapidated orchard situated in front of the castle, her face contorted with emotion.

Marchetta swiveled her head and felt her chest tighten at the sight of a shrouded body, lying motionless on a stone bench in the garden. She heard Cienzo's choked cry, and saw him scramble out of the cart and run to the still figure. Beside her, she felt Fiorita gasping for breath; Mama dropped the reins and wrapped her arms tight around the girl to keep her from jumping down and following Cienzo. The wail that went up from their stepfather confirmed their fears. *"She's past rescue now,"* Marchetta thought, blinking back the sudden tears that threatened to overwhelm her.

Marchetta glimpsed a man at the edge of the overgrown orchard, watching them intently from within the shadows. She looked over at Mama, but Venizia was too occupied with calming Fiorita to notice the stranger. Driven more by anger than sense, Marchetta stepped down from the cart and stalked towards the man.

She studied him carefully as she approached, wary of any sudden moves he might make. He was older than she, and to her eyes even less attractive than she found most men. His face was weary and burdened; one arm was thickly bandaged from elbow to neck, and the other carried a heavy pack slung over his shoulder. He watched her approach with a sad lack of interest, making no move to either flee or attack her.

"Are you the magician, then?" she asked caustically.

He hesitated at the question. "I suppose I am."

"You killed her?" Her hands were clenching and unclenching with anger. She folded her arms over her chest and stared at him.

"I ..." His eyes flicked over to the shrouded body being cradled gently by the sobbing Cienzo. "She was killed by a wolf," he said quietly.

Marchetta narrowed her eyes at him. "A wolf." Her voice was flat. "And not a magical beast?"

His body tensed and he stood a little straighter. When he spoke, there was an edge to his voice. "That's what I said. You're her family?"

"I'm her sister."

His eyes swept over her warily — *"Not what you expected, is it?"* Marchetta thought coldly — but at last he nodded. "I see," he said. His eyes flicked back to Bella and lingered for a long moment. "I'm glad you came. Please take her home and ..." His voice trailed off.

"Where are you going?" she demanded. "You've got a lot to answer for."

"You can't stop me."

"No?" She stepped forward, her arm outstretched to grab the wrist of his wounded arm, but he pulled back further into the shadows and she hesitated. *"I can't let him hurt Mama and Fiorita,"* she thought. She looked back for them, and panicked when she realized they weren't in the cart where she had last seen them; her heartbeat returned to normal when she registered that they were standing beside Bella's body, Venizia's arm wrapped protectively around Fiorita's shoulders.

When she turned back to the man, he was gone. She spun around in a quick, tight circle, her eyes darting over the misty castle lawns. *"There!"* she thought triumphantly; a thin outline, almost as insubstantial as the crumbling gate, trudged through the fog.

"Hey!" she shouted, and the outline trembled and resolved itself back into the color and shape of the magician. He didn't acknowledge her further, and continued steadily up the hill, clutching his pack with his un-bandaged hand.

"Wait!" Marchetta swung her head to see Fiorita stumble towards the man, one hand raised out to him in supplication. He paused and looked back at her — startled, perhaps, by the urgency in her voice. Fiorita took another step toward the road, but Mama caught her and held her firmly back.

"Flavio sends his love," she called up the hill. "He says you're always welcome with him, that you'll always be his brother."

The man frowned deeply and looked intensely puzzled for a moment before calling back, "He's a good boy. Tell him I won't be seeing him again." Then he turned and started up the road once more.

Marchetta took a step after him, but Venizia shook her head as she held Fiorita close.

"Let's ... get her on the cart," Venizia said quietly, and Marchetta understood. *"At least we can give her a proper burial,"* she thought sadly.

Between the two of them, they were able to gently lift Bella's pale body onto the cart. Marchetta helped Venizia into the driver's seat and handed her the reins; Fiorita, lost in her quiet sobs, allowed herself to be guided up to the seat next to Mama.

"Come on," Marchetta said sharply to Cienzo. "We're going." She walked quietly beside the slowly moving cart, bitterly wishing that it was a living, breathing Bella to whom she was giving up her seat in the cart, and not this cold shell that deserved so much better.

Behind her, she could hear Cienzo following, but she didn't care enough to look back at him. *"All this for your worthless life,"* she thought angrily, hurling the mental accusation at him. They were passing the evil-looking hedge of thorns, still dotted with wilting red roses.

"All this for a stupid rose," she thought, frustrated to tears. She brushed the back of her hand across her eyes, and then in a fit of pique she reached out and plucked a small rose from the hedge in passing. She cradled the

rose in her hand for a long moment before tucking the slender blossom gently next to Bella's cold, pale face.

Chapter 20 - Rosella

Rosella grinned as she walked away from the villa, the warm evening air punctuated by the crashes and screams that were such music to her ears. It was always fun to hear the humans run around in their overwrought panic.

She tilted her head back, relishing the scent of the nearby sea. "So inspirational," she murmured happily. She was particularly proud of the form she had given her latest human; there was so much more variety with what one could do with sea-beasts. Of course, occasionally they couldn't get to the water quickly enough to survive the transition from lungs to gills, but she couldn't be expected to coddle her humans. *"It wouldn't be punishment if I held their hand through it,"* she thought, giggling happily to herself.

Now the question was where to go next? Most of the humans at the coronation had appeared to be from the same coastal area as her target. As much as she loved the inspiration provided by the sea, she felt stifled if she worked with the same area twice in a row. *"Maybe a lakeside estate?"* she pondered. That could be the best of two worlds: the forest and the water. *"If I can find a girl, I can make a weeping willow,"* she thought, brightening considerably. Trees were always a great source of amusement.

Her thoughts were interrupted by a slight tingling that spread steadily through the vines that wrapped her arms. She frowned; someone was running out of their time, which shouldn't be possible. She'd only laid three curses since her last hibernation. Rosella pursed her lips — she didn't like to be interrupted — but curiosity won out over her irritation.

Closing her eyes in concentration, she plucked a single thorn from her vines, held it between forefinger and thumb, and used it to slowly cut the air in front of her. The air shimmered and rippled before resolving into a cool forest, deep with the shadows of the approaching dusk. She stepped quickly through the portal and felt it seal shut behind her with the soft sound of sucking air.

Rosella looked about her slowly, gathering her bearings and allowing her eyes, so recently dazzled by the bright seaside sunset, to adjust to the dusk of the forest. Turning to her right, she frowned to see the dark outline of a familiar castle; beside her stood a thorny hedge, as recognizable to her as her own handiwork as if she had signed it. And yet, something was not right here: every rose had been stripped from the hedge, leaving only bare thorn-covered branches.

Surprise was not a sensation that came frequently to the *fata*; Rosella stared at the hedge with increasing astonishment as she tried to work out the odd sight before her eyes. She'd seen her hedges destroyed by fire and lightning, but this one carried none of the blackened marks of fire. She'd similarly seen her creations stripped bare by swarms of insects and animals, but this hedge lacked the thoroughness of a feeding frenzy: here and there, clusters of ripped leaves poked pitifully through.

She heard a thick rustling noise that aroused her curiosity. She followed the bend of the hedge until the source of the noise came into view: a monstrous beast, tall and bony, stooped by the hedge. He clutched in the palm of his paw a single bright red rose, and as Rosella watched, he meticulously shredded the rose into a dozen tiny pieces that he flung contemptuously on to the ground.

"What are you doing?" Her voice was high and tight, and Rosella swallowed and cleared her throat. "I remember you," she said, recognizing the shape she had given the man. "You're not due yet."

The creature's head swiveled up in response to her voice; his black eyes locked with hers and burned with a hatred that she ignored. None of her creations could hurt her, and few bothered even to try. She was far more disturbed by his singularly strange attack on her roses, an attack that must have caused him a tremendous amount of pain as he felt each individual rose being shredded. Even now, she could see in the dim light small piles of rose shreddings heaped on the ground and trampled under his hooves.

"What are you doing here?" he snarled at her, a low growl that barely reached her ears.

"I sense when the last of the roses die," she said absently, still staring at him in astonishment. The beast wasn't wearing any clothes, and his fur was studded with hundreds of thorns. *"He must have got them while he was digging my roses out of their hedge,"* she realized, frowning at the black, matted blood that stained his body. "What are you doing?" she repeated her earlier question. "Don't you know that when the last rose dies, you'll remain a beast forever?" In all her centuries, this would be the first time a target had misunderstood the symbol of his time limit.

The creature spat at her, his vitriol falling short of the mark and landing at her feet. "I was already a beast forever," he growled. "Nothing you can do will ever make me less of one." His voice was trembling with emotion, building to a howling pitch. "At least I resemble what I am!" he yelled. "What's *your* excuse?"

Rosella blinked at him in bemusement. "What, you think *I* am a beast?"

"You're a monster." His voice had flattened out, but was still thick with conviction.

"For cursing you?" she asked, laughing at the accusation.

He snarled and snapped his teeth in a sudden fit of rage. Even knowing that he could not hurt her, Rosella recoiled a step back from the hatred that was packed into his movement. Usually her targets were cowed and defeated when she met them at this stage; never before had she seen one so enraged. "You sent Bella to me," he howled angrily. "She was the sweetest, most innocent girl — and she loved me!" His ears twitched spasmodically. "She loved me, and you made her sacrifice her life for me!"

Rosella stared at him blankly. "I don't know what you're talking about."

"You said she had to sacrifice everything," he spat the words at her. "You said it, it was a lie, we tested it to the final limit, and now she's dead."

Her eyes narrowed. "No, prince," she said, relieved to be on familiar footing again. "I said that *you* had to find that love which is willing to sacrifice everything. If you weren't able to make sacrifices for others as a human, you were to learn to do so as a beast," she finished triumphantly.

He stared at her, shocked and angry. Rosella met his gaze smugly. Now that she had popped his bubble of indignation, he would beg to be given a second chance. She smiled to herself and mused, *"I might just give it to him."* It could be interesting to watch: could he be truly selfless while absolutely knowing that he *had* to be selfless to get what he wanted?

"What was I supposed to do?" he asked her hoarsely. "I loved her," he insisted.

"Obviously not enough," Rosella retorted. "Not if you let her die." She smirked at him, suddenly amused by his little prank with her roses. "You're not even sacrificing for her *now*. You're doing this because you're angry, you're sad, you're upset — even now, you're completely focused on yourself."

She laughed again and was delighted to see the dull flash of pain in his black eyes. "You have no idea what I've sacrificed," he growled quietly, but the words lacked his earlier conviction and his shoulders slumped forward in despair.

"Not willingly. You're still lashing out in anger at the mess left on your doorstep." Rosella said with a grin. Sensing his defeat, she forced herself to smile more warmly at him. "Oh, don't look so sad. Everyone makes mistakes," she crooned, trying to sound sympathetic. "You just didn't understand. That's not your fault."

"*Everything* is my fault," he said, his voice thick with emotion. Tears welled in his black eyes and spilled over his matted cheeks.

"It will be all right," she said reassuringly. "I can give you a second try, another chance to redeem yourself." She held out her hand coaxingly to him, and she used just enough fairy magic to direct the last rays of sunset to play over her face and form. She wished she could see herself from his vantage point, but she could imagine how she must look: beautiful *fata* Rosella, the last bright spot of warmth and safety in a cold, dark world.

"*I haven't had so much excitement in decades,*" she realized joyfully. What an unexpected treasure this man was turning out to be, and such fun that she might even stick around to watch the curse play out this time. "*I could even hand-pick the girl myself,*" she thought, almost trembling with the anticipation of her fun.

The beast stared at her for a long time, as the sunlight dipped below the horizon and the darkness slowly shrouded them. His face was devoid of emotion, and Rosella shifted uncomfortably, wondering what he was thinking. When finally she could stand the silence no more, she smiled again and prompted him: "Well, my prince?"

He didn't answer. Instead, he dropped to all fours and padded like an animal silently around her, through the gap in the hedge and into the dark of the woods. "Prince!" she called after him, but with the setting of the sun on the last dying rose, her curse was finished and she could not restrain him. "Prince, come back!" she called, feeling her disappointment building. The only answer was a desolate howl from deep within the shadows.

Rosella stood rooted to the ground, shaken with surprise. No one, not a single human, had ever before completely refused to play her game. Glimpsing a trampled rose at her feet, she bent to scoop it up from the ground. An unfamiliar emptiness washed over her as she plucked the abused flower from the wet earth. "*I don't understand,*" she thought.

With a final glance back at the castle behind her, she turned and walked down the dark road out of the valley, cradling the dead rose gently in her palm.

Acknowledgments

I never realized just how many people it can take to write a book. There are so many people to whom I owe so much, and without whom this book simply would not exist.

I owe deep gratitude to my family. My dear Husband read each chapter as it was written, and then again several times over as I reworked the material. Throughout the entire process he was kind and encouraging and was frequently heard to say, "I don't like fairy tales, but I like this!" My Mother, too, devoted a great deal of her time to reading my book, providing invaluable corrections, and gratifying me deeply with her praise and support. I received a wealth of support from my Husband, my parents, and a number of blood- and marriage-relatives as I struggled through an exceedingly difficult year. While my writing supported me psychologically, it was my family who supported me physically and emotionally. Thank you.

I owe a tremendous debt to my friend and writing partner, J.D. Montague. She was my "shoulder cricket" for every step in my journey, and was always ready and willing to read another chapter, listen to another idea, and critique another proposed turn of phrase. J.D. had the skill to know when my writing was bad, the bravery to point it out to me, and the diplomacy and wit to do so in ways that invariably made me laugh. She helped me through my writing slumps and encouraged me no matter how much or how little I had written that day. J.D. has made me a better writer and a better person, and has been an invaluable friend.

I owe a chorus of thanks to all my beta readers, each of whom selflessly volunteered their time and effort to read my draft and provide invaluable feedback. I was overwhelmed by the sheer number of people who volunteered, and I was deeply touched by all the responses. The readers who loved my draft gave me the strength to keep going; the readers who didn't and yet bravely slogged through it anyway to provide crucial feedback gave me the vital tools I needed to improve. I owe my deepest gratitude to **Angela D, Cassandra, Charleen M, Danielle C, Elfwreck, Ian Pérez Zayas, Janell B, Jeanine Wood, Jeremy Janik, Jill Heather Flegg, Layne R, Marie L, mmy of mmycomments, Rachel Pumroy,** and **Sarah W.** I thank you all from the bottom of my heart.

I owe a very special 'thank you' also to my blog readers, whose witty comments and thoughtful insights motivate me to get out of bed every morning in the hopes that I will write something worthy of their time and attention. I am daily overwhelmed with humility and gratitude at the knowledge that there are people interested in what I have to say, and kind enough to give me the gifts of their time and attention. Thank you all, so very much. A very special mention must also go to readers **Dav** and **Rowen** for providing me with valuable links to historically appropriate cookbooks and gardening materials as part of my research.

I owe a final thank you to the artists and professionals who made this book possible. Emily Vreeland labored tirelessly over several months and a grueling scholastic period to provide the lovely portraits in this book. Clarissa Filice worked magic in her creation of the front and back covers, and turned my vague ideas into beautiful artwork. Thank you.

Each one of these wonderful people has touched my life and made it richer and fuller, just as they have touched this work and helped to shape and mold it. I thank you all, as deeply as I possibly can.

~ Ana Mardoll

About the Artists

Ana Mardoll

Ana Mardoll is an avid reader and writer. She loves cats, fairy tales, and intense navel gazing. She blogs on a near daily basis from an undisclosed location in the wild, untamed, and astonishingly dusty Texas wilderness. Her photo-realistic avatars are a gift from best friend and invaluable writing buddy, J.D. Montague.

Pulchritude is her first novel in a planned series of fairy tale retellings.

To read more of Ana's writings, including her snarktastic literary deconstructions, visit her website at www.AnaMardoll.com.

Clarissa Filice

Clarissa Filice is an widely talented multi-medium artist living in Portland, Oregon. She loves art, reading, chai lattes, and rainbow fried rice. However, oftentimes her brother has to remind her that to live you actually have to consume the latter two items.

Clarissa created the beautiful front and back covers for *Pulchritude.*

To view more of Clarissa's art, visit her gallery at FallingSarah.DeviantArt.com.

Emily Vreeland

Emily Vreeland is a student of Anthropology and Cross-cultural Leadership, working as an artist-for-hire so she can eat quasi-regularly and have her fancy teas. Besides keeping up with her art, and trying not to expire under the pressures of graduating, she relaxes with yoga, tree hugging, and volunteering. Her artistic style varies from realism to cartoony, and drives her to constantly cover everything she owns in a layer of paint.

Emily created the lovely character portraits for *Pulchritude.*

To view more of Emily's art, visit her gallery on Loving-Em.DeviantArt.com.

Character Portraits

Character Portrait: *Rosella*

When I started *Pulchritude*, the "Beauty and the Beast" story most firmly fixed in my mind was the Disney version, which starts with a curse. A beautiful fairy disguises herself as a beggar and then curses a prince for his selfishness when he refuses to give her lodging for the night.

The question that stuck in my mind, and the question that ultimately caused me to write the novel was, *"How could this go any way but wrong?"* And once I'd decided that a curse given in anger to a selfish prince not previously inclined to examine his actions for internalized privilege simply could *not* go right, it was a quick and easy slide to my interpretation of the fairy as something less modern-and-moralistic and more ancient-and-capricious. After all, the very word "fairy" is derived from the same root as "fate", and the fates are cruel as often as they are kind.

I gave my fairy the name "Rosella" because I had already decided on an Italian setting for the story and because the Disney version of the fairy gives the beast an enchanted rose to mark the time limit of the curse. I wanted to continue that idea of roses ticking down to an inexorable time limit, so I made roses a sort of signature for my fairy: she wears roses in her hair, has 'sleeves' of thorny vines covering her bare arms, creates a hedge of dazzling roses as part of her curse, and has a name derived from the Latin form of 'rose'. [22]

As much as I loved Rosella, her very existence seeks to create plot holes. I wanted a world where magic was possible, but not so common that skeptics couldn't still exist. As a result I had to do some heavy hand-waving to keep Rosella and the rest of her kind dormant for large chunks of the year and largely hidden during their active times. When Rosella proudly notes that she is the most active and most 'successful' of her kind, I'd hoped that would plant the idea that other *fata* act in invisible ways since they cannot emulate humankind and walk among them in the same way Rosella does. I'm far from certain that I succeeded, but I hope that my readers enjoyed the ride.

This portrait of Rosella was drawn by artist Emily Vreeland.

Character Portrait: *Ezio*

Every "Beauty and the Beast" story has a beast who traditionally starts out as a prince. What very few of the stories manage to agree on is his personality.

The original *La Belle et la Bête* features a kind and honorable prince who has been turned into a slow-witted lout by a vengeful fairy whose advances were spurned. Later retellings oscillated between an innately good prince who needed to be appreciated by a loving woman and an originally bad prince who needed to be redeemed by a loving woman. I knew starting out that neither of these approaches were ones I wanted to take, yet I didn't immediately have a clear picture of my own prince-beast.

I envisioned my prince-beast as a classic son of privilege: spoiled, entitled, selfish. I knew he had to lord over a very small pond since I couldn't keep the transformation quiet in-text if he was the crown prince of an entire country, but still I knew he would be a big fish in his small pond. He would have lived his life taking what he wanted and never thinking twice about satiating his needs at the expense of others.

And yet, I didn't want him to be a villainous person. I wanted to write a story about how patriarchal systems can ruin a person's ability for selflessness and empathy, and in order to do that, I needed my prince-beast to be a relatively decent person who — as a consequence of his birth, his parents, and his society — acted in ways that most of us would recognize as casually cruel and self-serving. And thus I ended up walking a fine line between a prince who thinks nothing of 'borrowing' his younger brother's wife and yet still has flashes of insight that perhaps his pretty prisoner may not always have had the easiest life, and I hope that his character will seem consistent throughout.

I chose the name "Ezio" for my prince-beast because the name derives from the same root as "eagle" and I felt that the name would be appropriate for the son of a royal family. [23] Later, one of my Beta Readers was kind enough to point out that my prince-beast shares a name with a popular video game assassin. [24] Ultimately, I decided to keep the name but I apologize to any readers who found the association distracting.

This portrait of Ezio was drawn by artist Emily Vreeland.

Character Portrait: *Guerrino*

The need for Guerrino impressed itself upon me very early in the planning process for *Pulchritude*: I simply could not imagine how the beast would otherwise survive without aid.

This isn't a new problem; the original *La Belle et la Bête* provides the beast with a fairy benefactress (separate and distinct from the vengeful fairy who cursed him) and she keeps him alive and well-fed. Later retellings sustain him through the efforts of his cheerful-and-resigned servants, who are variously turned into animals, invisible spirits, or sentient furniture until the curse is broken. I had initially wanted to dispense with the cheerful servants altogether, but I could not do so without creating an insurmountable hurdle: how does a previously pampered and now drastically cursed prince survive long enough for the beauty to turn up on his doorstep?

Thus was Guerrino born, named for the Italian derivative of "guard".
[25] And if I couldn't dispense with the cheerful servants, I could at least

dispense with the 'cheerful' part. To bridge the gap caused by the reduction of dozens of servants to a single old man, Guerrino was given an impressive array of magic (for a mere human), that he might help feed the beast, aid in the capture of the beauty, and facilitate her tragic death. Yet that talent for magic set him apart from the other humans and left him vulnerable without the sponsorship of a powerful royal family. As a result, he stays with Ezio not out of love or loyalty or laziness, but largely because he calculates that it's in his best interests to do so. I admired him for that, and I hope that my readers will feel the same.

I wanted Guerrino to be at least partly responsible for the beauty's death so as to reinforce my overarching theme that the beast is not the villain so much as the surrounding toxic culture that has created him. Guerrino is no more a villain than the beast is, but he *is* a product of his society and a product of the prejudice and biases within. Like the beast, he sees the beauty as the key to his freedom from a bad situation, and like the beast, he is willing to accept the possibility that the beauty may need to be sacrificed in order to beat the curse.

This portrait of Guerrino was drawn by artist Emily Vreeland.

Character Portrait: *Bella*

I first knew I wanted to write a "Beauty and the Beast" retelling when, in the course of a deconstruction blog post on "Twilight", I idly wondered what it would be like to live one's life being constantly called *Bella*, or "beauty". The thought then struck me that at least one other time-honored literary character was literally named *Beauty*, and I was immediately fascinated by all the expectations and insecurities packed into carrying that name around for an entire lifetime.

What would it be like, I wondered, for your very name to be a reminder that your most valuable asset was one you had zero control over? Would some sort of precarious balance be struck between a vain self-confidence and a deep insecurity? Almost every beauty in all the "Beauty and the Beast" stories I knew of were good and sweet and kind and loving and intelligent and practically perfect in every way, but what if life in a patriarchal society under a constant male gaze made a beauty less-than-perfect and deeply insecure about her own inner worth?

After much consideration, I set my beauty in Italy as "Bella" instead of in the original France as "Belle". I wanted a beauty who, from her first moment on the page, read as imperfect — sometimes selfish and vain, frequently insecure, yet capable of love and sacrifice — and I thought I had a better chance conveying that imperfection through "Bella" than through "Belle", which was the name given to the bookish Disney beauty who has been deeply branded on so many hearts.

The hardest part about writing Bella was conveying her as a complex human in a manner that was reasonable to the reader. Fairy tale women tend to be one-dimensional — either all good or all bad — and it was frequently difficult to convey that the insecurity that drives Bella to vainly examine every inch of her face for a blemish in need of more powder is the *same* insecurity that drives her to sacrifice her life for her father and her husband. I wanted to convey a young woman who does everything she can to be perfect for the patriarchy and, in the end, is used up and destroyed by the demands of the men who should have protected her.

This portrait of Bella was drawn by artist Emily Vreeland.

Character Portrait: *Cienzo*

I think Disney knew what they were doing when they had the beauty seek out her father and pro-actively make the offer to exchange her life for his: it's very hard to have much sympathy for the original *La Belle et la Bête* father who rides home to put his affairs in order after being sentenced to death by the beast and immediately lets it slip that his life can be saved if only one of his daughters goes back in his stead.

I didn't want any overt villains in my story and the merchant was no exception. I tried to write him as a product of his culture, in much the same way that I think the original tale tried to do. He is a jolly enough fellow in casual company, but he lives in a bubble of privilege that he makes no attempt to break out of. He gladly gives his daughter food and shelter and doesn't sell her into an unhappy marriage at the first sign of financial trouble, but at the same time he is quick enough to allow her to put her life on the line when his own is in danger.

In a small way, Cienzo orchestrates his own fate with his casual refusal to empathize with his fellow humans: though he is kind enough to pay a common innkeeper generously for his drink, yet he mocks the underprivileged man when he queries him about making much-needed trades with the village. When he then remembers Bella's request for a rose and asks the man he has insulted where he can buy ornamental flowers for "one of my ladies" back home, the man is disgusted enough with the privileged merchant to send him straight to the nearby castle and its recently-cursed inhabitant.

Cienzo's name was scavenged from a merchant's son in an Italian fairy tale of the same name. [26] But the merchant in my tale makes his living from others without fully realizing it or appreciating them. He lives in the house owned by his first wife, and he regains his business through the wealth and patronage of his second wife. His job does not revolve around the creation of goods, but rather the redistribution of same, and though his living is made from luxury items like jewelry and fine cloths, he criticizes his daughter for wanting the trinkets that he and his society have reinforced as crucial to a woman's existence. And of course, when facing the prospect of his own death, he makes his living literally from the exchange of his own daughter to his would-be executioner.

This portrait of Cienzo was drawn by artist Emily Vreeland.

Character Portrait: *Venizia*

There is no stepmother in the original *La Belle et la Bête*, but there are sisters to the titular beauty. I wanted my story to have those sisters, but I wanted *my* sisters to be black. I was intensely tired of fantasy stories that have dragons and fairies and demons and unicorns, and yet no black people for reasons of suddenly-very-important "historical accuracy". My mind was made up: my Italy was going to have black people living and working and marrying in it, and it was all going to be perfectly normal and no one was going to kick up a fuss about it. And since I wanted the beauty's sisters to be black, that meant marriage into the family, and *that* meant a stepmother. And by gum, I was going to have an awesome fairy tale stepmother.

I wanted Venizia to be a wealthy widow who married out of choice and love rather than necessity. I wanted her to be a loving mother who had tried to raise her daughters to be wise and cautious in passing judgment. She loves aphorisms and hands them down to her daughters, while still recognizing in her own life that some advice is easier to give than to follow. She's lived her entire life in a busy port city and as such has a very different perspective from the people in the small country village she has moved to. Even her name "Venizia" has been derived from one of our most famous Italian cities. [27] Her reliance on justice and the courts, her lack of interest in country royals, and her skepticism of magic have all been formed by her life in a completely different society. Like everyone else in this story, she's not perfect, but when she fails she does so in ways that I think are reasonable, given her background.

Once Venizia was created, I was pleased at how beautifully she entwined with the narrative. Her financial backing of the merchant allowed him to assert his claim to his ship's goods when it limped into harbor several years late. Her attempts to mold the family into a cohesive unit might have succeeded given a little more time. Her fierce defense of her daughters (both natural and by marriage) provided a striking contrast to the merchant's willingness to sacrifice them all to save his own skin. And I think that — had the beast been willing to let his beauty visit her family or allowed them to come visit her — things could have ended very differently under Venizia's sensible guidance.

This portrait of Venizia was drawn by artist Emily Vreeland.

Character Portrait: *Marchetta*

In the original *La Belle et la Bête*, the beauty has sisters who refuse to go to their deaths to save their father. The text treats them very meanly: the sisters are vain, the sisters are selfish, the sisters are cruel. And yet, just as I imagined that my beauty would not be a paragon of perfection, so too I imagined that my sisters might not be the heartless harpies portrayed by their predecessors. I had something else in mind.

My Marchetta is in many ways a deliberate foil to my Bella. By the standards of their world, she is just as conventionally beautiful; she is tall, slender, and with a lovely and pleasing face. The biggest way in which the two girls differ is with their respective parents: where a selfish father has consistently undermined Bella's confidence and sense of self-worth, a loving mother has carefully built up Marchetta's self-esteem.

Both girls are capable of biting wit, as when Marchetta snaps at the nosy storekeeper or when Bella teases the beast that he smells like an animal. Both girls know how to manage resources, as when Marchetta takes over the management of the kitchen and finances, or when Bella scavenges for makeup and money. Both girls have strong instincts for survival, and a strong willingness to sacrifice in order to please their parent. In another story, Bella and Marchetta could be friends, but yet here their histories have rendered them two entirely different people. Bella acts out of fear and nervousness, while Marchetta lives in a state of steely calm.

Had Marchetta been offered the chance to give her life for the doomed merchant, she would have refused. Not because of insufficient love or selflessness, as in the original tale, but because Marchetta would have recognized that the request was unfair and unjust. When the merchant asks his daughters who will die for him, he is in essence asking which of them loves him the most. *Sure,* he says, *you all claim to love me, but who will step up and prove that love with her life?* The request is not a fair one, and the daughter who steps forward is acting under duress: so anxious to 'prove' her love that all other considerations fall by the wayside. Marchetta has been given the tools to recognize that unfairness and to push back against it. Bella has not.

Marchetta's name, like her mother's, ties deliberately back into the port city home she misses so much, by attempting to invoke the history of our famous Venice. [28] Marchetta is also a lesbian, though unfortunately I never could find a way to work it into the story as overtly as I wanted.

This portrait of Marchetta was drawn by artist Emily Vreeland.

Character Portrait: *Fiorita*

When I decided to retain the sisters from *La Belle et la Bête*, I wanted one of the sisters to be younger than the titular beauty. If the older sister was a representation of what our beauty might have become under the guidance of a better parent, then the younger sister would be a picture of what our beauty might have been had not her father tried to mold her into the "perfect" patriarchal daughter.

Fiorita is lovely, but not conventionally so: she is heavy-set, as we see when Cienzo calls her his "chubby chipmunk" and later when one of the village children needles her about her weight. Because of this and because of the fierce protection of her mother and older sister, she's avoided some of the strong societal pressures that have assailed Bella. She does not, for instance, offer her own life in order to save the merchant, despite being a loving child and eager to please. Instead, she finds his request confusing and upsetting, and doesn't understand how he can ask someone he loves to suffer on his behalf.

Fiorita has not been shielded entirely from society. She is very conscious of what others think of her, and frequently self-censors in order to please. We see her nervously calculate what to ask as a gift when her stepfather solicits requests, before her mother comes to her aid with an appropriate suggestion. And because she is ostracized by the village children for her bodily appearance and general foreignness, she chooses to stay home and wait for (and then actively search for) her missing stepsister rather than trying to use the socially appropriate channels that her mother and sister are fruitlessly pursuing.

I had originally intended for Fiorita to be sixteen, in a stepping-stone arrangement of Fiorita-16, Bella-18, Marchetta-20, but my early readers felt that anything older than fourteen felt inconsistent with the character. Her cheerful exuberance and ready embrace of her standoffish stepsister seemed to speak of someone a little younger and more spontaneous. Accordingly, I adjusted her age in the text since I could not at that stage imagine how to alter her personality from what had already been written.

Fiorita's name, like her sister's, is borrowed from a family crest used in an Italian city. [29] Rather than evoke Venice, however, Fiorita's usage ties most closely in with the province of Bologna, which is famous for its sausages. This is, however, entirely a coincidence.

This portrait of Fiorita was drawn by artist Emily Vreeland.

Character Portrait: *Flavio*

Flavio has neither a picture nor a chapter to his name, as I genuinely did not expect to use him past his introduction in Chapter 2.

He was originally created as a characterization exercise for the prince: I wanted to conversationally convey the prince's frustration at his expensive banquet, tiresome guests, and financially-forced betrothal. I had planned for the prince to strike Rosella, but I wanted to set the scene sympathetically by highlighting that he is under a tremendous amount of social and financial pressure. At the same time, I wanted to clarify that this was a man steeped in birth privilege and casual selfishness; his proposal to set up his illegitimate half-brother in an arranged marriage so that the prince can 'borrow' his wife was a convenient way to foreshadow that the prince viewed women more as objects to be maneuvered than as people in their own right.

I didn't expect to see Flavio again after he fled into the night. I knew it was a loose thread in a story where all the other named characters were automatically important (the deceased Prince Domenico and Bella's friend Agata had not yet been granted names), but it seemed unavoidable as I couldn't realistically have a long conversation without granting the half-brother his own name. I gave him the name "Flavio", as the next letter in the alphabet after his older brother Ezio and meaning "golden", as per his sunny temperament. [30]

Fortunately for Flavio, the original *La Belle et la Bête* has the beauty make a visit home before returning to the beast out of love and concern for his safety. I had intended to preserve this aspect of the story in Chapter 12, but when the time came, it no longer worked within the narrative. The beast was supposed to let the beauty go, but Ezio was neither confident that she would return nor selfless enough to take the chance. The beauty was supposed to want to go home, but Bella was reluctant to leave a husband who claimed to love her for a father who very clearly didn't. The sisters were supposed to receive the beauty spitefully and thereby strengthen her resolve to return to the beast, but Marchetta and Fiorita would have received Bella with open arms and encouraged her to remain with them.

I had departed from the narrative so thoroughly in terms of characterization that I could no longer follow the plot as I had intended. And yet, I still needed a means of interaction between Bella and the outside world. I wanted her to learn that her father's life had gone on without her, and for her to feel a nadir of defeat that ultimately propels her to accept the situation and attempt to make the best life of it that she can. And if I couldn't send Bella home to have her illusions shattered, I would have to send someone from home to her.

Fiorita was the obvious choice: she had enough belief in the possibility of magic and the truthfulness of Cienzo to look for "the magician" who had taken her sister. But she needed a guide, and a mode of transportation would additionally be very welcome. I toyed with the idea of revisiting the innkeeper who had sent Cienzo to the castle in the first place, but then the thought struck me that I had a perfectly good half-brother holing up with his friends from the castle guard in their families' homes and additionally tortured with guilt and keeping his ears to the ground for any news of his brother's malignant condition.

And thus was my Chekhov's Gun born from a character I had originally conceived as a deliberate loose end.

Deconstruction

The Author's Afterword on "The Beauty and The Beast"
La Belle Et La Bête

I have held a passion for fairy tales since the first "Brothers Grimm" adaptation given to me in early childhood. I loved the stories with their heroes and heroines and their magical twists and turns.

But as I grew older, I started to balk at the black-and-white morality that was sometimes served alongside many of my fairy tale collections. I began to read the tales with a willingness to mentally compose my own modifications to the tales when I felt it was needed. If I felt particularly strongly about a story, I would dream of rewriting the tale entirely with my own personal spin. More frequently than not, the dream was dropped in favor of something more interesting in the moment, and nothing ever came of such fancies.

The idea that I might seriously attempt to write an adaptation of "The Beauty and the Beast" came simply enough one day. I was musing that many of the lovely ladies of fairy tale lore would possibly not in Real Life be quite so supremely well-adjusted after a lifetime of being *called* lovely all the time by everyone they met. "Beauty" of the classic *La Belle et la Bête* tale particularly intrigued me — in the original, she is simply known as *La Belle* everywhere she goes.

In the fairy tale, Beauty's identity is defined solely in terms of what others *see* when they look at her. Almost everything we know about her is simply that she conforms to the social standards of female attractiveness for her culture. As a character, she embodies the concept of Gaze [31], or the awareness that one's self is being viewed by external people as a physical object. Gaze holds a crucial place in both feminist theory and literary deconstruction, because the awareness of being observed can create a disturbance in a person's behavior. I wondered what kind of disturbance could result from Beauty's awareness that she is constantly being evaluated by everyone around her?

What would life be like for a girl spontaneously named "Beauty" by all her peers, even to the point that any prior name she bore now fades away? What kind of effect would such a name have on her personality? Would she be self-assured, possibly even haughty, in her unmatched beauty? Or would she tend towards the nervous and fretful as she strove always to live up to the expectations of others? Mightn't she possibly end up both vain *and* self-conscious at the same time?

If Beauty were a real person, I could imagine that an entire lifetime of being treated as a visible object might leave her anxious and lonely. I imagined her unable to connect with others, fearful that sharing her real feelings and inner thoughts might upset the delicate balance of being constantly beautiful to them. I saw her surrounded by friends and lovers and even superficially confident in their flatteries, and yet essentially alone and never fully understanding why.

That is the Beauty I wanted to capture in my story, long before I ever put pen to page.

Feminist Fairy Tale?

Unlike many of the fairy tales that we grow up with, "The Beauty and the Beast" is not an anonymous tale of unknown authorship. Whereas many classic fairy tales were handed down from multiple competing and collaborating sources and gathered up by folklorists, "The Beauty and the Beast" was an original tale written in 1740 by the Frenchwoman Gabrielle-Suzanne Barbot de Villeneuve, who chose older Animal Bridegroom legends as the inspiration for her story [32]. The original tale was exceedingly long (much longer than the short, archetypal version that Madame de Beaumont would later popularize) and explored in detail many social concerns of de Villeneuve's day.

The original *La Belle et la Bête* might be considered a feminist work for its time. Written by a woman, it explored the social problems faced by the women of de Villeneuve's day, and argued for the rights of women to determine their own fate apart from the whims of their fathers and husbands. Author Terri Windling argues eloquently that many of the Animal Bridegroom stories of the 17th and 18th centuries — de Villeneuve's tale included — were an especially valuable rhetorical vehicle for exploring the dangers faced by women who had no right to choose their own husband, no right to refuse their husband's sexual desires, and no right to own property or sue for divorce [33]. Even a privileged and socially-valued woman, like the fictional Beauty, had no way of knowing whether she would find herself married off by her father to a beastly monster.

Finding an English copy of de Villeneuve's original story is quite a hunt; for purposes of this deconstruction, I relied upon the version collected in "Four and Twenty Fairy Tales" translated by James Planché in 1858 and available online [34]. (The story itself is quite long, with my quotes covering only a fraction of the total story, but I hope to convey the most relevant pieces.)

The tale starts out simply and familiarly enough with the story of Beauty's family and their sudden fall from riches to rags:

In a country very far from this is to be seen a great city wherein trade flourishes abundantly. It numbered amongst its citizens a merchant, who succeeded in all his speculations, and upon whom Fortune, responding to his wishes, had always showered her fairest favours. But if he had immense wealth, he had also a great many children, his family consisting of six boys and six girls. None of them were settled in life: the boys were too young to think of it; the girls, too proud of their fortunes, upon which they had every reason to count, could not easily determine upon the choice they should make. Their vanity was flattered by the attentions of the handsomest young gentlemen.

But a reverse of fortune which they did not at all expect, came to trouble their felicity. Their house took fire; the splendid furniture with which it was filled, the account books, the notes, gold, silver, and all the valuable stores which formed the merchant's principal wealth, were enveloped in this fatal conflagration, which was so violent that very few of the things could be saved. This first misfortune was but the forerunner of others. The father, with whom hitherto everything had prospered, lost at the same time, either by shipwreck or by pirates, all the ships he had at sea; his correspondents made him a bankrupt, his foreign agents were treacherous; in short, from the greatest opulence, he suddenly fell into the most abject poverty.

He had nothing left but a small country house, situated in a lonely place, more than a hundred leagues from the city in which he usually resided. Impelled to seek a place of refuge from noise and tumult, he took his family to this retired spot, who were in despair at such a revolution.

In the tale, the fate of the family and the futures of its daughters are wholly dependent upon the fortunes of the father, the Merchant. The Merchant's luck turns ill when all his holdings are consumed in a series of accidents and outright theft from his trusted associates. The luck of his daughters turns in immediate response: they lose their home, their dowries, the clothes and jewels they need in order to be socially attractive, and in total every chance they once had for a comfortable future.

Whether or not this fate could have been avoided with more careful investments by the Merchant is ultimately a distraction from the fact that his children had no more say in their father's affairs than they did in being born to him in the first place. Their fates are inextricably tied to the father's and if a father's fortunes reverse, his children have no choice but to suffer alongside him.

The daughters of this unfortunate merchant were especially horrified at the prospect of the life they should have to lead in this dull solitude. For some time they flattered themselves that, when their father's intention became known, their lovers, who had hitherto sued in vain, would be only too happy to find they were inclined to listen to them. They imagined that the many admirers of each would be all striving to obtain the preference. They thought if they wished only for a husband they would obtain one; but they did not remain very long in such a delightful illusion.

They had lost their greatest attractions when, like a flash of lightning, their father's splendid fortune had disappeared, and their time for choosing had departed with it. Their crowd of admirers vanished at the moment of their downfall; their beauty was not sufficiently powerful to retain one of them. Their friends were not more generous than their lovers. From the hour they became poor, every one, without exception, ceased to know them.

In de Villeneuve's world, the only means by which a woman might disentangle her fate from that of her father's is by a change in her familial status. She may exchange the dependence on her *father* for a dependence on a *husband*, but in either case the woman is merely choosing into which basket to place all her eggs. In de Villeneuve's tale, the Merchant's daughters had not settled on suitors prior to the loss of their father's fortune. This is unfortunate for them, since now those opportunities are summarily withdrawn.

There is some sense in the text that the daughters have no one to blame for this ill fate but themselves. As profiteering speculators, they have played the market poorly by letting their vanity keep them on the marriage market for too long. They should have permanently selected a suitable suitor long before this misfortune occurred to rob them of their market value. And this marks the start of the villainization of the elder daughters, both as a typical fairy tale contrast to the virtuous Youngest Child, but also as a harsh embodiment of the rules of this world.

Because the text is so harsh in its treatment of the Merchant's daughters, the reader is propelled towards sympathy for the young women. No matter how vain they supposedly are, the bitter irony is that even if they *had* prudently settled upon husbands before their father's misfortune, there would still be no guarantee of a safe and happy life for them. A woman could be saved from poverty, only to see the fortunes of her husband reverse the very next day. And such a reversal would almost certainly leave her in a worse position than before: equally poor, but now dependent upon a new husband rather than a familiar father, and without the fantasy of marrying out of poverty.

The Merchant's daughters are ultimately in the unenviable position of having to choose which man to gamble their futures on, with no way to recover from a wrong choice and no way to know which choice is the right one.

Humility and Hubris

It is perhaps fortunate that the Merchant's daughters did not marry their suitors before their misfortune hits. Not only do the suitors lose interest in the young women in the wake of their impoverishment, but many of them also turn on the family with malicious rumors and gossip. The family is driven from the city by the ill-will of their former friends, to live out the rest of their years in humble circumstances.

This wretched family, therefore, could not do better than depart from a city wherein everybody took a pleasure in insulting them in their misfortunes. Having no resource whatever, they shut themselves up in their country house, situated in the middle of an almost impenetrable forest, and which might well be considered the saddest abode in the world. What misery they had to endure in this frightful solitude! They were forced to do the hardest work.

In their country home, only hard work and manual labor awaits the family. The boys work the fields from dawn to dusk while the girls toil at the chores that their former servants had previously performed for them. The older girls are miserable, but the youngest one accepts her fate and cheers the family with songs and music. Her labors are appreciated by her father and brothers, yet her sisters despise her for it.

The youngest girl, however, displayed greater perseverance and firmness in their common misfortune. [...] Every intelligent person, who saw her in her true light, was eager to give her the preference over her sisters. **In the midst of her greatest splendour, although distinguished by her merit, she was so handsome that she was called "The Beauty."** *Known by this name only, what more was required to increase the jealousy and hatred of her sisters? Her charms, and the general esteem in which she was held, might have induced her to hope for a much more advantageous establishment than her sisters; but feeling only for her father's misfortunes, far from retarding his departure from a city in which she had enjoyed so much pleasure, she did all she could to expedite* *it. This young girl was as contented in their solitude as she had been in the midst of the world. To amuse herself in her hours of relaxation, she would dress her hair with flowers, and, like the shepherdesses of former times, forgetting in a rural life all that had most gratified her in the height of opulence, every day brought to her some new innocent pleasure.*

In the characterization of these sisters, de Villeneuve is following an old and established fairy tale tradition, that of the Youngest Child being more beautiful and desirable than her older sisters [35]. Here, the text argues that the universal preference for their younger sister is more than enough to render the older sisters bitter and angry. After all, everyone has spontaneously given her the appellation "La Belle", or "The Beauty", to the point where no other name or designation is even hinted for her in the text. Nor is she simply "Beauty" in the sense that one might name a girl "Hope" or "Charity". Rather, she is **The** Beauty, which begs the question: **the** beauty of what? The beauty of the family, surely, since all the sisters' suitors publicly and openly prefer the youngest girl to her older siblings. The beauty of the town, perhaps, given that she outshines with such relative splendor every person she meets.

If we take the older sisters not as *characters* but as *concepts*, their dislike of their younger sister reflects the flaws of the society in which they live. Since women cannot earn their own living by talent or trade, their only hope for a secure and happy future is to "win" the most eligible suitor as a husband. Because of this, all the sisters are necessarily in competition with each other. Personal feelings and family loyalties fade before the reality that the youngest has an immeasurable advantage over her sisters: an apparent accident of birth has left her valued at a far higher price on the almighty marriage market that hangs over all their heads.

With this in mind, it is easy for the readers to sympathize with the Sisters and their dislike of Beauty. Though the Sisters have been abandoned by their lovers, Beauty's impoverished state has not diminished the number of *her* suitors. Though the spurned Sisters have been driven to the bleak countryside by a lack of viable alternatives, Beauty's presence is wholly motivated by a filial devotion to their father. Is it surprising that Beauty's cheerful songs and daisy-chain making might grate on the nerves of her hard-working Sisters, when she alone has the freedom to leave that life at any moment? Where the Sisters are prisoners of fate, Beauty is by contrast free.

After two years in country exile, the Merchant receives news that he may not be as poor as he previously thought. One of his ships thought lost at sea has arrived unexpectedly in port, bursting at the seams with riches ripe for the collecting.

Two years had already passed, and the family began to be accustomed to a country life, when a hope of returning prosperity arrived to discompose their tranquility. The father received news that one of his vessels, that he thought was lost, had safely arrived in port, richly laden.

The Merchant is immediately counseled by friends and family that if he does not make the trip at once to take his goods in hand, the vultures at port will pick him clean and he will not see a cent of his earnings. He readies for his journey to the port while his children's hopes are raised for a restoration to the lifestyle they were once accustomed to.

His daughters, with the exception of the youngest, expected they would soon be restored to their former opulence. They fancied that, even if their father's property would not be considerable enough to settle them in the great metropolis, their native place, he would at least have sufficient for them to live in a less expensive city. They trusted they should find good society there, attract admirers, and profit by the first offer that might be made to them. [...] They requested him to make purchases of jewelry, attire, and head-dresses.

It is easy for the reader to mistake the Sisters' requests for "jewelry, attire, and head-dresses" as a useless vanity. Here their father has not yet seen a single cent from his newly returned ship, and yet they are already spending his earnings on worthless trivialities. Haven't they learned from their time in the country what is important in life and what is not?

And yet, to condemn the Sisters for their vanity is to understandably fail to comprehend their world. Their requests are completely logical and sensible, just as soon as we accept their frame of reference. They have learned a painful lesson: they missed their chance at forging an advantageous marriage once before, and they are anxious not to repeat the same mistake. Their first order of business — and a decision that benefits both themselves *and* their father — is to place themselves back on the marriage market at once, with the intention of taking the first reasonable offer presented. And in order to get back on the marriage market, money *must* be invested to cultivate their social attractiveness: the right clothes, jewels, and hair pieces must be bought and worn to signify that they are desirable and worthwhile. The Sisters are not dressing to appease their vanity; they are costuming as part of an elaborate social mating dance.

Their haste is perfectly sensible given their circumstances, and yet at the same time is palpably tragic. The text implies that the Sisters do not have faith that their father will be able to keep his riches long enough for them to shop carefully for suitable husbands. Considerations such as a suitor's business sense or his genial attitude or their mutual compatibility must be discarded in favor of sealing a deal as quickly and permanently as possible. Once again, we are given the sense that in the Sisters' world, the transition from a father's house to a husband's home is as much a gamble for a better future than a meeting of hearts.

Beauty, who was not the slave of ambition, and who always acted with prudence, saw directly that if he executed her sisters' commissions, it would be useless for her to ask for anything. But the father, astonished at her silence, said, interrupting his insatiable daughters, "Well, Beauty, dost thou not desire anything? What shall I bring thee? What dost thou wish for? Speak freely."

"My dear papa," replied the amiable girl, embracing him affectionately, "I wish for one thing more precious than all the ornaments my sisters have asked you for; I have limited my desires to it, and shall be only too happy if they can be fulfilled. It is the gratification of seeing you return in perfect health."

This answer was so unmistakably disinterested, that it covered the others with shame and confusion. They were so angry, that one of them, answering for the rest, said with bitterness, "This child gives herself great airs, and fancies that she will distinguish herself by these affected heroics. Surely nothing can be more ridiculous."

The text indignantly tells us that Beauty is not "the slave to ambition" and that she holds back any requests from the realization that if her father purchased all the items required by her Sisters, then he would have nothing left to spend on her. And yet, there's a subtext to this passage that the reader simply cannot ignore.

Beauty may not be a slave to ambition, but she has the distinct privilege of not *needing* to be. The text has already noted that she is universally loved and valued by her community, on account of her adherence to the local social standards of physical beauty and personal amiability. She is completely dependent for her livelihood on the whims of her father and brothers and suitors, yet even in her powerless state, she is probably the most "empowered" woman for miles. She can, at any moment, decide that the shepherdess life is for the dogs and petition her father to make a mutually beneficial match between her and any eligible bachelor in the community.

Though Beauty sardonically notes that her Sisters' requests will consume the entirety of her father's fortune, with none left over for her, it is a fact that she does not *need* anything from her father. And this is a difficult aspect of the text, because once again the reader must remember that the Sisters' "jewelry, attire, and head-dresses" are not vanities but necessities. If they are to escape their current status as a burdensome mouth to feed in their father's household and install themselves as ambassadors in a family that can help the Merchant and his sons prosper in their trade, they *must* invest in the necessary trappings to augment their attraction. Beauty needs no such augmentation, and as such has no real *needs* to request of her father.

Is it fair that the Sisters upbraid Beauty for her request? Yes and no.

Beauty's request that their father come home safely and in good health need not, in the context of their society, automatically be a sentimental request. As bad as their current social station is, it would almost certainly plummet farther if the Merchant were to die while the daughters are still unwed. The brothers have been explicitly stated in the text as too young to think of marriage, so it seems likely that in the event of the Merchant's death, the responsibility of disposing his daughters in marriage would fall either to the oldest of the young brothers or to a distant relation. The father, for all his faults, seems to genuinely care for his daughters; it stands to reason that a transition to an orphaned state with no equally doting older male relative to shelter them would leave the girls in a precarious social situation.

Of course, Beauty's request is not meant to be interpreted as a practical one. She is very clear in her request as to the motive: her father is more precious to her than any jewelry, attire, or head-dress could ever be. And yet this framing immediately casts aspersions on her Sisters for failing to ask for the "more precious" and yet inherently obvious 'gift' of their father's safety. Beauty does not humbly ask simply for her father's safe return, nor does she ask for nothing at all; instead she makes a proud production of her request, singling out her Sisters' requests and deliberately contrasting them with her own. Her statement evaluates and judges both explicitly the *requests* and implicitly the *requesters*.

But the father, touched by her expressions, could not help showing his delight at them, appreciating, too, the feeling which induced her to ask nothing for herself, he begged she would choose something; and to allay the ill-will that his other daughters had towards her, he observed to her that such indifference to dress was not natural at her age — that there was a time for everything. "Very well, my dear father," said she, "since you desire me to make some request, I beg you will bring me a rose; I love that flower passionately, and since I have lived in this desert I have not had the pleasure of seeing one." This was to obey her father, and at the same time to avoid putting him to any expense for her.

Though the Sisters are primed by their toxic society to view Beauty as a competitor first and a dear sister last, it would seem in text that Beauty is not intentionally trying to hurt her Sisters with her request. And yet, already the reader can see the tiny fissures in this complex family. The Merchant reacts with immediate and obvious pleasure at Beauty's 'selfless' request, and then immediately back-pedals in an attempt to prevent family conflict. He strongly pressures her to make a 'real' request of him, and in doing so he effectively seals his own fate. Beauty asks for a gift of his time, effort, and attention rather than one simply of his money: a single rare rose.

Children as Collateral

When the day comes for the Merchant to leave for the port, he does so with a heavy heart and an unwillingness to separate from his family. When he reaches the city, he learns that his trip is a waste of time; the bulk of his riches have been stolen by his business partners, and he wastes the last of his wealth in fruitless litigation. Discouraged and depressed, he sets out for home in the dead of winter and almost immediately becomes lost in a thick snowstorm.

The Merchant stumbles through the storm in imminent danger of death, when suddenly he reaches a beautiful castle that seems to invite him in as master of the house: the castle doors open before him, and invisible servants serve him warm food while he rests deeply in comfort. In his astonishment, the Merchant begins to believe that the house is a gift from a good spirit, and he travels through the marvelous castle taking stock of his new home. Almost at once, he comes upon a little alleyway lined with roses, all of which bloom brightly in spite of the cold winter outside the castle estate.

He had never seen such lovely roses. Their perfume reminded him that he had promised to give Beauty a rose. He picked one, and was about to gather enough to make half-a-dozen bouquets, when a most frightful noise made him turn round. He was terribly alarmed upon perceiving at his side a horrible beast, which, with an air of fury, laid upon his neck a kind of trunk, resembling an elephant's, and said, with a terrific voice, "Who gave thee permission to gather my roses? Is it not enough that I kindly allowed thee to remain in my palace. Instead of feeling grateful, rash man, I find thee stealing my flowers! Thy insolence shall not remain unpunished."

The good man, already too much overpowered by the unexpected appearance of this monster, thought he should die of fright at these words, and quickly throwing away the fatal rose. "Ah! my Lord," said he, prostrating himself before him, "have mercy on me! I am not ungrateful! Penetrated by all your kindness, I did not imagine that so slight a liberty could possibly have offended you." The monster very angrily replied, "Hold thy tongue, thou foolish talker. I care not for thy flattery, nor for the titles thou bestowest on me. I am not 'my Lord;' I am The Beast; and thou shalt not escape the death thou deservest."

In a manner consistent with his characterization thus far, the Merchant has squandered the good situation he found himself in. Despite being in an obviously magical castle, he has let his pride get the better of him and has fancied himself the owner of the fine things that surround him. What he doesn't know — and what the reader will not know until the lengthy final chapters — is that the entire castle was a trap for him. The Beast wanted him to pick the roses, because the Beast wanted to demand Beauty be brought to him as prisoner.

Pleading for his life, the Merchant describes how charming Beauty is and that the rose he plucked was for her alone. He hopes that by explaining his motives, the Beast will understand his actions and will allow him to return home to the charming daughter who asked for nothing from him but a single rose. The Beast seems unmoved by his tale, and insists that a life must be sacrificed for the loss of the rose. Either the Merchant can die, or one of his daughters can donate her life willingly in his stead.

The Beast considered for a moment, then, speaking in a milder tone, he said to him," I will pardon thee, but upon condition that thou wilt give me one of thy daughters — I require some one to repair this fault."

"Just Heaven!" replied the merchant; "how can I keep my word? Could I be so inhuman as to save my own life at the expense of one of my children's; under what pretext could I bring her here?"

"There must be no pretext," interrupted the Beast. "I expect that whichever daughter you bring here she will come willingly, or I will not have either of them. Go; see if there be not one amongst them sufficiently courageous, and loving thee enough, to sacrifice herself to save thy life."

It is interesting that the Merchant first asks how he could possibly be expected to sacrifice one of his own children, and then in the same breath asks how he could trick a daughter into coming under some pretext. Possibly the question is a rhetorical protest against the Beast's proposal — "I could never feasibly trick anyone into coming here, so it's not even worth asking me to" — and yet the Merchant will return home with the intention of proposing the trade, so it's hard to believe that the question of pretext was entirely an incredulous attempt to refuse the deal. The reader is left with the impression that the Merchant would prefer that 'willingness' not be a prerequisite for the sacrifice.

The good man, although quite convinced that he should vainly put to the proof the devotion of his daughters, accepted, nevertheless, the Monster's proposition.

Out of fear, the Merchant agrees to the Beast's terms: he will ask his daughters to sacrifice their lives for his, and either he or they will return in one month for their death sentence. Though he has no faith that any of his daughters will accept the offer, still he resolves to ask and know their answer.

Halfway to his home on a magic steed supplied by the Beast, the Merchant suffers a pang of guilt. He decides he will not torment his children with the knowledge of his bargain, and resolves that the best course of action is to return immediately to the Beast for his death. The horse refuses to veer from its course, however, so the Merchant amends his plans; he will remain silent about his bargain and use his month to put his affairs in order. From the moment he is deposited at his house, however, his resolve flees him and he spills the whole tale.

Already he saw his house in the distance, and strengthening himself more and more in his resolution, "I will not speak to them," he said, "of the danger which threatens me: I shall have the pleasure of embracing them once more; I shall give them my last advice; I will beg them to live on good terms with their brothers, whom I shall also implore not to abandon them."

In the midst of this reverie, he reached his door. His own horse, which had found its way home the previous evening, had alarmed his family. His sons, dispersed in the forest, had sought him in every direction; and his daughters, in their impatience to hear some tidings of him, were at the door, in order to obtain the earliest intelligence. As he was mounted on a magnificent steed, and wrapt in a rich cloak, they could not recognise him, but took him at first for a messenger sent by him, and the rose which they perceived attached to the pummel of the saddle made them perfectly easy on his account.

*When this afflicted father, however, approached nearer, they recognised him, and thought only of evincing their satisfaction at seeing him return in good health. But the sadness depicted in his face, and his eyes filled with tears, which he vainly endeavoured to restrain, changed their joy into anxiety. All hastened to inquire the cause of his trouble. **He made no reply but by saying to Beauty, as he presented her with the rose, "There is what thou hast demanded of me, but thou wilt pay dearly for it, as well as the others."***

"I was certain," exclaimed the eldest, "and I was saying, this very moment, that she would be the only one whose commission you would execute. At this time of the year, a rose must have cost more than you would have had to pay for us all five together; and, judging from appearances, the rose will be faded before the day is ended: never mind, however, you were determined to gratify the fortunate Beauty at any price."

"It is true," replied the father, mournfully, "that this rose has cost me dear, and more dear than all the ornaments which you wished for would have done. It is not in money, however; and would to Heaven that I might have purchased it with all I am yet worth in the world."

These words excited the curiosity of his children, and dispelled the resolution which he had taken not to reveal his adventure. He informed them of the ill-success of his journey, the trouble which he had undergone in running after a chimerical fortune, and all that had taken place in the palace of the Monster. After this explanation, despair took the place of hope and of joy.

The Merchant cannot resist giving his youngest daughter the rose she asked for, along with a cutting barb blaming her for his as-yet-unknown-to-them fate. And thus does Beauty's request — which he previously valued as a sign of her devotion and humility — become something that he hates and blames her for.

In this family of competing love and competing resources, her Sisters seize the opportunity for filial favor to go on the offensive. They point out that their requests of jewelry and clothing, once despised as being less precious than his safety and more expensive than a single rose, are now in retrospect altogether harmless. Beauty can only protest in vain against the general clamor that a request for a rose in the summer cannot be reasonably foreseen to culminate in the plucking of a magic rose in the dead of winter from an enchanted castle occupied by a vicious beast-monster.

Notwithstanding this, they sought for expedients to save his life; the young men, full of courage and filial affection, proposed that one of them should go and offer himself as a victim to the wrath of the Beast; but the monster had said positively and explicitly that he would have one of the daughters, and not one of the sons. The brave brothers grieved that their good intentions could not be acted upon, then did what they could to inspire their sisters with the same sentiments. But their jealousy of Beauty was sufficient to raise an invincible obstacle to such heroic action.

"It is not just," said they, "that we should perish in so frightful a manner for a fault of which we are not guilty. It would be to render us victims to Beauty, to whom they would be very glad to sacrifice us; but duty does not require such a sacrifice. Here is the fruit of the moderation and perpetual preaching of this unhappy girl! Why did she not ask, like us, for a good stock of clothes and jewels. If we have not had them, it has at all events cost nothing for asking, and we have no cause to reproach ourselves for having exposed the life of our father by indiscreet demands. If, by an affected disinterestedness, she had not sought to distinguish herself, as she is in all things more favoured than we, he would have, no doubt, found enough money to content her. But she must needs, by her singular caprice, bring on us all this misfortune. It is she who has caused it, and they wish us to pay the penalty. We will not be her dupe. She has brought it on herself, and she must find the remedy."

What is most interesting here is the immediate fracturing of the family. The sons leap to offer their lives in the place of their father's, but they conveniently offer their lives well after the Merchant has already told them that only a daughter's life will suffice. Their offers are therefore not genuine, but they quickly use their counterfeit offers as leverage to urge their Sisters to go willingly to their deaths on behalf of a father who has consistently valued them less than the rest of their siblings.

The Sisters, sensing the dangerous position they are in and the animosity of their brothers, lash out at Beauty. It's not their fault their father stumbled into a magic castle and started defacing the rose hedges, so why should they have to volunteer to fix it? Either their father can take his lumps and pay the price for his favorite daughter's rose-gift, or Beauty can step up and sacrifice herself in his stead. Either way, the Sisters maintain their refusal to be sacrificed on the altar of their father's folly or their sister's sainthood.

As harsh as their words are, their attitudes underscore just how dysfunctional this family has been for a long time. For the last two years of their exile, both father and brothers have nagged and harried the Sisters for failing to possess Beauty's humility and frugality. Why were the Sisters doing hard work around the house instead of singing cheerfully and stringing daisy-chains like the Beauty? Why were the Sisters spending their brothers' inheritance in an attempt to secure their futures instead of asking for flowers and rainbows like Beauty?

And now, when that 'innocent' and no doubt much-needled request for a rose has spelled doom for their father, the Sisters are being loudly called upon to give their lives to a monstrous Beast. Their father has ridden up to the doorstep and asked point-blank for one of the Sisters to die for his foolish mistakes. Their brothers have made obviously counterfeit offers of their lives in an attempt to bully the Sisters up to the chopping block. By lashing out at Beauty, the Sisters are fighting dirty, but they are fighting for their lives.

Beauty, whose grief had almost deprived her of consciousness, suppressing her sobs and sighs, said to her sisters, "I am the cause of this misfortune; it is

I alone who must repair it. I confess it would be unjust to allow you to suffer for my fault. Alas! it was, notwithstanding, an innocent wish. Could I foresee that the desire to have a rose when we were in the middle of summer would be punished so cruelly?"

Beauty accepts the situation and steps forward to die in her father's place. This is another one of those acts that could be equal parts sentimental and practical. Of course, it is very noble to sacrifice one's life for a loved parent, but at the same time there is perhaps nothing to be gained living as an impoverished orphan in a home filled with bitter siblings who blame you for your father's death.

Then, also, there is the fact that the Merchant *asks* Beauty to sacrifice herself for him. He does not ask her alone, of course — he, like her brothers, would prefer that one of her less-pretty and less-amiable Sisters take on the death sentence. But neither does her father refuse her when she steps up to the plate. His reluctance has nothing to do with a *love* for her, and everything to do with a *preference* for her.

By asking Beauty to die in his place, the Merchant demonstrates that he does not love her as much as she loves him. Beauty loves her father enough to die in his place; the Merchant does not love his daughter enough to do the same. His request underscores the inequalities in their relationship: as parent and male, the Merchant has far more power over Beauty than she could over him, as child and female. In this light, regardless of how good and noble and loving Beauty may or may not be, the conclusion here was always foregone. One of the Merchant's daughters must sacrifice herself for him, and the task falls to the one most traceably at 'fault'.

The father alone would not consent to the design of his youngest daughter; but the others reproached him insolently with the charge that Beauty alone was cared for by him, in spite of the misfortune which she had caused, and that he was sorry that it was not one of the elders who should pay for her imprudence.

It is noteworthy that the Merchant would happily sacrifice one of his children to save his life, and that it only matters to him *which* child will pay the price for his indiscretions. The boys he could part with if he had to, and the Sisters he would be glad to see the back of, but he grieves that Beauty will die for his sake. He just doesn't grieve enough to put up any meaningful resistance to her offer.

The Merchant, in his position as head of the family, is willing to spend his children to settle his debts. It's true that his response to poverty wasn't to immediately sell his sons into slavery or send his daughters to work in the brothels. At the same time, though, he doesn't consider the loss of one child to be an unacceptable price to pay when it comes to saving his own life. He sees his children as collateral: property that he can use to secure his loans and, if necessary, pay his debts entirely.

This barbarous decision is accepted by the other children without horror. Indeed, they strongly counsel him to seal the decision over any lingering doubts he might have. Though his decision to trade the life of a child to settle his debts sets a rather dangerous precedent for the other children, yet still they urge him on. Why? It seems that they truly consider their difficult future as poor orphans to greatly outweigh the loss of a single sibling. And as for the Merchant, he seems to honestly consider the death of his youngest daughter to be preferable to his own untimely demise.

Submission and Refusal

On the appointed day, the Merchant and Beauty both mount the magical horse sent to summon them to the Beast's castle. Upon reaching the castle, the Beast meets and greets the family with an almost macabre politeness. With a sudden intensity, he begins to question Beauty on the particulars of her visit: does she come willingly to this place and is she prepared to place her life in the hands of this monstrous being?

"Do you come here voluntarily?" inquired the Beast; "and will you consent to let your father depart without following him?" Beauty replied that she had no other intention. "Ah! and what do you think will become of you after his departure?"

"What it may please you," said she; "my life is at your disposal, and I submit blindly to the fate which you may doom me to."

"I am satisfied with your submission," replied the Beast.

The Beast has not yet mentioned marriage — his only stipulation was that a daughter be brought to him and left for dead by her father — yet still his words contain a double meaning here that is apparent to the reader. The situation in which Beauty now finds herself is not materially different from that of a marriage arranged to pay her father's debts. Her father will leave, she will remain behind, and what happens to her then is completely in the hands of this new stranger.

In a world where a woman has no right to refuse a marriage and no right to flee from an abusive husband, her fate is truly in the hands of her father and the man he gives her to. In every meaningful sense of the word, she is owned by the men in her life. They determine when and what she may eat, when and how she will have sex, where and how she will live, and they can dispose of her (her father by marriage and her husband by an asylum) at any moment they see fit. She may hope that the men who own her will take pity on her and treat her kindly, but ultimately she has the same legal recourse as, say, an unhappy horse or dog — and she may be significantly less able to defend herself from abuse.

Knowing this, the reader can see that though Beauty "submits" to the wishes of the Beast who now owns her, her submission is less of a choice and more of a reality of the world she lives in. The Merchant and the Beast can have their theater and pretend that Beauty has been given a choice to make, but ultimately the 'choice' she has been offered is no choice at all. She can give up her life as forfeit to the Beast, or she can let the Merchant be killed in her stead, only to return home and be married off in a match created by resentful brothers laden with debts. Either way, the only hope Beauty can have for the future is that her fate be quick and relatively painless.

The Merchant, in contrast, is in high spirits. Laden with riches by the Beast and encouraged by the fact that the monster has not chewed on his daughter in his presence, the Merchant has decided to convince himself that the Beast is a man of quality who will care for Beauty. Why, he might even someday reverse his stern decree that the father and daughter may never meet again! Why not?

He would have departed without concern if the Beast had not had the cruelty to make him understand that he must not dream of seeing his palace again, and that he must wish his daughter an eternal farewell. There is no evil but death without remedy. The good man was not completely stunned by this order. He flattered himself that it would not be irrevocable, and this hope prepared him to quit his host with tolerable satisfaction.

Beauty was not so well satisfied. Little persuaded that a happy future was prepared for her, she feared that the rich presents with which the Monster loaded her family was but the price of her life, and that he would devour her immediately that he should be alone with her, or at least that a perpetual prison would be her fate, and that her only companion would be this frightful Monster.

Beauty is understandably less enthused. The mere fact that she has not yet died does not automatically auger a happy, carefree future for her. The contrast between Beauty and the Merchant is striking. The Merchant decides that his daughter will be fine as long as her physical needs are met and her 'womanly' desires for wealth and comfort are satisfied. As the Beast is well-mannered enough not to murder her, then she should be safe; as the Beast is obviously wealthy, then she should be happy. What more could a woman ask for than physical safety and comfort?

Here, more so than anywhere else in the story, Beauty represents the feminist perspective. She has needs and wants and desires beyond simply 'safe from murder' and 'safe from poverty'. She doesn't want to live out her life with no company but an ill-mannered, boorish, frightening stranger. She doesn't feel compelled to view with charity a creature who arranged for her to be sold to him as a prisoner. Tellingly, the future she anticipates for herself is the *exact same future* that her father imagines for her: forced to endure for eternity the captivity of this gilded castle around her. But where the Merchant views this prospect with delight on her behalf, Beauty feels only dread.

At the usual hour, Beauty found her supper served, with the same delicacy and neatness as before. No human figure presented itself to her view; her father had told her she would be alone. This solitude began no longer to trouble her, when the Beast made himself heard. Never having yet found herself alone with him, ignorant how this interview would pass off, fearing even that he only came to devour her, is it any wonder that she trembled?

But on the arrival of the Beast, whose approach was by no means furious, her fears were dissipated. This monstrous giant said, roughly, "Good evening, Beauty."

She returned his salutation in the same terms, with a calm air, but a little tremulously. Amongst the different questions which the monster put to her, he asked how she amused herself? Beauty replied, "I have passed the day in inspecting your palace, but it is so vast that I have not had time to see all the apartments, and the beauties which it contains." [...]

At length he asked her bluntly if she would marry him. At this unexpected demand, her fears were renewed, and uttering a terrible shriek, she could not help exclaiming, "O! Heavens, I am lost!"

"Not at all," replied the Beast, quietly; "but without frightening yourself, reply properly. Say precisely 'yes' or 'no.'"

Beauty replied, trembling, "No, Beast."

"Well, as you object, I will leave you," replied the docile Monster. "Good evening, Beauty."

"Good evening, Beast," said the frightened girl, with much satisfaction. Extremely relieved by finding that she had no violence to fear, she lay quietly down and went to sleep.

At dinner, the Beast proposes to Beauty: will she marry him? The irony, not lost on the reader, is that the immediate appreciable difference between her *current* state and a *married* state is not clear. Beauty is his prisoner — she cannot leave the grounds nor can she return to her family without his express permission and aid. Her safety and comfort are wholly dependent on the Beast's goodwill, and he can harm her at any moment without fear of reprisal.

Marriage, of course, implies sole sexual access, but the truth of the situation is that the Beast has as much of that as he is willing to take. Locked up as she is in his enchanted castle, Beauty is not free to give herself to a rival; and inasmuch as the Beast is free to harm her, starve her, or beat her while she lives as his prisoner, so too does he have the ability to rape her — a fact that de Villeneuve must have known her audience would seize upon. However, just as the Beast required that Beauty submit willingly to live as his prisoner, so too does his curse require that she 'willingly' acquiesce to marry him.

And yet, the reader will question whether such willingness is even possible in the context of the situation. While the Beast's mild behavior and unwillingness to force Beauty's decision is meant to be reassuring, her status as prisoner is not something that can be completely swept aside. She is his prisoner and can neither leave nor choose another suitor to marry. He is dangerous to her, and while he does not fly into a rage and tear her apart with his teeth at the dinner table, yet still Beauty is constantly aware that this is a possibility. Nightly, the Beast will return to ask this question, only to be nightly refused. Each time, Beauty must fear that this time may be the end of his patience, that *this* time may end in her rape or her death.

But even if the Beast never intends to harm her, even if he can accept her refusal night after night for the rest of her life, Beauty is still not well cared for in her new 'home'. She is a prisoner, doomed to live out the rest of her life being hounded by the same question nightly. She is caught eternally between the submission of her will to the man who controls her entire life and her refusal to pretend that she loves him.

Stockholm Seduction?

Beauty is given free rein to wander the enchanted castle and enjoy its magical sights and sounds. Animal servants are provided to wait on her every need and they show her magic portals that allow her to watch stunning plays and remarkable theater productions. Yet even with these intellectual delights, as time passes she begins to feel more isolated and lonely. Both the Merchant's hopes and Beauty's fears have been realized: though she is safe and enjoys the comforts of wealth, still she longs for human companionship. The only conversation offered to her is the nightly interrogation that invariably culminates in a marriage proposal.

She took great pains to conceal from the Beast the sorrow which preyed upon her; and the Monster, who had frequently surprised her with the tears in her eyes, upon hearing her say that she was only suffering from a headache, pressed his inquiries no further. One evening, however, her sobs having betrayed her, and feeling it impossible longer to dissimulate, she acknowledged to the Beast, who begged to know what had caused her afflictions, that she was yearning to see her family.

Though she has not accepted the Beast's marriage proposal, still there is a bitter similarity between Beauty's confinement and an unwanted marriage. Beauty feels compelled to hide her sorrow out of fear that candor will worsen her situation. She lies to protect the feelings of her captor, concerned of what he might do if she admits to being unhappy with the life he has forced on her. After all, the Beast was willing to kill her father over a single rose; mightn't he 'give her something to cry about' if she admitted that her tears were anything other than a symptom of illness? And when finally she can hide her feelings no longer, she reflexively sugar-coats the truth. Her problem is **not** that she doesn't love her new prison, nor is it that she doesn't enjoy the companionship of her captor. No, her sorrow is simply born out of a deep longing to see her family. Filial devotion motivates her, not physical revulsion.

This is, on the face of it, not entirely a lie. The reader may be forgiven for seeing the Merchant in a vastly different light than Beauty does; though we despise him for leaving his daughter with a monster while telling himself comforting lies, Beauty's love for her father has not been wholly extinguished by his bad behavior. She misses his company, and hopes to reassure her father that she is safe and unharmed. And again the reader is struck by the analogy between captivity and marriage: Beauty must plead for permission to leave the Beast's home that she might visit her family and reassure them that she is safe in her new surroundings. She does not blame the callous father who made this disastrous bargain she now labors under; she is resigned to the belief that her father simply did what he had to.

The Beast, however, does not see value in Beauty's filial devotion. He only dwells on how her conflicting loyalties between captor and father affect him. Flying into a fit of pique at her request, he casts himself as the victim and Beauty as the cruel abuser.

At this declaration the Beast sank down without power to sustain himself, and heaving a deep sigh, or rather uttering a howl that might have frightened anyone to death, he replied, "How, Beauty! Would you, then, abandon an unfortunate Beast? Could I have imagined you possessed so little gratitude? What have I left undone to make you happy? Should not the attentions I have paid you preserve me from your hatred? Unjust as you are, you prefer the house of your father and the jealousy of your sisters to my palace and my affections. You would rather tend the flocks with them than enjoy with me all the pleasures of existence. It is not love for your family, but antipathy to me, that makes you anxious to depart."

"No, Beast," replied Beauty, timidly and soothingly; "I do not hate you, and should regret to lose the hope of seeing you again; but I cannot overcome the desire I feel to embrace my relations. Permit me to go away for two months, and I promise you that I will return with pleasure to pass the rest of my days with you, and never ask you another favour."

While she spoke the Beast stretched on the ground, his head thrown back, only evinced that he still breathed by his sorrowful sighs. He answered her in

these words: "I can refuse you nothing; but it will perhaps cost me my life. [...]
If you break your word you will repent it, and regret the death of your poor
Beast when it will be too late. Return at the end of two months, and you will
still see me alive."

In this single exchange, the Beast hits every area except one on the
"Power and Control Wheel" of domestic violence. [36]

- His **Privilege** allows him to make the final decision on when and
  how she will leave.
- He **Threatens** to commit suicide if she does not return, and
  insists that his death will be her fault.
- He **Intimidates** her with his nightmarish howls that "might have
  frightened anyone to death".
- He **Emotionally Abuses** her by calling her ungrateful and
  making her feel guilty for her request.
- He **Isolates** her by keeping her contained in his castle and hidden
  from her friends and family.
- He **Minimizes** the abuse and belittles her needs as ingratitude
  and a peevish refusal to be happy.
- He **Economically Abuses** her by denying her resources that she
  may use to pursue happiness.
- The only spot on the "Power and Control Wheel" that the Beast
  didn't hit was **Using Children**.

The Beast has not physically attacked Beauty in response to her request.
But he has attacked her emotionally and psychologically for the crime
of requiring more out of life than the home and company of her captor.
And thus we see that Beauty was prudent to keep her sorrows to herself
and excuse them as a symptom of illness; she has correctly judged that
her captor is not interested in her psychological well-being, and she has
instinctively recognized that her needs will not be taken seriously and
treated with respect here. The Beast's professed 'love' for her is a meager

love that asks only what she can do for him, and never what he can do for her, since any answer she could give would imply that she is not already happy with the life he has 'given' her.

With the aid of a magic ring, Beauty lies down to sleep and awakens in the house of her father. She embraces her father and siblings, and then she and the Merchant retire privately to discuss all that has happened since she left them to live with the Beast.

Beauty, in her turn, related to him all that had happened to her since they parted. She described to him the pleasant life she led. The good man, enraptured at the charming account of his daughter's adventures, heaped blessings on the head of the Beast. His delight was much greater still when Beauty, opening the chests, displayed to him the immense treasures they contained, and satisfied him that he was at liberty to dispose of those which he had brought himself, in favour of his daughters, as he would possess, in these last proofs of the Beast's generosity, ample means to live merrily with his sons. Discovering in this Monster too noble a mind to be lodged in so hideous a body, he deemed it his duty to advise his daughter to marry him, notwithstanding his ugliness. He employed even the strongest arguments to induce her to take that step.

"Thou shouldst not take counsel from thine eyes alone," said he to her. "Thou hast been unceasingly exhorted to let thyself be guided by gratitude. [...] Therefore, the next time that the Beast asks thee if thou wilt marry him, I advise thee not to refuse him. Thou hast admitted to me that he loves thee tenderly: take the proper means to make thy union with him indissoluble. It is much better to have an amiable husband than one whose only recommendation is a handsome person. How many girls are compelled to marry rich brutes, much more brutish than the Beast, who is only one in form, and not in his feelings or his actions."

It's interesting that the Merchant exhorts Beauty to be guided by "gratitude" to the Beast. A classic aspect of Stockholm Syndrome is the tendency for victims to view a lack of overt abuse from their captors for an act of kindness. [37] The Merchant, once sentenced to death by the Beast and now generously bribed several times over by him, seems completely under his sway and characterizes the Beast as brutish "only in form, and not in his feelings or actions".

The reader recognizes that this is not true. The Beast has failed to physically attack Beauty, but he has not prevented himself from controlling, isolating, threatening, and abusing her emotionally and psychologically. His brutishness is not a lust for violence, but it is one of disgusting selfishness, prizing his own needs and wants and feelings entirely over Beauty's. Since he is an enchanted prince, awaiting the resolution of the curse that plagues him, his selfishness is entirely *understandable* to the reader, but that does not make it *commendable*.

It is little surprise, though, that the Merchant might not understand that. He is the human mirror of the Beast: not once did he seriously consider it immoral for him to use Beauty to better his own life. Since the Merchant sees no conflict between his abuse of his daughter and his professed love for her, naturally he sees no similar conflict between the Beast's abuse of his captive and his offers of marriage. The Merchant therefore urges Beauty as strongly as he can to submit to marriage with her captor, and without reservation.

Beauty admitted the reason of all these arguments; but to resolve to marry a monster so horrible in person and who seemed as stupid as he was gigantic, appeared to her an impossibility. "How can I determine," replied she to her father, "to take a husband with whom I can have no sympathy, and whose hideousness is not compensated for by the charms of his conversation; no other object to distract my attention, and relieve that wearisome companionship; not to have the pleasure of being sometimes absent from him; to hear nothing beyond five or six questions respecting my health or my appetite, followed by a 'Good-night, Beauty,' a chorus which my parrots know by heart, and repeat a hundred times a day. It is not in my power to endure such a union, and I would rather perish at once than be dying every day of fright, sorrow, disgust, and weariness."

Beauty enumerates her continued objections to marrying her captor. She neither loves nor likes him, and finds both his body and mind repugnant. She is provided with no mental distractions, no human companionship, and no means by which she may leave her home at will. Beauty is so unhappy with the situation that she would rather die now than continue living in the isolation being imposed on her against her will.

Yet there is also a problematic aspect to this text. Beauty *does* accept the framing that the Beast's lack of overt physical abuse denotes great love and strength of character on his part. And I think it likely that de Villeneuve would like *us* to accept this framing as well, at least enough for us to cheer the mismatched couple onward to a 'happy' ending together.

Does this framing stem from a gulf of culture between author and reader? After all, it seems reasonable for Beauty to accept her father's words when such "logic" has formed the entire basis of her relationship with her father. In the same way, perhaps we cannot criticize de Villeneuve for pushing inexorably towards a 'happy' ending if her society maintains that a bare minimum of physical safety and conversational civility is all that one is entitled to expect from a good husband.

And yet, I wonder if what we really have is a gulf not of culture but rather between fantasy and reality. The Beast is manipulative, controlling, and callous but in carefully structured ways. As a lover in the real world, he would pose a serious emotional and psychological threat to Beauty. But as a fictional lover, he represents a very specific fantasy: a lover whose abuse is motivated entirely out of deep love and pained yearning, and whose abuse will be literally magically erased at the end of the story, when Beauty rises from her position of weakness and marginalization to stand beside her lover as a powerful equal.

The difference between reality and fantasy is simple. Real abuse can linger in the victim's memories forever, and more often than not is afflicted by an abuser who will always be dangerous. Fantasy abuse, on the other hand, can roll off the victim without impact, and the abuser will be magically redeemed and totally reformed. But there is another fantasy here, often overlooked: by the end of the tale, Beauty will raised to a position of power equal to or greater than the position occupied by her lover.

Return and Rescue

Beauty stays with her family for the full two months allotted to her visit, but as the time comes closer to return to the Beast, she hesitates. She doesn't have the resources or privilege to visit her family again the next time she feels the need for their company, and so she knows every time she tries to say goodbye that this may be the last time she sees any of her family. She is drawn to fulfill her promise to the Beast out of 'gratitude' but though he has grudgingly given her leave to see her family, she has no promise from him that she will ever be allowed to do so again. Small wonder, then, that she hesitates to return.

The two months had nearly expired, and every morning she determined to bid adieu to her family, without having the heart when night arrived to say farewell. In the combat between her affection and her gratitude, she could not lean to the one without doing injustice to the other. In the midst of her embarrassment, it needed nothing less than a dream to decide her.

She fancied she was at the Palace of the Beast, and walking in a retired avenue, terminated by a thicket full of brambles, concealing the entrance to a cavern, out of which issued horrible groans. She recognised the voice of the Beast, and ran to his assistance. The Monster, who, in her dream, appeared stretched upon the ground and dying, reproached her with being the cause of his death, and having repaid his affection with the blackest ingratitude.

In a dream, Beauty sees that the Beast is languishing near to death and blaming her for being the cause of his destruction. The reader who skips ahead will find that this is not quite the case. The Beast is not dying because of some quirk of magic that ties his life to hers and causes him to wither in her absence. Instead, he is dying because he refused to eat while she was gone. He is practicing grievous self-harm, ostensibly because he cannot bear to live without her, but his cause seems markedly less noble when he chooses to blame Beauty for his 'death' both prior to her leaving and now at the dangerous culmination of his hunger strike.

Beauty does not have this advance knowledge, though, and she reproaches herself as the sole cause of the Beast's mortal suffering. She returns to his home immediately and takes up a prolonged search for him through the empty rooms of the castle.

Divided through hope and fear, her mind agitated, her heart a prey to melancholy, she descended into the gardens, determined not to re-enter the Palace till she had found the Beast. No trace of him could she discover anywhere. She called him. Echo alone answered her. Having passed more than three hours in this disagreeable exercise, overcome by fatigue, she sank upon a garden seat. She imagined the Beast was either dead or had abandoned the place.

She saw herself alone in that Palace, without the hope of ever leaving it. She regretted her conversations with the Beast, unentertaining as they had been to her, and what appeared to her extraordinary, even to discover she had so much feeling for him. She blamed herself for not having married him, and considering she had been the cause of his death (for she feared her too long absence had occasioned it), heaped upon herself the keenest and most bitter reproaches.

It is a common trope in fairy tales for the seeker to lose hope before they find what they seek, and this moment of self-reflection allows Beauty to reflect on what she has lost and truly appreciate the Beast now that he seems irretrievably lost. It is interesting, though, that her reflection is tinted with the knowledge that she has hitherto been able to come and go from the castle entirely by the Beast's magic. If he is dead and gone, will she be trapped in the castle alone for the rest of her days? How long can she live here in this castle without starving to death or being driven to despair in her loneliness?

We have seen that Beauty's earlier 'gratitude' to the Beast was shadowed by her natural rationalization as a victim to expect the worst from her captor and consider neutral or 'less abusive' actions to be kindness. Now we see that Beauty's revelatory 'appreciation' for the Beast is still tinged with a survival reflex: she appreciates the Beast at least in part because he keeps her alive when she fears and expects death.

In the midst of her miserable reflections she perceived that she was seated in that very avenue in which, during the last night she had passed under her father's roof, she had dreamed she saw the Beast expiring in some strange cavern. Convinced that chance had not conducted her to this spot, she rose and hurried towards the thicket, which she found was not impenetrable. She discovered another hollow, which appeared to be that she had seen in her dream.

As the moon gave but a feeble light, the monkey pages immediately appeared with a sufficient number of torches to illuminate the chasm, and to reveal to her the Beast stretched upon the earth, as she thought, asleep. Far from being alarmed at this sight, Beauty was delighted, and, approaching him boldly, placed her hand upon his head, and called to him several times; but finding him cold and motionless, she no longer doubted he was dead, and consequently gave utterance to the most mournful shrieks and the most affecting exclamations.

The assurance of his death, however, did not prevent her from making every effort to recall him to life. On placing her hand on his heart she felt, to her great joy, that it still beat. [...] She cheered him with her voice and caressed him as he recovered. "What anxiety have you caused me?" said she to him, kindly; "I knew not how much I loved you. The fear of losing you has proved to me that I was attached to you by stronger ties than those of gratitude. I vow to you that I had determined to die if I had failed in restoring you to life."

Is it a declaration of love or practicality that Beauty would seek to join the Beast in death? After all, Beauty is in an enchanted castle, the only exit from which is a magic ring granted by the Beast which may not function in his absence. She has already anticipated with dread the fate that awaits her should she find herself unable to leave this place and now with even less company than before. Even if she could escape, the reader can imagine that this strange interlude as the captive of a magical beast may mark her permanently, both emotionally and socially. Even if she were physically able to return to her father's home, would she be able to live any semblance of a normal life now that all this has happened to her?

Still, the Beast's wishes have come true. He has come close enough to death to frighten Beauty into realizing that she would miss him if he were gone. For better or worse, she accepts this tenderness that she feels towards the Beast as love — or as near as she is likely to experience, given the hand that has been dealt to her — and when their daily routine resumes and the Beast picks up his usual nightly marriage proposal, Beauty answers in the affirmative.

The Beast briefly thanked her, and then being about to take his leave, asked her, as usual, if she would marry him. Beauty was silent for a short time, but at last making up her mind, she said to him, trembling, "Yes, Beast, I am willing, if you will pledge me your faith, to give you mine."

"I do," replied the Beast, "and I promise you never to have any wife but you."

"Then," rejoined Beauty, "I accept you for my husband, and swear to be a fond and faithful wife to you."

It is significant, I think, that Beauty's acquiescence to marriage does not occur in the same scene as her declaration of love. To the movie-maker, the delay and change in scene from "declaration of love over the Beast's dying form" to "later the next day, at dinner" lacks value and must be cut to save every precious second for the 'real' story. And yet, to the author, I think this delay was invaluable for carrying her message. Beauty declares her love for the Beast when she realizes how much she missed him, but this sudden rush of emotion is *not* what causes her to decide to wed him. Her love for him is just one piece of that decision.

Throughout the novel, the theme has been reiterated that a husband who is outwardly a bad match but inwardly loving and gentle is far more worthwhile than a husband who is outwardly a good match but inwardly brutish and cruel. This, in itself, is not a revolutionary idea, but what de Villeneuve hoped to convey was the revolutionary idea that it is the *woman* who has to live with the decision who should be given the right to make the choice.

Over their time together, Beauty has had the opportunity to observe the Beast minutely in his words and actions. Slowly, she has come to two separate and distinct decisions. First, that she loves him. This love is crucial, because it marks the place where Beauty is no longer disgusted by him and can then fairly evaluate the second, which is that, based on what she has observed thus far, he would make a good husband. The two decisions *together* propel her towards marriage with the Beast, and by placing them in different scenes, on entirely different days, I think the author is deliberately trying to keep the two concepts very separate.

The second part of Beauty's decision — the evaluation that the Beast would make a good husband — is possibly the most controversial part of every "Beauty and the Beast" tale. Knowing what we do now about human psychology, we may question that Beauty is in a position to fairly evaluate a person who holds the power of life and death over her. Then, too, we may question Beauty's criteria for 'good husband' material. Yes, the Beast is kind and gentle and patient and giving in certain ways, but he is also undeniably cruel and harsh and childish and selfish in other ways. Since we know that hers is a choice made essentially under duress, should Beauty still be given this choice to make for herself?

I think de Villeneuve would argue that she should. Is Beauty's situation a perfect one, free from problematic considerations? No. Beauty is the daughter of a man who was willing to give her life in order to save his, and who encourages her to wed a beast knowing nothing more about the creature than that he liberally showers wealth on his prospective father-in-law. She is a member of a society that prizes her for her beauty alone, and where her unattractive sisters are cruelly taunted and slandered by their former suitors for the 'crime' of being unable to invest the necessary money to maintain their social attractiveness. She is the captive of a creature who does not take her needs seriously and begrudges her requests to visit her family, yet who is comparatively a good and kind suitor in her society.

If Beauty *must* marry in order to survive — and in a society that prevents her from earning her own living or owning her own property, she does — then regardless of her extenuating circumstances, de Villeneuve believed that Beauty should hold the final decision on who her husband will be. Not because she necessarily holds all the tools to make the best decision, but because she may be the only one in this world who holds her well-being in any kind of serious regard. Beauty should make the decision because it will be Beauty who will ultimately be affected by her choice.

Social Security

When Beauty agrees to marry the Beast, there is an instant magical reaction. The Beast does not change into his Prince form just yet, but there is a celebratory firing of artillery outside and the sky lights up with fireworks decorated with symbols of love and marriage.

> *She had scarcely uttered these words when a discharge of artillery was heard, and that she might not doubt it being a signal of rejoicing, she saw from her windows the sky all in a blaze with the light of twenty thousand fireworks, which continued rising for three hours. They formed true-lovers' knots, while on elegant escutcheons appeared Beauty's initials, and beneath them, in well-defined letters, "Long live Beauty and her Husband."*

The enchanted castle is immediately decked out with escutcheons, or decorative shields which display a coat of arms. [38] It is an important point that the shields bear Beauty's initials alone, and not those of the Prince, and that the inscription names Beauty first, and the Prince second as a possessive article. The shields do not say "Long live Beauty and *the Prince*", but rather "Long live Beauty and *her Husband*". The Prince exists in relation to Beauty, as her husband and eclipsed by her station. The couple, if the escutcheons are to be believed, will not be styled "Mr. and Mrs. Prince", but rather "Ms. and Mr. Beauty".

This is a crucial point in the narrative because, for de Villeneuve, the story is only half finished. Almost every later "Beauty and the Beast" retelling will reach its literary climax at this moment — at the declaration of love and/or marriage and the restoration of the Beast into the Prince — but for this original feminist version of the tale, there are still two very important points left to be settled. It is not enough for de Villeneuve that Beauty has been allowed to make her choice independently of her father. Now, the Prince must be allowed to make *his* choice, and to choose unencumbered by any curse laid upon him. And after the Prince has affirmed his choice, Beauty must be raised to a status such that no one — not even her royal husband or his family — can sever their union.

After the celebratory magic has run its course, Beauty hears another sound from outside and looks out the window to see two distinguished ladies ride up to the castle in a chariot pulled by four white stags.

By the noise, which became louder, she was aware that the ladies had nearly reached the ante-chamber. She considered it right to advance and receive them. She recognised in one of them the Lady she had been accustomed to behold in her dreams. The other was not less beautiful. Her high and distinguished bearing sufficiently indicated that she was an illustrious personage. She was no longer in the bloom of youth, but her air was so majestic that Beauty was uncertain to which of the two strangers she ought first to address herself.

She was still under this embarrassment, when the one with whose features she was already familiar, and who appeared to exercise some sort of superiority over the other, turning to her companion, said, "Well, Queen, what think you of this beautiful girl? You owe to her the restoration of your son to life, for you must admit that the miserable circumstances under which he existed could not be called living. Without her, you would never again have beheld this Prince. He must have remained in the horrible shape to which he had been transformed, had he not found in the world one only person who possessed virtue and courage equal to her beauty. I think you will behold with pleasure the son she has restored to you become her husband. They love each other, and nothing is wanting to their perfect happiness but your consent. Will you refuse to bestow it on them?"

The Queen, at these words, embracing Beauty affectionately, exclaimed, "Far from refusing my consent, their union will afford me the greatest felicity! Charming and virtuous child, to whom I am under so many obligations, tell me who you are, and the names of the sovereigns who are so happy as to have given birth to so perfect a Princess?"

The "familiar" lady in the chariot is the benevolent Fairy whose magic maintained the enchanted castle, guided the Merchant to the castle gates, and kept Beauty and the Beast alive and entertained during their long confinement together. She has also been a regular feature in Beauty's dreams and has counseled her frequently on matters of love.

The second lady is the Prince's Queen Mother, who has mourned her cursed son all this time and now embraces Beauty with warmth and gratitude. But her gratitude notably hinges on a single point: she desires Beauty to be a princess of noble blood, and her first action on receiving her potential daughter-in-law is to inquire as to the purity of Beauty's lineage.

"Madam," replied Beauty, modestly, "it is long since I had a mother; my father is a merchant more distinguished in the world for his probity and his misfortunes than for his birth."

At this frank declaration, the astonished Queen recoiled a pace or two, and said, "What! you are only a merchant's daughter? Ah, great Fairy!" she added, casting a mortified look on her companion, and then remained silent; but her manner sufficiently expressed her thoughts, and her disappointment was legible in her eyes.

Beauty does not attempt to dissemble or sugar-coat the truth. She does not trot out the great-uncle on her mother's side who always claimed to be related to royalty in obscure ways. She lays out the bad news to the Queen Mother directly: Beauty's mother is dead and her father is a poor Merchant. She has no pedigree whatsoever, and she doesn't try to hide that fact.

Many fairy tales don't concern themselves with this aspect of marriage. The poor, clever boy marries the princess with no obstacles whatsoever to him joining the royal family, or the humble, virtuous girl marries the king without a single objection raised to her suitability as mother of the next ruler. When fairy tales do bring up pedigree, it's usually to add an extra layer of challenge to the story: the brave boy may have passed all the *king's* tests, but now the proud princess has a few of her own to dish out. And thus the story can continue a little longer.

The pedigree in this tale, however, is not a stalling device to draw out the story. There is a point here: by the standards of Beauty's society, she is utterly unsuited to marriage with the Prince. It doesn't matter if they love each other; love is what mistresses are for, not wives. Wives are for bearing legitimate children whose traceable lineage grants them power and protection from kings and emperors. Beauty has no pedigree, no power, no connections, and no wealth. She was valuable as a bride for the *Beast* because the curse merely required that any maiden submit willingly to marry him. She is valueless as a bride for the *Prince* because there is no longer any material benefit that a union with her will bestow.

Beauty knows this. The Queen Mother knows this. And the Prince knows this.

"It appears to me," said the Fairy, haughtily, "that you are discontented with my choice. You regard with contempt the condition of this young person, and yet she was the only being in the world who was capable of executing my project, and who could make your son happy."

"I am very grateful to her for what she has done," replied the Queen; "but, powerful spirit," she continued, "I cannot refrain from pointing out to you the incongruous mixture of that noblest blood in all the world which runs in my son's veins with that of the obscure race from which the person has sprung to whom you would unite him. I confess I am little gratified by the supposed happiness of the Prince, if it must be purchased by an alliance so degrading to us, and so unworthy of him. Is it impossible to find in the world a maiden whose birth is equal to her virtue?"

The Queen Mother has her mind so set in this matter that she is willing to push back against a very powerful Fairy. This is not something to be done lightly; it was at the whim of an offended Fairy that this curse was first laid on the royal family. And yet, so set is the Queen Mother on Beauty's pedigree that she is willing to risk the wrath of this Fairy, willing to risk even the Prince's life all over again, rather than give her blessing for him to enter into a union that she sees as beneath him.

But what does the Prince think? Has he inherited the prejudices of his mother and his society? Will he value Beauty less now that he needs her no more? The Fairy calls the Prince to the conversation.

"Your mother," said she, "condemns the engagement you have entered into with Beauty. She considers that her birth is too much beneath yours. [...] It is for you, Prince, to say with which of us your own feelings coincide; and that you may be under no restraint in declaring to us your real sentiments, I announce to you that you have full liberty of choice. Although you have pledged your word to this amiable person, you are free to withdraw it. [...] What say you, Beauty?" pursued the Fairy, turning towards her; "have I been mistaken in thus interpreting your sentiments? Would you desire a husband who would become so with regret?"

"Assuredly not, Madam," replied Beauty. "The Prince is free. I renounce the honour of being his wife. When I accepted him, I believed I was taking pity on something below humanity. I engaged myself to him only with the object of conferring on him the most signal favour. Ambition had no place in my thoughts. Therefore, great Fairy, I implore you to exact no sacrifice from the Queen, whom I cannot blame for the scruples she entertains under such circumstances."

Both the Fairy and Beauty offer the Prince an easy out: any oath he swore to Beauty as a Beast has no hold over him now that he is a Prince. The Fairy's exchange with Beauty is especially key; the Fairy asks if Beauty would accept a husband who doesn't want her as wife.

The circumstances of the curse are now ironically reversed. Before, the Beast was the party at a disadvantage, cursed to be monstrous, frightening, and slow-witted. The onus was on Beauty to look past the outward manifestation of a bad husband to see the real value within. But now that the curse is broken and the Prince is restored to his full form and rightful place in society, he is the most powerful party in their relationship. Beauty is still lovely and virtuous and good, but she is also impoverished and low-born and a tremendous social handicap for the royal family. If they are to have a happy marriage, the Prince must look past social prejudices and cherish the rare goodness of his bride.

In both cases — both when Beauty was choosing whether to wed the Beast, and now that the Prince is choosing whether to wed Beauty — the decision must be entered into willingly by the two parties most affected by the decision. Their choice must be made without duress and without the prejudices of their parents, again, not because they are magically best suited to make the right choice, but because it should be their right to make this one decision that will guide the rest of their lives.

The Prince, who, by order of the Fairy, had been silent throughout this conversation, was no longer master of himself, and his respect for the commands he had received, failed to restrain him. He flung himself at the feet of the Fairy and of his mother, and implored them, in the strongest terms, not to make him more miserable than he had been, by sending away Beauty, and depriving him of the happiness of being her husband.

At these words, Beauty, gazing on him with an air full of tenderness, but mingled with a noble pride, said, "Prince, I cannot conceal from you my affection. Your disenchantment is a proof of it, and I should in vain endeavour to disguise my feelings. I confess without a blush, that I love you better than myself. [...] It is enough for me to know who you are, and that I am to renounce the glory of being your wife."

"Generous Fairy!" exclaimed the Prince, clasping her hands in supplication, "for mercy's sake, do not allow Beauty to depart! Make me, rather, again the Monster that I was, for then I shall be her husband. She pledged her word to the Beast, and I prefer that happiness to all those she has restored me to, if I must purchase them so dearly!"

It is not enough for de Villeneuve that the Prince choose to wed Beauty despite her low birth. Such a choice would not truly be comparable to the choice that had been put before Beauty. The Prince, by marrying Beauty, would give up some degree of social standing, but it is easy to imagine that the unsettling news that he has spent the last several years as an enchanted beast-creature would probably eclipse the shame of his marriage to a low born woman. Then, too, Beauty is in all things good and beautiful and pleasing and charming; she would no doubt be integrated into his society in time, by the virtue of her personality and the power of his influence.

Beauty had to give up far more than a degree of social standing when she made her choice. She gave up her family and her freedom, knowing that her husband the Beast would probably not allow her to travel any more than before when she was his captive. She gave up her future, her chances to bear children, and all her ties to friends and society. She sacrificed everything she had out of fondness and love for a creature who arguably did not deserve either — not because of an accident of his birth, but because of the wrongness of many of his actions.

And thus we come to this moment of redemption for the Prince. He is able to match Beauty's choice in every point. If she will not have him as a Prince, let him be returned to his beastly, slow-witted form. Let him give up entirely his family, his future, his legacy, his friends, and his society to live in happy isolation with Beauty. He would rather return to the suffering he felt under his curse than be restored to the form he craves as a man, if the difference is whether or not he may marry Beauty.

No one spoke for some minutes, but the Fairy at length broke the silence, and casting an affectionate look upon the lovers, she said to them, "I find you worthy of each other. It would be a crime to part two such excellent persons. You shall not be separated, I promise you; and I have sufficient power to fulfill my promise."

The Fairy — and de Villeneuve — is satisfied. The Prince has chosen Beauty, and has chosen her in such a way that truly conveys his willingness to sacrifice everything to be with her. He has passed essentially the same tests as Beauty, and has been willing to make the same sacrifices that she was, and now the choices of the two lovers will be honored. And if society or the Queen Mother or the Merchant or anyone else has anything to say about it, the Fairy is there to lay down the law.

Changelings and Changes

And as it turns out, there is someone who *does* have something to say about the Fairy's decision, namely Beauty.

Beauty, at these words, embraced the knees of the Fairy, and exclaimed, "Ah, do not expose me to the misery of being told all my life that I am unworthy of the rank to which your bounty would elevate me. Reflect that this Prince, who now believes that his happiness consists in the possession of my hand may very shortly perhaps be of the same opinion as the Queen."

"No, no, Beauty, fear nothing," rejoined the Fairy. "The evils you anticipate cannot come to pass. I know a sure way of protecting you from them, and should the Prince be capable of despising you after marriage, he must seek some other reason than the inequality of your condition. Your birth is not inferior to his own."

To the impatient reader, this must seem like yet another delay to the inevitable happy ending, but de Villeneuve has one last unhappy reality to address. She and Beauty both recognize that while the Prince currently values Beauty more than the good opinion of his family and society, that position is subject to change. Just as the Queen Mother considered Beauty worthless once the girl was no more use to the family, the Prince may come to value Beauty less over time as he gains distance from his time as a Beast. Thus we come to de Villeneuve's final feminist argument: Beauty must be raised to a position as powerful and privileged as the Prince's own in order to protect her from the whims of him and his family.

And so Beauty, we are about to discover, is a Fairy Princess by birth, and the niece to this good guardian Fairy standing before her. She was switched as an infant with the Merchant's youngest daughter (who had died of crib-death) in order to protect Beauty from a malicious Fairy. But now that her birth-right has been revealed as the daughter of a King and a powerful Fairy, her pedigree is even greater than that of the Prince and his Queen Mother. The Prince — as foretold by the escutcheons — will be "Beauty's

Husband", rather than she "The Prince's Wife".

At first glance, this seems like something of a contradiction after the impassioned argument moments before that Beauty's birth is immaterial and only her virtue and goodness is required to make the match suitable. Is de Villeneuve trying to have her cake and eat it too by arguing in the same breath that Beauty's birth is immaterial but that she's also a Fairy Princess? I don't think that's the case.

It seems to me that the raising of Beauty from a low-born state to a high-born one isn't the result of simply wanting a good pedigree as icing on the cake that is Beauty's perfection. Rather, I think the point here is to raise Beauty to a position of power so that she has the tools to defend herself. After all, the Queen Mother and the Prince (should the mood take them) can taunt and torment a low-born Merchant's daughter to the point of misery, but they would not dare do so to a powerful Princess protected by a high King and a good Fairy. And this, I think, marks the point at which this fantasy stops being about protection and starts being about power.

The fantasy of being protected and valued by a powerful creature is a meaningful ideal for many people, but it has a double-edge. In order to need protection, one must also be vulnerable. And in order to be protected, one must necessarily be weaker than the protector. This is all well and good within the setting of the fantasy, until we ask *what then?* Will the protector continue their protection forever? Will they never slip up, never fail, never grow tired, never get weary? Will the vulnerable one be vulnerable for a lifetime, both to their attackers and to the protector, should they break faith down the line?

I do not think it is a coincidence that many "protection fantasies" eventually evolve into "power fantasies" where the protected ends up surpassing the protector. This evolution of vulnerable-to-powerful has the effect of rendering the vulnerable partner ultimately on an equal footing with the protector. The protector's job becomes not to protect the vulnerable party forever, but merely to facilitate them on their way to power. The appeal of this fantasy seems to lie in the *accessibility* at the start: anyone who has ever felt vulnerable can step into the shoes of the protected and then enjoy the ride to a climax of privilege and strength.

Beauty started this tale in the most vulnerable of positions. She was the youngest child in a society that disproportionately favors the elder children. She was a woman in a society that disenfranchises women to the point that not a single objection or investigation is raised when she disappears from her father's home the night he leaves her with the Beast. She was a daughter in a household that valued her life and her worth as so much less than that of her father that she was expected to give her life in his place in order to settle his debts. She was a prisoner to a captor who demeaned her wants and needs to the point where she was forced to hide her feelings lest she be emotionally and verbally abused.

From this position of vulnerability, Beauty gained the love and protection of the Beast and his guardian Fairy. And that protection evolves now into power of her own: without the Beast, Beauty would never have known her hidden lineage as a Fairy Princess, but now that she knows her heritage, her whole life will change. She is the eldest child of a King and a Fairy, and the inheritor of all their power and privilege. She is the lost daughter of a doting family who has been mourning her loss since the moment she was taken away as an infant. As the descendant of fairies, the daughter of a king, and the wife of a prince, she is possibly the most powerful woman in the land.

Now is the story truly over. Beauty has broken free from the rules of society and exercised her own choices. The Beast-Prince has done likewise, and has shown himself a better man than the Merchant by his willingness to make the same sacrifices for Beauty as she would have made for him. And Beauty has been raised from her initial place as the most marginalized to her final destiny as powerfully privileged. All that remains is tying up a few loose ends, specifically the movement from her old family to her new one. The Fairy conjures the Merchant and his children to the castle to greet Beauty.

The moment he perceived her he ran to her with open arms, blessing the happy moment that presented her again to his sight, and heaping benedictions on the generous Beast who had permitted him to return; he looked about for him in every direction, to offer him his most humble thanks for all the favours he had heaped on his family, and particularly on his youngest daughter. He was vexed at not seeing him, and began to apprehend that his conjectures were erroneous. Still, the presence of all his children seemed to support the idea he had formed, as they would scarcely have been all assembled in that spot if some solemn ceremony, such as that marriage, were not to be celebrated.

These reflections, which the good man made to himself, did not prevent him from pressing Beauty fondly in his arms, and bathing her cheek with tears of joy. After allowing due time for this first expression of his feelings, "Enough, good man," said the Fairy. "You have sufficiently caressed this Princess. It is time that, ceasing to regard her as a father, you should learn that that title does not appertain to you, and that you must now do her homage as your sovereign. **She is the Princess of the Happy Island, daughter of the King and Queen whom you see before you. She is about to become the wife of this Prince. Here stands the Prince's mother, sister of the King. I am a Fairy, her friend, and the aunt of Beauty.** [...]

The merchant could not help weeping, without being able to tell whether his tears were caused by the pleasure of seeing the happiness of Beauty, or by the sorrow of losing so perfect a daughter. His sons were agitated by similar feelings. Beauty, extremely affected by this evidence of their love, entreated those on whom she now depended, as well as the Prince, her future husband, to permit her to reward such tender attachment. Her entreaty testified the goodness of her heart too sincerely not to be listened to. They were laden with bounties, and by permission of the King, the Prince, and the Queen, Beauty continued to call them by the tender names of father, brothers, and even sisters, though she was not ignorant that the latter were as little so in heart as they were in blood. She desired they would all, in return, call her by the name they were wont to do when they believed her to be a member of their family.

The fate of the Merchant is not a happy one. As much as he loved Beauty, he must now deal with the fact that she is a changeling, and that his biological daughter has been dead, unknown and unmourned by him all this time. And now his adopted child is being taken from him and given to a royal family, with the title of 'father' taken from him.

We might pity another man, but the Merchant has not conducted himself well over the course of this tale. It is almost karmic that his daughter is ultimately taken from him after he has been so eager to throw her away, once to a violent monster to save his own life and then again to a boorish beast out of gratitude for the riches sent his way. The Merchant has consistently valued Beauty less than he has his own wealth and safety. Now as a favorite of the Princess he will have both, but too late he recognizes that he has carelessly sacrificed "so perfect a daughter".

Beauty and the Prince immerse themselves into the pleasures of their wedding and each other's company.

Enraptured with the scenes around them, entranced by the pleasure of loving and expressing their love to each other, they had entirely forgotten their royal state and the cares that attend it. The newly-married pair, indeed, proposed to the Fairy that they should abdicate, and resign their power into the hands of any one she should select; but that wise being represented to them clearly that they were under as great an obligation to fulfill the destiny which had confided to them the government of a nation as that nation was to preserve for them an unshaken loyalty.

They yielded to these just remonstrances, but the Prince and Beauty stipulated that they should be allowed occasionally to visit that spot, and cast aside for a while the cares inseparable from their station, and that they should be waited on by the invisible Genii or the animals who had attended them during the preceding years. They availed themselves as often as possible of this liberty.

And they lived Happily Ever After.

Modern Spins

When I first set out to write a retelling of "Beauty and the Beast", I had never read the original *La Belle et la Bête*. Indeed, despite my best efforts, I could not even find the original until after I had penned my first three chapters — and then only because a dear friend sent me a copy. And yet even without reading the text, I knew something of the tale. How could I not? Our culture is saturated with it.

At the time of writing this, Wikipedia lists no fewer than ten film versions of the tale, four television tie-ins, and twenty prose adaptations. [39] *Pulchritude* will, I suppose, mark the twenty-first, and yet I have no doubt that dozens of other adaptations exist that simply have not been added to the Wikipedia database. For whatever reason, this tale has resonated deeply with our society. So what more was there to be done with a story that can be abridged into a few pages and yet has been repeated endlessly over film, television, books, and musicals? Did the world really *need* another "Beauty and the Beast" adaptation?

I hoped so. I started from the standpoint that the tale as I knew it — a cursed man desperately waiting on a young woman to realize her love for him and restore him to humanity before the time limit runs out — could not possibly end well. Not because the Beast was beastly or because Beauty was damaged by an abusive home or any other reason relating directly to the characters themselves, but rather because the society that shaped them was fundamentally toxic. I saw the tale as one in which privilege damages us and prevents us from having nice things in general and healthy relationships in particular.

It's ironic that I hope to use de Villeneuve's classic story to tell a feminist tale, and yet I depart so wildly from her happy ending. I knew, even before I had read her original text, that she meant the story as a commentary on the social ills of her day, and I hoped to replicate that. But where she was able to embrace the difference between Fantasy and Reality and take her story to a place where abusers can be suddenly redeemed and victims can be magically elevated to positions of ultimate power, I couldn't.

She followed a path that she hoped would map out how much better the world could be if society gave women choice, agency, and equal power in their relationships. I followed one that I hope will demonstrate how good people can meet terrible ends when society isn't willing to give those tools to the disenfranchised.

Trigger Warnings

This novel contains potentially triggering content. A list of that content is provided here, or you may return to the Technical Details page. Please note that lists of triggers may be seen by some as "spoilers" for book content.

The following potentially triggering content is included in this novel:
Descriptions of violence, spilled blood, and animal-on-human attacks.

Allusion to the fear of potential rape in frightening situations.

Depiction of captivity and emotional manipulation within captivity.

Discussion of mental illness, including ableist terminology.

Abusive parenting, including verbal abuse and emotional abuse.

Involuntary and painful body transformation.

Patriarchal societies and their detrimental effect on the inhabitants.

Endnotes

1. "pul-chri-tude. noun; physical beauty, comeliness."
   Source: Dictionary.com
   Link: http://dictionary.reference.com/browse/pulchritude

2. Creative Commons Attribution-NonCommercial-NoDerivativeWorks License human-readable explanation.
   Link: http://creativecommons.org/licenses/by-nc-nd/3.0/

3. Creative Commons Attribution-NonCommercial-NoDerivativeWorks License full legal code.
   Link: http://creativecommons.org/licenses/by-nc-nd/3.0/legalcode

4. Ana Mardoll email.
   Link: mailto:anamardoll@gmail.com

5. Acacia Moon Publishing email.
   Link: mailto:acaciamoonpublishing@gmail.com

6. Brooke Mixon email.
   Link: mailto:bmixon@hallmixon.com

7.   Elaine Kennedy email.
     Link: mailto:elaine.p.kennedy@gmail.com

8.   Emily Vreeland email.
     Link: mailto:envree@gmail.com

9.   Clarissa Filice email.
     Link: mailto:irish_mint@yahoo.com

10. Black Jack font.
     Link: http://www.dafont.com/black-jack.font

11. Shonar Bangla font.
     Link: http://fontzone.net/font-details/Shonar+Bangla/

12. Estrangelo Edessa font.
     Link: http://fontzone.net/font-details/Estrangelo+Edessa/

13. Calibri font.
     Link: http://www.ascenderfonts.com/store/search.aspx?q=Calibri

14. doc format.
     Link: http://en.wikipedia.org/wiki/DOC_%28computing%29

15. 52 Novels e-book design shop.
     Link: http://www.52novels.com/

16. Author's website.
     Link: http://www.anamardoll.com/

17. "Just like its English and French counterparts, the Italian word
     fata comes from Latin Fatae, which is the feminine form of
     Fatum, 'fate, destiny.'"

Source: Raffaella Benvenuto
Link: http://www.endicott-studio.com/rdrm/rrItalianF.html

18. "A portative organ (from the Latin verb portare, "to carry")
is a small pipe organ that consists of one rank of flue pipes,
sometimes arranged in two rows, to be played while strapped to
the performer at a right angle. ... The instrument was commonly
used in secular music from the twelfth to the sixteenth
centuries."
Source: Wikipedia.org
Link: http://en.wikipedia.org/wiki/Portative_organ

19. "...a myriad of different magical creatures: not only fate, but
also the diminutive beings usually called folletti, the Italian
counterparts of the various sprites, gnomes, leprechauns and
pixies encountered in the folklore of western and northern
European countries."
Source: Raffaella Benvenuto
Link: http://www.endicott-studio.com/rdrm/rrItalianF3.html
Folletto is rendered as elf in the Google English translation.
Source: Wikipedia.org
Link: http://it.wikipedia.org/wiki/Folletto

20. "Like most spirits of this type, monachicchi are tiny, extremely
lively, and wear red hoods; they also stand guard over a treasure
(usually a pot of gold), and exact revenge on anyone trying to
steal it by turning the gold into lumps of coal."
Source: Raffaella Benvenuto
Link: http://www.endicott-studio.com/rdrm/rrItalianF3.html
Monachicchio is rendered as gnome in the Google English
translation.
Source: Wikipedia.org
Link: http://it.wikipedia.org/wiki/Monachicchio

21. "An example is the Mazapegol of the north-eastern, coastal region of Romagna (formerly inhabited by Celts), described by folklorists as a cross between a goblin and an incubus."
Source: Raffaella Benvenuto
Link: http://www.endicott-studio.com/rdrm/rrItalianF3.html
Mazapégul is rendered as goblin in the Google English translation.
Source: Wikipedia.org
Link: http://it.wikipedia.org/wiki/Mazap%C3%A9gul

22. Rosella's name.
Link: http://www.behindthename.com/name/rosella

23. Ezio's name.
Link: http://www.behindthename.com/name/ezio

24. Ezio of Assassin's Creed.
Link: http://assassinscreed.wikia.com/wiki/Ezio_Auditore_da_Firenze

25. Guerrino's name.
Link: http://www.behindthename.com/name/guerino

26. Cienzo's name.
Link: http://en.wikipedia.org/wiki/The_Merchant_%28fairy_tale%29

27. Venizia's name.
Link: http://www.thinkbabynames.com/meaning/0/Venizia

28. Marchetta's name.
Link: http://www.houseofnames.com/marchetta-family-crest

29. Fiorita's name.
   Link: http://www.houseofnames.com/fiorita-family-crest
30. Flavio's name.
   Link: http://www.behindthename.com/name/flavio

31. "Gaze is a psychoanalytical term brought into popular usage by Jacques Lacan to describe the anxious state that comes with the awareness that one can be viewed. The psychological effect, Lacan argues, is that the subject loses some sense of autonomy upon realizing that he or she is a visible object."
   Source: Wikipedia.org
   Link: http://en.wikipedia.org/wiki/Gaze

32. "Beauty and the Beast (La Belle et la Bête) is a traditional fairy tale. The first published version of the fairy tale was a rendition by Gabrielle-Suzanne Barbot de Villeneuve, published in La jeune américaine, et les contes marins in 1740. The best-known written version was an abridgement of her work published in 1756 by Jeanne-Marie Le Prince de Beaumont, in Magasin des enfants, ou dialogues entre une sage gouvernante et plusieurs de ses élèves; an English translation appeared in 1757."
   Source: Wikipedia.org
   Link: http://en.wikipedia.org/wiki/Beauty_and_the_Beast

33. "The story she came up with was uniquely her own, however, and addressed issues of concern to women of her day. Chief among these was a critique of a marriage system in which women had few legal rights -- no right to choose their own husband, no right to refuse the marriage bed, no right to control their own property, and no right of divorce. Often the brides were fourteen or fifteen years old, given to men who were decades older. Unsatisfactory wives risked being locked up in mental institutions or distant convents. Women fairy tale writers of

the 17th & 18th centuries were often sharply critical of such practices, promoting the ideas of love, fidelity, and civilité between the sexes. Their tales reflected the realities they lived with, and their dreams of a better way of life. Their Animal Bridegroom stories, in particularly, embodied the real-life fears of women who could be promised to total strangers in marriage, and who did not know if they'd find a beast or a lover in their marriage bed."
Source: Terri Windling
Link: http://www.endicott-studio.com/rdrm/forbewty.html

34. "Four and twenty fairy tales : selected from those of Perrault and other popular writers."
    Source: Archive.org
    Link: http://www.archive.org/details/fourtwentyfairyt00planiala

35. "Youngest Child Wins: A common Fairy Tale situation. Whenever multiple siblings are portrayed, the youngest is the hero; the older ones are either evil or just boring."
    Source: TVTropes.org
    Link: http://tvtropes.org/pmwiki/pmwiki.php/Main/YoungestChildWins

36. The "Power and Control Wheel" contains the following categories: Coercion and Threats; Intimidation; Emotional Abuse; Isolation; Minimizing, Denying, and Blaming; Using Children; Economic Abuse, and Male Privilege.
    Source: National Center on Domestic and Sexual Violence
    Link: http://www.ncdsv.org/images/PowerControlwheelNOSHADING.pdf

37. "In psychology, Stockholm Syndrome is an apparently paradoxical psychological phenomenon in which hostages

express empathy and have positive feelings towards their captors, sometimes to the point of defending them. These feelings are generally considered irrational in light of the danger or risk endured by the victims, who essentially mistake a lack of abuse from their captors for an act of kindness."
Source: Wikipedia.org
Link: http://en.wikipedia.org/wiki/Stockholm_syndrome

38. "In heraldry, an escutcheon is a shield which forms the main or focal element in an achievement of arms. The word is used in two related senses. Firstly, as the shield on which a coat of arms is displayed. Escutcheon shapes are derived from actual shields used by knights in combat, and thus have varied and developed by region and by era. [...] Secondly, a shield can itself be a charge within a coat of arms."
Source: Wikipedia.org
Link: http://en.wikipedia.org/wiki/
Escutcheon_%28heraldry%29

39. "The tale has been notably adapted for screen, stage, prose, and television over the years."
Source: Wikipedia.org
Link: http://en.wikipedia.org/wiki/Beauty_and_the_Beast